BOTTOM LINE

BOTTOM LINE
John Chaloner

SEVERN SH HOUSE

First published in Great Britain in 1984 by
SEVERN HOUSE PUBLISHERS LTD of
4 Brook Street, London W1Y 1AA

Copyright © 1984 by John Chaloner

British Library Cataloguing on Publication Data
Chaloner, John
  Bottom line.
  1. Title
  823′.914(F)   PR6053.H283

ISBN 0 7278 1025 1

The names of characters and locations in this book are wholly invented.

Printed and bound in Great Britain by
Anchor Brendon Ltd, Tiptree, Essex

1

When Rupert woke there was soft bright light waving on the ceiling. He thought he was on the boat. Then he turned his head the other way and saw that Lady Madeleine Bair, still pink and naked, slept next to him. No nightie was a signal.

'Are you awake?'

Last night they had both fallen asleep instantly after two drinks parties and a dinner party. Maddy, he now saw, had not even dealt with her face. She had two mascara-black eyes and looked rather like a sleeping panda. The panda in the London Zoo had been one of his first loves. Was there much difference in the feelings he had now? He tried a mating call.

'Maddy!' No answer. 'Darling, you're uncovered!' Maddy had thrown back the single sheet covering in the heat of the summer night, and lay twisted and serpentine. The same soft light rippled on a pale, raised hip. Rupert realised it was not movement but the transferred reflection through the gap in the curtains from the Thames six storeys below. It was a beautiful curvature. But the signal, he had discovered rather sadly over a year, was unreliable and not the same in the morning as at night. Sometimes signal lights stuck. Go or stop. You never knew with Madeleine. You could only try. Carefully.

Rupert slid one arm over the bare shoulder. He always wore pyjamas unless told not to. Long ago nanny had said no gentleman would sleep without pyjamas. Without them, he still felt sinful. And if the sense of sinfulness rose nothing else would. Perhaps that was what nannies had in mind.

His hand encountered and closed upon a deliciously full and shapely breast. He recognised it as Madeleine's left breast. Larger than the other one. Why this was so, had never been really clear, but he found the fact in the flesh faintly erotic. The owner of the unequal bosom claimed that it was because her only child, a daughter, was 'leftish' and a proper revulsion against the child's father who was so 'rightish' – and, to make things worse, had divorced Maddy in order to marry a Mexican princess. One who had not only orderly breastworks, but large and shapely assets of all kinds that would appeal to a man who was not only a peer but a banker.

The breast pulled gently out of Rupert's hand. One black panda eye opened and a husky voice gave the ubiquitous greeting: 'Hi!'

Rupert was more definitive. He slipped the other hand round the palely illuminated hip and shifted his own to close the small distance between them.

'I love you!' It was going to be all right, even if delayed.

The telephone rang its brisk British, nannylike double tone. Instantly Maddy Bair sat up, with an effortless tightening of her visible stomach, and although the two panda eyes had both closed again, one hand unerringly located the receiver and brought it to her ear. With the other she tucked the loose sheet around her torso as though the telephone caller could see her. The movement also served to roll Rupert aside.

'Gugi, darling! *Good* morning!' Eyes flashing wide open now, she gave Rupert a warning glance.

'That Swiss cuckoo!' Rupert whispered. He was suffering. 'Get him off the phone or I'll give you two real black eyes! I mean it! It's too *early*. Nobody can call at this hour! It's the middle of the night! Oh, my God!' He

8

flung himself to the side of the bed and sat up. Then, grandly gloomy, he got up and pulled his pyjama trousers on again.

He made for the window, wrenching the curtains apart so that bright, white reality flooded the room. Below the endless traffic on the Embankment was silent. Dolphin Square's fitted double-glazing ensured that the Thames beyond continued to shimmer in the early sunlight. A lone tug hauled three barges up river. Rupert could almost feel the weight of them, the drag of the tide going the wrong way was for him too.

'Gugi, listen! No listen to me!' Maddy always said listen. Even if the other person was listening. It made the conversation more pointed, urgent. As usual, Rupert felt the force of it and hung around listening.

'You just said it isn't complete. OK. Only one? How many? They're making one. What is it? Certificate of authentic? OK. Authenticity! Yeah, yeah, I know. That's OK. *Listen*. Who does that? I mean who issues that? Is that genuine? Dated *what*? Amazing. OK, I'll call him. If you get them in today – yes, after eleven. I'll be there. Listen, any news of the Sèvres? He's waiting. I agreed the price. Sweety, there is no insurance charge. You know you can't insure that stuff. OK. Sure. Bye!'

Sitting there with pale, naked shoulders hunched to look specially helpless, wrapped in the whiter-than-white sheet, she turned to look at Rupert and gave her maddeningly Maddy smile. He knew it so well. The pretty, thin lips went in a tiny vee shape, shining sweet, spellbinding. It was the young witch's smile. The magic spell of the coven.

'Sorry, darling! That was Gugi with the Italian chess sets. Bless his cotton socks he's actually got them here!'

'Even a middle-aged Swiss queer doesn't wear cotton socks – not the kind you mean! And why do you have to call him sweety if it's business? Here in our bedroom? I don't want to know anything about your deals! Then I shan't be an accessory after the fact.' Putting on a feigned criminal leer, Rupert leapt across the distance that

9

separated them and grabbed for the top of the sheet.

'Pot, don't!' Maddy squealed, breathless.

'You can call me Mr Potter! Or darling. Or buster. But you might as well give in.'

'Darling Pot!' Maddy said still breathlessly clutching the sheet at the level of her nipples. 'You know Audrey will be in! And Nancy and – '.

'Why don't you get that lock mended?' Rupert asked. 'They both know what it's all about anyway. I won't have this All-American-Girl Saturday Evening Post stuff. Totally artificial –'

The telephone rang again. With an instant sweep of one pale arm, Maddy had the receiver off, scarlet nails rattling on the white ivory of the receiver. As one breast became exposed and Rupert was happily diving for it, the bedroom door was flung open. He continued to move, from years of playing rugby, rolling dexterously on to the carpet, eyes closed and clutching the front of his pyjamas. A stunningly beautiful small girl of about twelve, long dark hair framing an angel face, wearing an angel's white nightie, came in with a rush, and finding Rupert helpless on the floor, pulled at his pyjamas and hair, crying with feigned terror: 'Mummy darling! What was he doing? What has happened to Pot? Is he dead?'

'I'm on the phone, darling! *Listen*. No. I mean yes, I am listening! Rudi, you're an angel! Just bring them round.' She put a hand over the receiver and yelled: 'For Pete's sake, will you all shut up a minute! Hello, yes, I'm here!'

A new figure appeared in the doorway carrying a small tray with orange juice and a miniature cup of coffee.

Rupert, struggling up, saw that it was Nancy, the buxom *au-pair*. Shaking her dark ringlets, part of the Elizabethan serving maid act, she quite capably made a curtsy even with the tray. 'Good morning, Mr Potter!' Rupert observed that beside the miniature cup was another tiny receptacle. The millionaires' one ounce of caviar, open, with a silver salt-spoon stuck in it. Nancy, he knew, also worked in Fortnum's food hall which made her, as Maddy was always telling friends, worth her pay in what purported to be left-overs.

'I've brought you a little breakfast, too, Mr Potter!'

'*Lucky* Pot!' the dream child said with an adult purring voice. She still had a hand on Rupert's pyjamas.

'Allow me,' Rupert said, with what dignity was still possible. 'My dressing gown is in my room. I must get it. Put Lady Bair's breakfast on the bed, Nancy.' He pushed past her towards the open door. The telephone talk was still going on.

'Listen, Rudi! Be a pet! I'm busy. I'll call you when I get into the gallery!' He heard Maddy's happy scream as he left but, looking over his shoulder, he saw that she was hugging her daughter and Nancy was completing drawing the curtains. He turned back to join in. Maddy was now pretending to see him for the first time.

'Good morning, darling! Good morning, Nancy! Hi, everybody!' The phone began to ring again. Rupert groaned, and swung out on to the landing and into the darkened, unused anonymity of the spare bedroom next door. A strange clumping sound began on the staircase off the landing. He recognised the steps of Mrs Deere, the daily cleaner, dragging up the vacuum cleaner. She, too, would gain entry into the bedroom with some dismal tale. Maddy's part-time secretary would be next, and then the Morning Court would be fully assembled. To escape, he crept across the landing into the emptiness and sunlight of the big drawing room.

The windows also looked out over the Thames and the tall chimneys of factories and Battersea power station on the far bank. It could not really be called a living room, nor rightly a drawing room, but perhaps a receiving room. There were bottles permanently on the corner table. The arrangement of sofa, frilled chairs and low tables was unmistakably purposeful. It was a room for the regular drinks parties that Maddy loved. At that hour of the day it looked rather forlorn but Rupert always felt happy there because it was so much Maddy's room and where he had first met her. The tangerine-coloured carpet and the cream-white walls and loose covers were essentially Maddy. He could still hear her voice on the telephone and waited while the sunlight chased across the tangerine carpet. It made an audio-visual symphonic effect with the sound of her laughing.

They drove to Maddy's Gallery in her *Deux Chevaux* which, in the style of the salon, was also bright orange with a cream cloth roof. She drove while Rupert cleared rubbish and various *objets* from the front on to the back seat.

'You'll have to put some money into the account, Pot!'

'OK.'

'It was nothing but bills in the mail.'

'I'll do it in the morning.'

'You can't be a kept man, Pot!' Maddy wore glasses for driving. She looked serene.

'It would undermine my entire character. Have you noticed this car is what you call out of gas?'

'It keeps going for ages even when the gauge says Zilch.'

'Like me!'

'Ahhh!' Now Maddy flashed him one of her warm, dark-eyed looks from under her fringe. The Citröen bumped gently against the kerb and off again.

'What do you run on, Pot darling? Scotch?'

'Love. And alcohol, I agree. If you look at me like that, and we both get killed in the process, I wouldn't even mind.'

'Let's not get killed!' Her hands flashed about on the steering wheel for a moment. An emerald and two diamond rings sparkled wildly. She missed a cyclist and turned the car into Sloane Square. 'Listen, don't forget about the account. And, by the way, you can't stay tonight, Bella's coming.'

'Now you tell me!' said Rupert bitterly.

'Darling, I only knew this morning on the phone. I have to put up my sister-in-law when she's in town!'

'She isn't your sister-in-law,' Rupert said pointedly.

'You're not married to Lord Bair any more, had you forgotten? You're living with me. Listen, as you say. Why don't we get married? Then it would be OK.'

'Darling Pot! So practical. Isn't Sloane Square looking super! I love Sloane Square, the flower stands and that little fountain, don't you?'

'No. I don't like anything. Why do I have to get out?'

'We've gone through all that.'

'But if it's OK for your daughter and domestics, why...?'

'I get alimony. That's what keeps us. If Desmond chose to get rough he could cut us off. You couldn't put that sort of money into the bank. I don't say Bella would tell, but I feel embarrassed.'

'Like a loose woman?'

'Sort of.'

Rupert looked at her, searching for signs that this was true. The little pointed, pretty face was tilted up to peer at the traffic through the very grubby windscreen. She always dressed demurely in oddly old-fashioned flowered dresses that clung to her slim body, but in a way their gentle respectability enhanced the loose woman image. Rupert laid a hand on a flowered silken thigh as it moved, operating the clutch pedal, and squeezed.

'I shall miss you dreadfully. Will you miss me?'

'We've got drinks first, then dinner at home with the Bealeys. You'll see lots of me!'

'Where the hell am I to stay after that?' Rupert said desperately. 'I'm not going to pay for an hotel. That's too late to go down to the boat. Besides my employer is over here this week. Suppose he wants me for dinner?'

'He'll be at the Bealeys. Pam told me. So I asked him to dinner for your sake. And Polly will put you up. She'll be there. Sweety, don't make a fuss, be a good boy!' Now it was Maddy eyeing Rupert critically. 'Why do you wear those sort of country suits? That mud colour I mean. Aren't you going into the City?'

'I'm sorry you don't like them,' Rupert said stiffly. 'I'd sort of forgotten. It is an old ploy, to look as though I had private means and a country estate and didn't give a damn! It will impress my employer. But don't worry. Tonight I will pour myself into your favourite inkwell blue. I shall *oil* my way across the floor!'

'Oozing charm from every pore!'

'That I can't guarantee. I'm not very keen on drinks parties.'

'I know. Where do you want to get out?' Maddy asked shortly. As she got nearer to her gallery in Knightsbridge she became, as always, absent and intense.

'Right here!' said Rupert. 'I'll take the Tube.'

Once again the *Deux Chevaux* nudged the kerb, rocking and making a snuffling, grunting noise, like a pig approaching its trough, as Maddy worked the engine. It was nearly out of fuel Rupert reckoned as he kissed her on the neck just below the swinging gold earring and was rewarded with the special look in the glowing azure eyes under the dark fringe.

'Be good, Pot!'

'You look out in that Clockwork Orange!'

Lady Bair's gallery was a small shop with its own ornamental front door, situated in the choice and useful area between Belgrave Square and Lowndes Square. There was never much in the window space, which had an eau-de-nil velvet backdrop. The things were taken out at night and rearranged every morning, generally by her efficient assistant and personal friend, Ruthy. She and Ruthy had been at Vassar together and, by quite different routes, had met up again in London. Ruthy, married to a mineral company executive, had always been efficient and had gone on to get her degree. Maddy herself had failed to get one.

'Oh shoot!' said Maddy Bair as she looked in the window of her very own Knightsbridge Gallery. This pause before she walked through the door was ritual. The puritan streak inherited from her distinctly dull middle-west parents still inhibited her from using the real bad words. Her reflection in the gallery window was more vivid.

14

People said she looked like the Princess of Wales: older and with dark hair, but with unmistakable similarities. Was she a failure? The gallery was great. Her own, real proof that she could stand on her own feet without Desmond. Well, nearly on her own feet, since the awful day Desmond, the Lord Bair, had told her he no longer loved her. Quite suddenly and strangely in his thick, rich voice. And then he was gone. And the great house near Donegal was lived in now by his sister and he had married a Mexican princess with untold wealth, which was all that bankers thought about – money. Except that the princess was ravishingly beautiful, too.

Perhaps she could find a fabulously wealthy Mexican prince. That would torture Desmond. But also poor Pot. Darling, lovable, not-very-well-off Pot, who was so gentle in bed and so solemn at drinks, and as quietly bossy as her father had been. He made her pay parking fines and turned off the radio at breakfast. God! He was so English!

The door of the gallery opened. Maddy loved the handsome door with its golden oak panels and in the middle the great, old, dark green metal knob she had found in Italy. A small woman, almost a dwarf with orangey hair and a tissue-paper white face looked out.

'Maddee! You going to stay out on that sidewalk all day?'

'Ruthy sweety! No, just admiring that window of yours, that's all! But how do we get some new stuff?'

'Same window as yesterday.' The auburn-haired dwarf agreed, but blushed with pleasure. Then quickly scowled suspiciously, putting a cigarette reached from a capacious pocket into her small lipsticked mouth. She lit it with an equally bright-red throw-away lighter, whose jetting flame was nearly two inches long.

'You're going to set light to yourself!' Maddy said, following her in. She knew why Ruthy needed big pockets: king-size cigarettes and a torch-lighter flame. Early on she had once told Ruth Hoken that she was worth her weight in gold. And the little woman had burst into tears and screamed that everyone made fun of her size and weight, and every other goddamn thing. She told Maddy all about Joe, and how he made her do dreadful things, and also locked her in the closet when she wouldn't. And how she could never leave him, any more than she could leave Maddy, because love was all a mixed-up thing and because art and antiques were beautiful, and they and Maddy's friendship were all that made the world less ugly.

'While we're both right here, give me the cloth and I'll shine up the plate!' Maddy Bair said crisply. This was another routine she secretly loved doing. She dumped her handbag and briefcase on the step. 'Maybe we get no passing trade in this backwater, Ruthy, but one day that plate will bring in the crown jewels! Thanks!'

She took the tin of polish and the duster from Ruthy and went to work on the discreet brass plate on the door. The lettering said simply: Art Acquisitions in straight Times Roman. Maddy Bair still loved that plate, the name and all it represented – her own commercial talent, knowledge and connections. She dined out on it and politicians were surprised, tycoons looked at her with respect, foreigners gave her their cards. 'It's AA!' Maddy told them. 'Not alcoholics, and nothing to do with automobiles but lots to do with me. Do come and buy things!' And she gave them her young witch's smile. They were bewitched. Some did come, and bought things.

With the brass plate glittering, Maddy stepped back inside and shut the door. There was not much space in the gallery where Ruthy sat.

'Listen, Maddy,' Ruthy said. 'I've done the figures again. We're going bust! You must know! You've put in two thousand of Desmond's money this month. But how do we get onto some real stuff? And if we do, how do we buy it?'

'Gugi is due now,' Maddy said calmly. 'If he wants to come into my office it means he's got something. We might give him some champagne.'

'Two halves in the ice box.'

'The place *looks* empty, you're right. We've *got* to get some stock!'

In the space behind the window in which they both now stood, only a few various small items stood on a French reproduction table. Round the gallery were two Chippendale chairs, some sad little oils on the walls, an ikon and a Victorian chaise longue.

As Lady Bair turned round, there was a knock on the front door which was kept locked. It added to real security as well as giving the impression of precious things within.

'Such ambiance!' cried Gugi stepping in and kissing Maddy's hand. 'Charisma!' Ruthy scowled and lit another cigarette while she turned on the bugging switch under her little table.

'Gugi, you're quite the most unswissy Swiss I've ever known!' Maddy put out a sweetly dramatic straight arm to him and gave the azure eyes and the coven smile.

Gugi, who was perhaps forty and looked thirty, had a thin, tanned face with quick, boot button eyes. His figure was slim to the point of being almost emaciated. He was obviously neither Zurich gnome nor Alpine guide, in his oversize black silk beret, a collarless evening shirt with frilled front and jeans so tight they wrinkled up his calves, leaving an exposure of pale, hairy ankle above the Gucci lizard shoes. His manner and appearance had cost a lot of inattentive people more gold than most of the gnomes made. Equally some of the matters in which he dealt were of a slipperiness that would have earned respect on any Alp. Maddy Bair was also fond of Gugi. She walked ahead of him into the small office and shut the door.

'Show me!'

Gugi put the bulky English-French dictionary he had been holding since he came in on to the small, exquisite ormolu table between them and they both sat down. He opened the cover, fluttered a few pages and the rest of the book became a hole. In the hole, on a bed of cotton wool, rested a small, beautiful object like an egg in a nest. It was in fact an egg.

'Fabergé,' said Maddy, resting her exquisite chin on

17

one hand. 'But a copy.'

'*Exactement*.' Gugi knew Maddy liked French, providing the words were of the Franglais kind. '*Mais parfait*!' He lifted the golden egg with long, bony fingers, turned it over to show the design and dropped it back into the nest.

'And you have a certificate? One that looks real?'

Gugi tipped the book, flicked the loose pages again and took out a crisp, folded sheet of paper, only faintly brown at the edges.

'So *fidèle*! Your friend will like it?'

'He might. I wish we could get some *real* stuff, Gugi! The big money!'

'A real Fabergé! *Puf*!'

'How much for this?'

Outside, behind her little table, Japanese doll's eyes almost shut behind her cigarette smoke, Ruthy moved the recording tape switch.

'Five thousand? Pounds, not francs.'

'The usual for me,' Gugi said. 'But in francs, sweety.'

Maddy nodded. Tapes don't pick up nods but Ruth outside knew she had nodded. When you are very small and not very pretty, and get knocked about and locked in cupboards, you got to tell what people were doing, even on the other side of the door.

Rupert's office where he functioned as UK editor of *Midas* magazine, the international monthly of finance and business, was, compared with the gallery, completely lacking in either ambiance or charisma. It had to have location kudos, a quality delineated by Mr Curt Epoch, the president and publisher, whose own office in Washington DC was twenty times as big.

Rupert's predecessor, who had two months ago gone to work for an oil protectorate bank for ten times the money Mr Epoch paid, had found the cupboard off the Strand. It was OK for 'lk', Mr Epoch's abbreviation, being better in that respect than a similar cupboard in Holborn (too near the Museum) or one in the City (too

18

near the readers).

With a desk not much larger than a tea table, it was quite difficult for Rupert to get round the filing cabinet and into his chair. He had to shut the door first. On the other hand, the publisher's philosophy was quintessential. 'I can either pay you the dough or the tax guy.' He had explained this and more, Rupert recalled, as he opened the mail. When Epoch engaged him, an interview arranged by Maddy who knew Epoch through Lord Bair and the bank, Curt Epoch had first told him most of his own life story, seeming almost uninterested in Rupert's. Epoch was seventy, a real gnome. Sitting in a chair, his shoes did not quite touch the hotel carpet. The interview had taken place in the Connaught where the publisher always stayed. Not to have lunch, Rupert remembered sadly as the interview passed two o'clock. He had been perceptive enough, in spite of hunger pangs, to ask for a lager when Epoch ordered Perrier water for himself.

'You will send your expenses into me personally, monthly. You'll find I give a free hand. *Midas* is not tightwad. But sprats to catch a mackerel, bread on the water. OK? You tell me who you bought lunch for, with details. And a story or a column item follows, OK?

'OK,' said Rupert. It was the first firmish indication that he had got the job. He noticed the publisher did not say dee-*tales* but a more European *ditells*.

'Why you leave IMF, Mr Potter?'

'They kept sending me to unhealthy places.'

'Men or microbes?' Rupert recognised the *Midas* headline style.

'Both. I was part of a team checking out situations and aid schemes. It was all right here in London, or back in Washington. Except for the endless drinks parties.'

'You gotta go, but you don't haf to trink!'

'Well, apart from the climate, when I eventually got to some of these places, the information didn't add up. Not the figures, not the people, together or separately, if you follow me. And politics came into everything. I saved up a bit. I quit!'

Mr Epoch seemed happy with quit. He had tapped Rupert on the knee. 'At *Midas* we know all about politics. You send us everything you pick up and we vet it. We try you for six months.'

That was four months ago. Now Epoch was staying at the Connaught again. There was nothing that mattered in the mail so Rupert picked up the telephone and called the hotel. He was connected immediately. As soon as he heard the publisher's cautious throat clearing, Rupert could visualise him. Epoch called so often from Washington he seemed more real on the telephone than in the flesh.

'I've been trying to call you since nine!'

'I was working late.'

'Like with vot?'

'A dinner party given by Lady Bair. The wife of the merchant banker, you know. Lots of useful stuff.'

'Of course I know her. She got you the job!'

Rupert had not forgotten, but he said: 'I try to keep my private life private.' It seemed to him sometimes that London life, at a certain level, was a kind of American country club.

'*Midas* finds out most things!' He could hear the aged dwarf's obscene cackle. 'Remember the cover by-line?'

'It's What you know about Who you know that turns to Gold,' Rupert recited obediently.

'We see each other this evening! I've got three things for you to work on. What have you got by yourself?'

'Four things,' said Rupert, who had made a list in preparation for this moment. '*Private Eye* says you are over here to buy the crown jewels for Saudi Arabia.'

Epoch chuckled happily. 'And?'

'Rothschilds have most of the SS wartime gold in their vaults.'

'Next?'

'It is genuine dried blood that is used to colour the *Financial Times* newsprint pink.'

From the other end the telephone sighed resignedly. Rupert visualised the small, grey unsmiling face. 'More,

Potter!'

'Bair Brady's could be overstretched – the merchant bank.'

'I heard it. Any more?'

'The Treasury's main computer has disc swivel.'

'It's American gear, so kill that one.'

'OK. How about this? The French have found oil in Alsace but they're scared to tell the Germans. I got it from their commercial attaché at a party the other night.'

Epoch was sighing again. 'It's the Swiss. They're drilling in the Alps. Can you beat that? Now listen, Potter. I'll say this, you try. And your expenses are reasonable. Not like all my editors. But you are not turning the stuff into copy. The *Midas* touch! I want gold from every one. Get into the Bair Brady story. We haf the feelink all the banks are in trouble. I'm working on it myself. Anything else?'

For a moment Rupert felt like babbling into the telephone like a tape recorder on back-run. Anything else indeed! How about the Bair-Potter story that Epoch seemed to know about? And that he had nowhere to go that night. Not even to his little boat at Beaulieu, where the mooring charges were overdue. And that his ex-wife, who was as mad as a hatter, was yelling for money. And the overwhelming desire he had to be working for *Poets and Poetry* instead of *Midas Magazine*. Or, a more recent thought, one of the better Champagne Houses. That would be gold of a kind that would lift the spirits.

'A medical friend of mine says they have found more mercury in champagne than in Tuna fish,' Rupert tried. 'Do you have contacts in Rheims or Epernay?'

'I don't drink.'

'Is there any way I can help you at all, sir, before we meet?'

'You don't help me, young man. I help you!'

The phone went dead. For a while Rupert sat. Perhaps Maddy knew some champagne people. She knew almost everybody.

'Epoch phoned this morning. He wants me to do a profile of your ex and his beastly bank! He says things aren't so good at Bair Brady.'

Maddy sat at her dressing table fastening a tiny emerald earring, looking in the glass and smiling the young witch's smile up at him. But back to front.

'I've put on the ink suit. For you! Is that good news?'

'How about this dress?'

'Sort of old-fashioned. I mean, I wouldn't look at it twice on the peg, but with you inside it, yes, yes!'

'*Darling!*' Maddy got up, uncoiling swiftly and he followed her out as she tried to find a coat in the muddle that was in the hall cupboard.

'You've changed all the pictures again,' he said accusingly, looking round. 'That one's from the loo and those two belong to the landing, and where is the Irish scene? I liked it where it was!'

'In the bedroom.'

'Whose bedroom?'

'Yours, that's why I put it there.'

'So that Bella can enjoy it!'

'Bye Audrey darling! Bye Nancy!' Maddy screamed. Audrey came hurtling from somewhere, bouncing over the tangerine carpet like an overgrown puppy, ringing her arms round her mother's neck, insisting on kissing Rupert. Duty done, she returned with speed to television and they were on the other side of the front door.

'Have you cigarettes?'

'Have I ever failed you?'

'Carry a lipstick for me?'

'Haven't you a bag?'

'Didn't have time to change it.'

'And I've had to pack a whole night bag,' Rupert said moodily, swinging it about in the elevator. 'Suppose Polly isn't there, or can't have me?'

'I expect someone'll put you up; don't be tiresome about it, Pot. And *don't* say anything to Bella!'

'I doubt if she'll even talk to me. I don't think any of your relations approve of me.'

22

In the car Maddy drove as usual while Rupert, hunched in the passenger seat, felt the constrictions of his best suit. The trousers were unpractically tight fitting. Maddy, with her chin tilted up as she drove, looked sparkling and pretty, with a secretive aura of well-being. Rupert knew the look.

'Is the gallery really going bust? Or is a drinks party enough to make you look happy?'

'Gugi came up trumps. And Rudi came in with a really fabulous ikon. I wish you could have seen it. Sakavoshek.'

'You know I've no idea what that means.'

'Nearly quarter of a million dollars. To a German account.'

'And how much do you keep?'

'One per cent!' Maddy pulled suddenly on the steering wheel, her slim white hands like butterflies. The *Deux Chevaux* rolled sickeningly. 'Christ, these zebra crossings! Less Rudi's cut,' she went on calmly. 'Less the bank's special account cut.'

They entered Chelsea Square. 'Wowee! Look a parking space! Hop out and stand there while I reverse in!'

To Rupert Chelsea Square looked like the part of Basle he had known when working with the IMF where every other building was a bank. But these were houses where people actually lived and had drinks parties.

'What a price, just to feel secure,' he said as they crossed to the Bealeys' house.

'You be nice to my friends – the whole evening!' Maddy warned.

The heavy panelled door was opened by a middle-aged lady in a black dress who, acting the rôle of housekeeper, was really the children's nanny.

'Good evening, Lady Bair!'

'Why doesn't she say anything to me?' Rupert muttered as they were drawn in by a *son-et-lumière* effect of well-bred uproar. Candelabra gleamed on glasses and jewellery, dresses and hair styles, bright young faces, important old ones. The uproar was already overflowing into the hall.

Rupert drew a deep breath. It was the deck of the Titanic.

A bobbing silver tray offered a selection of drinks, and he took a glass that might be champagne. Even if they were all going down, it was Nearer My God to Veuve Cliquot.

But not nearer to Maddy, who was already surrounded by those who had reserved places in the last lifeboat. Rupert could already hear ten conversations at once, but he was forced to focus on a tall young man with a sun-tanned face and what was certainly a more expensive inkwell suit than his own.

'Hello, I'm Tim Bealey! You're Rupert, aren't you? Maddy's fella. Glad you came. Got a drink? I hear you've left IMF and gone to *Midas*.' Bealey gave him a sharp look. 'I ride on his Lordship's coat tails – Maddy's ex, you know. Bair and Brady. Just met your boss! So you're the bloke that's going to come and see us! Profile of Bair and Blarney, as they call us!'

'Polly, darling!' Rupert turned to grab her. 'Did you know I'm staying with you tonight?'

'Maddy just told me!' The Hon 'Polly' Flinders, warm and cuddly and one thing to all men, with tangled blonde hair restrained by pushed-up black sunglasses, sipped her orange juice and dragged at a cigarette that had gone out. Tim Bealey flicked a lighter for her.

'Have you and Maddy split?'

'God, no! It's her purity line. Bella is staying with her tonight. She only told me today.'

'You can have the spare bed. There! One of the girls is with her Pa.'

'Where are you? I've no transport.'

'Right here in the square, sweety! You're forgetting.' Polly laughed and rolled her eyes. 'Tim is one of *my* ex's! Sadie's Daddy! Before he married Pam. I have, as a result, rights! Like parking rights.'

'Your first was Flinders though, wasn't it?'

'Sure – so I get called Polly, don't I, instead of Pauline!'

'And Tim's wife doesn't mind?'

'Pam? Hell, no! Here she comes. Pam, darling!'

'So much noise! Suchamucha people!' Pam Bealey also had piled hair, ebony with tendrils that fell over marble shoulders. She looked thoughtfully at Rupert with green cat's eyes. 'You're Maddy's fella! Why do we have so many people? I told Tim I can't get to talk to anybody!'

'Yes, I'm Rupert Potter. Thanks for including me.' But she wasn't interested. Her face, like the others, kept revolving round, like lights at a disco, to make sure they were not missing the ones that mattered. There were still sixteen conversations going on nearby. Rupert took a fresh glass of champagne that appeared alongside and tried to listen.

'As we say at *Midas*, it's what you know about who you know that matters. Did you say Senator Quiggs was on that Inquiry?'

'Darling Rudi simply brought this man in just when I was giving up, and he looked at it through a glass and telephoned Switzerland. Do you know Ruthy? She's vice-president of Arts Appreciation. Yes, that's my gallery!'

'How my eye got that way? I was just looking over a piece of modern sculpture at Christie's and it kind of struck out at me. Bill? He's gone to New York. Last night.'

'*Mon cher Rupertte!*' It was Gugi, close enough at hand to cut out the rest of the noise. 'If you are here, Maddy cannot be far be'ind!' His thin, neurotic face was almost hidden by a straw hat with corks dangling from the brim. 'So I go to Melbourne tomorrow. Do you like it? I find it is like wearing a veil. No wonder the ladies are so fond of veils. How do you say? *Allure!*'

'Alors!' cried Pam returning. 'Isn't French beautiful? Gugi, you must come with me and meet Tristram Tweed. He wants lots of discount Swiss francs for ski-ing.'

'Who is that prick?' a man with a golf club face asked no one in particular.

'Darling, *don't*! There's the Bealey child!'

25

A very beautiful small boy with a black velvet jacket and frilled jabot offered smoked salmon canapés.

'You must be Sean!'

'No, I'm Bladon.'

'Where are you going to school?' asked the golf club.

'Arlington House. Then Harrow.'

'A Banking House of which Harrow can be proud. B and B's!'

'Darling, sometimes you're quite clever!'

'Not original.'

'Jasper went to Eton, that's why.'

'Maddy, honestly darling, does the gallery *pay*? I mean pay?'

Rupert wondered whether it did people any harm to receive more or less sixteen programmes at once. Or whether the microchips in the brain were different. And eyes swivelled round, looking like radar scanners. He tried to ignore the people and with his own to see round the room. It was large, delicate in colour, with lit alcoves and a few expensive pictures. At the far end, the garden through neo-Georgian glass doors, also looked painted.

'Do you think manicured would be a kind word?' Someone close by was envious.

'Lacquered, darling!'

Rupert pushed out into the hall where the party had already spilled over, and where a few couples were already sitting on the broad staircase. Rupert found Maddy. She was busy.

'If you really think its original, I'll have a look at it. No, honest, I'd love to! Do you know Rupert? This is Gilly Denman. Her man has just walked out and gone to live in Mauritius so that he doesn't have to pay her anything. Isn't that great?'

'I shall have to live on what you can get for all my lovely treasures, Maddy sweet.'

'Sir Michael Denman. Diamond Denman?'

'Do you know him?'

'Pot works for *Midas*,' Maddy said absently. 'He knows all that stuff.' Her large eyes swept the room like questing lasers.

The deserted Gilly twirled so that her tiny, exquisite pointed face disappeared beneath a cloud of soft red hair. 'Do you see that man?'

'Darling, so many men!'

'Well, hear him then!'

'Rather a loud laugh for a beard,' Rupert said, remembering too late that Maddy had once told him not to make that sort of remark. 'Beards should be seen but not heard!'

'Do you think those gold pillars holding up the stairs are real?' Maddy cried.

'Twenty-two carat!' Tim Bealey, towing with him a waitress with a loaded tray, handed round glasses in exchange for empties and kissed Maddy. 'Simply terrific you look! How's the gallery game?'

'So-so.'

'We have a rich client at the bank coming to see you. He wanted a personal introduction to a top gallery. Of course Lord Bair has pointed him your way.'

'My ex is so kind!'

'You kissed Maddy when she came,' muttered Rupert who didn't like the way Bealey was holding Maddy's hand.

'We melted down Krugerrands to make the pillars,' Tim Bealey said. We hold them in escrow at the bank. Does Rupert *want* a kiss? There are lots of kissables here.'

'Who *is* the beard?' Maddy asked. 'He certainly seems to be doing the Georgie Porgie bit.'

'Who? Oh, that's Norman Crimp. He came with one of Pam's chums. Editor of *Groin*.' Tim Bealey looked sideways at Rupert. 'So many publishing people. That's why its so noisy.'

'You mean the magazine?' Maddy looked interested.

'Not for you, darling. *Groin* is the biggest circulation mag in that trade.'

'What trade?'

'He does full-frontals, but just of Debretts' best. No

27

pros. No models. And they queue up to get in.'

'Can I meet him?' The tiny, pointed face under the diaphanous red cloud looked up hopefully.

'Not really for you, Lady Denman.'

'Oh, get stuffed Tim Bealey. What does he pay?'

'Thousands, I believe.'

'Pot, darling, we must go!' Maddy was whispering now, close to his ear. 'Listen, I must get back. Will you bring Polly and Bella – if you see her – she has a car. Your Mr Epoch is coming, I was desperate for a single, and Gugi.'

'He can't eat anything. He's corked.'

'Don't be horrid to Gugi.' Maddy disappeared.

Uneasily Rupert moved closer to the pornographer with the beard. A kind of fascination gripped him. The man was positively surrounded by talent, bare shoulders, wide eyes, red mouths parted like beds of geraniums. How did he do it?

'It depends what you mean by pubic hair, of course.' The laugh was an acquired, cricketing padré's laugh. 'The camera chaps are very expert. And, of course, the whole *genre* has changed since Heff started it and the Calcutta vintage. If you deal in the top – in anything – pubics or whatever it is, well you get to be the best.'

'Did he say beast?'

'I can't hear in this din.'

'Base?'

'Bella!' Rupert saw and pounced on Maddy's pudding-faced ex-sister-in-law. 'Let's go – we're late for dinner!'

When they got back to Maddy's flat, Rupert, who had had little to drink, nevertheless felt light-headed. The drawing room, the fabulous view over the Thames, all the furniture seemed larger, the ceiling higher, the tangerine carpet brighter.

'Good God! You've moved some more pictures!' he said to Maddy who was now wearing a frilly apron.

'Gugi helped me. We put all the moderns in the big room. And some little ones that might sell in the dining room.'

'I didn't realise it was a business evening.'

'Every time it's a potential fixit evening, darling! Now get some drinks ready. Gugi is making his *sauce fantastique*. After all that's why I asked the Epoch to come. You can improve your shining future with him.'

'He doesn't drink and he hardly eats. I don't know why he comes out to dinner.'

'You're being a bore, Pot.'

'I'm just so *hungry*. Why does everyone have to eat at nearly midnight now? This isn't Spain. Couldn't we give High Teas? I'm faint. I'm hallucinating.'

'It's just post-cocktails, darling. Like jet-lag.'

Maddy returned to the kitchen and Rupert wandered onto the landing looking for the bathroom. Bemused by changed landmarks – a picture of Maddy's grandmother had become a rather Munch-like nude, sitting pregnant on a truckle bed – he pushed open a door, one hand at his trouser zip. It was his old bedroom. He backed out instantly, mostly because Bella in a black petticoat, was squirting lacquer on her hair and screamed at him.

In the kitchen, when she joined her ex-sister-in-law, she said: 'You can't possibly marry him, you know.'

'Pot?'

'Is that what you call him? Do grow up, darling! Desmond always said you were a child wife. Couldn't take anything seriously.'

Lady Bair looked at her former husband's sister with suddenly bleak eyes. She put dishes into a warmer and slammed the door. 'After your own disastrous little marriage, darling, I will take anything you say on the subject with authority! There, that's everything. I hear people arriving. How is Desmond's *ménage* anyway?'

'At the moment somewhere in South Africa, checking out her diamond mines or selling some hotels or something.'

'Do you think they play Monopoly in the evening together? Come on, I want you to meet a darling old Duke who's coming. I think he owns all of two chicken coops in Leinster. Then there's a trade-union MP who might buy some *objets*. Just peep through the hatch.

Hasn't my Nancy made the table lovely?' But Bella was offended, flounced away, and Maddy checked the table alone.

How she loved dinner parties! It was an empty world without them. The great Game, home or away, people, food, ambiance and the lovely tingly tension, the feeling that she looked beautiful, the men who told her she did. It was like a tiny first night play. She peeped at herself in the little mirror kept in the kitchen. There were the fancy dress parties when you were small, a guessing game of charades. Of course this evening was a shadow of what it had been when she had first learned to do it for Desmond, at the two big houses, and with the help of servants. Even that had changed in such short time. That little dago princess, for all her tiaras, didn't even care for entertaining, from what she had heard. Rupert jumped at her by the drinks table.

'Maddee, you are having secret thoughts and looking unbelievably witch-like.' He gave her a whispery kiss on her ear and pulled the earring off with his teeth.

'Give it back!' He palmed the earring into her hand as a visitor came down the passage.

'Eamon, have you met Mr Potter? May I introduce him?'

The ancient aristocrat turned a craggy smile in all directions, wavering white eyebrows and gently clawing the air as he kissed Maddy slowly and carefully on both cheeks.

'Bella, my former sister-in-law, you know! Now this is Sir Reginald Sharp, who manages all of the sewage workers' union, so if you ever want to go underground, he's your man! My dearest friend, Gugi Mizzli, who's just going to fill your glass again and Polly Flinders you know.'

'Spent the night with Polly once!' said the Duke happily.

'Eamon the demon lover!' Polly cried and took the Duke's arm and walked him round. The Duke was glad to be introduced to people all over again.

'I hear you're called Midas,' he said to Curt Epoch.

'Wish I was.'

Everybody was happily placed for dinner. Maddy waved pale hands with a finger pointing downwards like the conductor of a small orchestra, and without fuss the round table was seated. She never needed a plan, nor even hesitated. The candle flames in the central silver holders fluttered, everyone drew their napkins over their laps, the first course of shrimps in garlic sauce shone in their ramekins with the white wine that had already been poured. Maddy was trying it quietly, knowing wines better than anyone else present.

'Always like a round table,' the Duke mumbled. 'No damn nonsense about who's at the head. What do I say to the lady on t'other side?'

'Ruthy,' said Maddy shortly. 'She's my vice president.'

'I have so many vices.'

Eamon ought to do better than that, but Maddy's attention was being distracted. It was Sir Reginald on her other side and she felt his hand on her knee under the tablecloth. 'Darling, have you got any tomato ketchup to go with these shrimps?' She knew he had been hopeful, since they had met at a Foyles Literary lunch. Shortly after that his wife had eloped with a member of a visiting Australian sewage delegation.

'Eat up your nice dinner, Reg! We haven't any ketchup.' She looked round the table and smiled brightly. It really was a successful table and the next course was easy. Nancy and the hired help were dependable. Audrey had gone to bed without fuss. She had been admired by several men at the drinks party the other night. And now, across the table, Rupert was looking at her over a raised glass. He knew she was happy. Maddy laughed, the young witch's laugh, as she raised her own glass. Darling Pot! He really looked quite handsome in his ink blue with the bow tie. Tomorrow night he would be back in her bed. Neatly she speared her shrimps, one by one.

'Lucky bastard!' said Sir Reginald almost inaudibly, in his flat Balham accent.

'Do you know about pictures, Eamon?' Maddy asked

brightly. 'Gugi hung these only this evening!'

'Didn't paint them, did he?' asked the aged peer. 'Bloody awful mess all of them, if you'll allow me. What happened to the others you had? Sold 'em I suppose. Got to pay taxes like the rest of us. Sewage, you said was his line?'

Maddy emptied her glass and smiled even more brightly. The evening was going to be a little harder work after all.

Rupert sitting between Ruthy and Polly had already come to that conclusion. Curt Epoch on Polly's far side was drinking Perrier water, and spoke across her.

'I made a list for you!'

A business evening, Maddy had said. He tried to look interested and, as a large casserole had arrived on the serving table, this was not difficult.

'Sent it round to the office this evening. I fixed the interview with the Bair Brady outfit. Give it the *Midas* treatment!'

'The way we've got the town halls, they can't move,' Sir Reginald was saying. 'Tied hand and foot.'

'How's that?'

There was a sort of snuffling noise between the two men where Ruthy was crouched in her chair. Rupert was reminded of the dormouse at Alice in Wonderland's tea party. Suddenly Ruthy's chair was pushed back and she was gone, scuttling unhappily for the door, choking wretchedly.

'Tied hand and foot,' repeated Sir Reginald.

Curt Epoch waved away the steaming plate put before him. 'Thanks, I don't eat that much. Just let me pass. Maybe she's not well.'

Maddy Bair, who had seen Ruthy go, took back the plate. She had been far too confident far too early. From the other side she felt the claw-like fingers of the Duke fumbling for a suspender button through her dress.

'Always said you were the prettiest damn woman in London! I suppose that sewage fellow has made a pass at your little friend and she didn't like it?'

When Rupert stood with Polly Flinders under the street

32

lights on the silent Embankment he felt tired.

'How do we travel? Or do we go to sleep on this bench?'

'The river is beautiful. Look at it! Water, boats, lights! Silver! Black! Purple sky, moon, colour signs, fairy bridges. A stage set!'

'Polly! Please! It's two o'clock. I'll try and get a taxi.'

'Scooter, sweetheart. Little folding Felix. Here, look! Put your bag on here.'

His arms round her waist, his head resting on her shoulder, Rupert slept until they reached Chelsea Square again. He dreamed he was flying on a bumble bee.

Staggering about under more street lighting, he stared wearily at the small single-decker bus parked between a row of cars at the kerb. It, too, was gently technicoloured like the Embankment view.

'Home sweet home!'

Polly took his hand and climbed two steps, opening a door opposite the driving side with a key that hung on a gold chain round her neck. Inside it was dark and warm with interesting smells and the quiet sound of sleeping children breathing. A tiny bulkhead light burned by the driving seat. Sleepily, it was almost familiar – like being in his boat.

'There you are – it's the top berth that side.' Polly was pushing him up. 'And listen! Don't get up when we move in the morning, unless you want to. Two of the kids have got to be in school by eight-thirty. Then we'll have breakfast in Battersea Park.'

2

Once again afloat, again a dappled, moving light pattern on the low ceiling above his face. But also the sound of an uneven motor, the feel of a hard berth. Surely afloat.

Then Rupert heard the Hon Polly Flinders, felt the bus swing hard round a corner and heard her cry. From her helm in the bows came a stream of instructions to various offspring to get up, get dressed, get fed.

It was the moments in bed, first thing in the morning, when Rupert remembered the sounds. How it had been with mad Marge. Two kids, two jobs, mad marriage, *au pairs*, no *au pair*, no job, no marriage. Marge had gone back to South Africa to ride horses, the children with her, and finally re-married. Rupert had slept with the *au pair* for consolation, then she had gone. The IMF seemed a nice alternative way of living, because you were not supposed to have a home life. Only a briefcase.

So perhaps with Polly Flinders, who had four children by three fathers and otherwise only a bus.

'Where are we?'

'Battersea Park. One of the capital's nicer parking lots! Free, friendly, yogi bear, rangers! Just right for breakfast now the kids have gone.'

'Bananas?' said Rupert, looking round from his bunk.

'And coffee. And as it's a nice morning we can put the canvas chairs outside.'

He rolled out of his berth and into a pair of socks and trousers to see Polly's back as she hauled on the hand-brake. Outside the windows, daylight, trees, the River Thames. Familiar, but different looking from the opposite bank.

'I'll do that,' said Rupert. He put his feet into shoes and rummaged in his overnight bag. 'Are there washing arrangements? By the way, did you sleep OK?'

'Sure, always do.' Polly was switching on an electric kettle. 'Jelly Bean had some sort of nightmare about his Dad, but that's normal. I thought it might have woken you. Say listen – the razor plug is on the blink. Or at least, so I was told.' Polly giggled. That was one of the nice things about Polly. She did still giggle. 'Here's some hot water.'

Rupert tried the plug and it was as reported. 'I must say you do keep a marvellous hotel, Polly – much better than a lot I've been in. Looking glass, lights, comfortable beds, hot coffee, terrace, TV, fridge, ice in the drinks, infinitely variable view.'

'I do like tug boats, don't you?' Polly flashed him her grateful, warm smile. 'They're sort of a comfortable shape.' She was already dressed: Russian suede boots and cossack breeches, full blouse and head scarf. With one hand she poured the rest of the hot water into mugs and with the other hitched up a bra strap.

'I dropped that girl of mine off to do some shopping. Said I'd see her here in an hour. What do you do today?'

'I've got the rather weird job of interviewing Maddy's ex,' said Rupert. 'For *Midas*. He's chairman of Bair Brady.'

They sat outside on the two upright canvas chairs and had coffee, rolls and bananas. Pigeons and a few sparrows pecked around on the grass that surrounded them. The river was busy and various craft passed peacefully before them in both directions. A breeze stirred the trees over-head. A middle-aged jogger in a bright blue track suit panted past.

'Maddy's well rid of him. Whether she'll have you is another matter,' Polly said.

'I've only met him once or twice – he came to pick up Audrey one evening, and Maddy made me stay. I don't suppose he'll remember. He's that sort.'

'Won't Maddy give you some leads, or whatever you call them?'

'I wouldn't try. She's a bit clammed up about previous life. As a matter of fact, I think I'll stroll across there now,' said Rupert. 'It's only a walk across the bridge to the other side and I think I must get into another suit. I expect Maddy's already away with bitch-Bella who was to catch an early plane.'

'Yeah, I must say I don't get the you-or-Bella bit. And I will add you do look more like a real international journalist, not having shaved and without a tie. I like it!'

Polly gave him a buttery kiss, holding her coffee mug in one hand and putting the other on his shoulder.

'Remember the old bus always needs a conductor!'

To Rupert's surprise, Maddy was still having breakfast in the kitchen. She was wearing the tangerine house coat with large white flowers on it. She seemed pleased to see him.

'Darling Pot!' She kissed him exactly where Polly had. 'You smell greasy. Did Polly give you breakfast?'

'Coffee and sympathy.'

'Smoked salmon here – thanks to Nancy. Would you like a fried egg on it?'

'Amazing!'

'Cognac in the coffee?'

'Darling!' said Rupert. 'Has Bella gone?'

'Does this sound her kind of breakfast?'

'No,' said Rupert. 'But I want to ask you about your ex-husband. So I need to know his sister isn't lurking.'

'I never tell the Press anything.'

'I am not the Press. I am your lover. No! I am your suitor. We are in fact engaged. The *Daily Express* said so.'

'By the time you're through the bathroom and look

36

more as though you had spent the night with me and not with Polly Flinders, I might accept the idea.'

'You want it every which-way!'

When Rupert returned to the kitchen, Maddy was folding back the pages of her favourite tabloid. She smiled the beautiful witch's smile. 'I see that Polly Flinders is in the news again as it happens. How does that breakfast *surprise* look?'

Maddy reached out a pale arm to put the plate in front of him. The tangerine house coat slid aside and revealed a meringue of breast with pink cherry tip.

'Life with you is all *surprise*,' Rupert said gratefully.

'Sin Mother in Commons Car Park Rumpus,' Maddy read out, closing the house coat.

'Polly told the magistrate that having four offspring by three different fathers was not a sin, even if parking their mobile residence in the House of Commons yard was breaking the law.'

'What was she doing at the House of Commons?'

'Trying to hand over one of the children to its father – what's his name? Nigel something. He was on a late sitting.'

'Where did the Squeals on Wheels park last night?'

'Outside the Bealey's. He's another father. Pre the Flinders, of course. Then Battersea Park.'

Maddy was reading something with intense interest. Rupert moved about and waited for a piece of toast to pop up. He liked Maddy's large, sunny kitchen more than any of the other rooms. Even so there were a few disconcerting things about it. On the windowsill, a coloured fretwork screen meant to resemble a Californian Morn with the sun rising like a great yellow spider. There was pop corn on the table, pop art on the walls and pop music on the radio. Even the toaster popped too enthusiastically and hurled its contribution to the floor.

'That damn thing!' Maddy said absentmindedly. She licked a finger and spun sheets of newsprint. 'Can't you fix it, Pot?'

'I don't think one can fix toasters.' Rupert sat down.

'You live with them. They're like some kind of women – unreliable, mysterious, essential, functional – you push something in and something pops out after a while. Amazing!'

'Clever Pot!' Maddy looked up and gave him a long, strange, sad stare. She shook her short dark hair so that the fringe swung over her green eyes. 'Sometimes I think you're wasted. On *Midas* certainly. On me probably. Oh, Pot, what are we to do? The gallery isn't making, you know, and you're not making enough. But I'm happy and you're happy. And there's my stupid ex-husband and his princess with millions and they're unhappy.'

'I told you, I'm going to meet him today. It's Epoch's idea. He wants a profile of Bair Brady and has fixed up for me to go along. He sort of hinted, here the other evening, that BB are maybe in some sort of difficulty and *Midas* magazine will be on the ball with a ready piece.'

'I don't think I like your boss. He's a scheming, Wall Street high-priest, meddling with that damn magazine. In a way, I'm sorry I helped you get the job.'

'I don't like the idea of spending time with your husband. When I look at him I shall think of him making love to you and breathing on you. And Rolling About!'

'*Darling*!' Maddy looked at him over the rim of her coffee cup with more interest than understanding. 'A barbaric, jealous, silly sort of Pot! When do you see Desmond?'

'At eleven-thirty.'

'Tell him I hate him. And I adore you.'

'Does he really know about us?'

'I think so. Not so that he knows it's you and me, together sort of in bed.' Maddy loved playing fake shy. She blushed beautifully, and fluttered her eyelashes. The house coat began to slip again.

'How about *now* ?' Rupert said.

'*Darling*! I can't – I've just got to be at the gallery!' She began to get round the table.

'Maddy. I love you!' cried Rupert. 'Let's get married this week!'

'Potty Pot! Lovely Pot!' She whirled from the table, evading his reaching hand, and out of the kitchen. He heard her scampering along the passage, shutting the bathroom door.

There are taxi drivers who are not quite sure where Prawn Passage EC2 is. They may pretend that it does not exist. The newer, younger ones. The older cabbies, like a lot of people in the City of London, know Prawn Passage only because Bair Brady are there. The bank's new offices, rebuilt after World War Two's blitz, are sizeable. There is not much room for anyone else in the cramped city lane. A small café, a shop selling regimental ties and that is about all. But a great number of people all over the world who did business with Bair Brady, merchant bankers, themselves lived in some very quaint places.

It was one of the older cab drivers who got Rupert to Prawn Passage without trouble, and pulled up in front of the bank's entrance with its sweep of stone steps and tall columns. Rupert started to work even as he paid the driver.

'How d'you think this place got its name?'

'Dunno.' The cabby glanced down with a watery eye at his tip. 'Near to Billingsgate, ain't it? Used to get the prawn and whelk sellers down this bit, see? You got Hake Lane and Cod Street. Mind you, this isn't the old bank. Got clobbered during the war.' The elderly driver coughed and croaked and chuckled as he rang up his meter. 'All a bit of a fishy business if you ask me! Prawns and banking!'

Rupert turned to face the wide stone steps. At the top, a porter in thick blue serge uniform swung open the door. Inside, a dozen or more were grouped around the reception desk, watchful while at ease, like a naval gun crew. There was, in fact, a small and ancient cannon in the hall to add to the effect. One of the walls was plain blue-red brickwork and hung with tapestries of ancient seafaring scenes. The general design was early Georgian, with white paint, plain pillars and, in the background, a fine mahogany staircase with a curling banister.

Rupert's eye, trained to bank interiors by his time with IMF looked at all this curiously. It was different. Oddly it was an atmosphere in which he felt at home.

'Did you wish to see someone, sir?' The leader of the gun crew had brass tabs on his lapels and a red sea-faring face.

'Mr Bealey.'

'Misther Bealey!' The senior gunner glanced down at the dim light behind his mahogany desk top that was like a miniature ship's poop. The slight Irish accent was a proper part of the antecedents of Bair Brady, Rupert realised. 'Tom, take the gentleman up to Conference Three!'

'Will you come this way, sir!'

Rupert followed the brisk blue uniform along a stone flagged passage into a small, trim elevator.

Upstairs, where they alighted in the corridor, there were elegantly suited young men with long hair and pale poet's faces, clever looking older women and younger ones who might easily have appeared in the beagling features of *Country Life* rather than *Midas*.

Rupert was put in a small room with an oval table laid out with notepads and sharpened pencils and a blank view out of the window over a courtyard. On the wall one lonely painting looked like a foetus. Was it a symbolic prawn?

Behind him the door opened and Tim Bealey slid in soundlessly. He shook Rupert's hand limply. They sat down.

'Listen old chap! We've known each other – through Maddy. Well, you see Lord Bair doesn't like the Press. No, not at all!'

Tim Bealey in daylight still had a pale and amorous look, as though he belonged more to the poets than the gunners. His suit was black mohair and he wore a bright purple tie. His tawny eyes shifted unhappily.

'Is he going to see me?'

Tim Bealey picked up one of the sharpened pencils

and broke the point on his pad. 'Oh, no! Don't get me wrong. He's going to see you. What I mean is, God help us if it goes wrong.'

'What goes wrong?'

'It's not you I'm worried about, it's his lordship. He doesn't like any of the media. Somehow your publisher – what's his name – Pockmark? – he got at him. I don't know how. I'm detailed off to handle the media here. So if I could see the piece before you send it in –'

'Not allowed,' said Rupert firmly. 'It's the one thing Curt Epoch – that's his name by the way – won't have. No censorship.'

'Oh Lord!'

'Do you think,' Rupert paused, 'Desmond – I mean Lord Bair – knows about Maddy and me?'

Tim Bealey looked thoughtful. The tawny eyes flickered. 'We don't need to remind him, do we? Now look, I've brought you all the glossy bits about BB.' He slid papers and brochures across the oval table. 'That's got all the basic stuff, and I expect you've done some homework. Now I know what you fellows want: colour, inside stuff, profiles, personalities. Right?'

'This crest?' said Rupert, looking at the first folder.

'The famous shamrock. Those who don't love us call it the three balls. Sign of the usual business. The money-lenders. Any cracks about that hurt Lord Bair.'

'What about Brady?'

'Dead. Fell out of a helicopter some years ago. Thought it was down when it was still up. Motto, never drink Guinness and play with the oxygen mask at the same time.'

'Can I use that?'

'No! Listen – there are younger ones, nephews and so on, coming along. There's a lot of family at BB, and the old man will be glad to tell you about that. The thing is, don't ask him too much about the business. I can introduce you to other directors for that. Know what I mean?'

A telephone on a side table began winking a small green light.

'Three!' said Bealey. 'Yes, he is. I'll bring him up,' he rang off. 'There you go!'

It was a different elevator, but again had one of the uniformed men with the moneylenders crest on his lapels. Repeated, Rupert noticed, in a pattern along the mahogany walls of the passage which was lined with oil paintings of rainy Irish landscapes, alternating with pictures of ancient sailing vessels on unfailingly stormy seas.

'This approach is known as making the stormy passage,' Tim Bealey said helpfully. 'You could use that I suppose. Anecdote? Colour?' Another green light shone above splendid double mahogany doors in front of them.

Inside, at two unevenly facing desks, sat two middle-aged ladies with strong faces, somehow giving Rupert the impression they were rowing a boat together. The light over the inner door was red.

'You'll have to wait a minute. This is Jane Faughsquar, Lord Bair's personal assistant. Ten years in the Wrens,' said Tim. 'Colour, anecdote. What are the signals, Commodore?'

'Fair on the whole I would say, bar rising. The chairman has a fully submerged lunch, so maybe something good is on.'

'In-house code,' said Bealey shortly, 'that means a deal is in the offing, but client requests strict secrecy so any director is bound by that and works like a submarine until he's allowed to break surface. No questions asked. Green – in we go!'

Lord Desmond Bair advanced on them across the deep blue carpet with a powerful, silent movement. If he recognised Rupert he was not saying so.

'Mr Midas, I believe?'

'Potter, sir.'

Lord Bair looked suspicious. He stood for a moment with his head jutting forward. It was a strong, patrician profile rendered imperfect by a redeemingly pudgy nose. 'I've met you before! I know everybody in this business. You sit there!' He poked Rupert in the chest with a blunt forefinger. 'Tim, you're there. Now!' He went round to the other side of a vast expanse of dark polished wood desk and sank into a huge, buttoned-back chair. 'Shoot! Isn't that what you chaps say?'

Rupert did a quick look round the collection of desk-top items between them. Cigar boxes, calculators, ink-wells, pieces of nautical brass work, pennants on masts, photographs of yachts in silver frames.

'Not shoot?' Lord Bair produced a pair of half-spectacles with brass frames and put them on. He pulled at the bottom of his waistcoat and leaned back. 'Shoot is for the TV chaps. That's it!'

'Potter has come to do a useful report on BB for *Midas Magazine*, sir!'

'I know that, Tim! I hope I know the difference between a journal and a television set. A lot of my younger directors think I'm not really with it on some of the stuff, and of course it's true.' Lord Bair looked at Rupert with lowered eyebrows over the half glasses. 'I can't keep up with everything! That's why Tim here looks after you chaps. Who's Eunuch?'

There was a stunned silence.

'Epoch,' Rupert said uncertainly. 'You mean my employer? The president. He owns the magazine.'

'Well, he thought of sending you along. Foreign. Clever little bugger in his way. I don't trust him, but he's useful! So what do I say to you, eh? Scoop?'

'We'd like that,' Rupert said. 'Anything exclusive, new, different. The way you see the merchant banking world. Do you read *Midas*?'

'Of course I bloody well do!' roared Lord Bair. 'Have to spend half my day reading the bumph that pours into this office.'

'I see *Midas* on your desk, sir.' Tim Bealey, who had arranged to have it put there, nodded. Lord Bair searched around amidst the twinkling silver and brass until he found the bulky, gold-covered current issue of the magazine.

To his surprise, Rupert felt a strange sense of affinity breaking through his carefully pre-prepared indifference

43

to the man. Maddy as his wife. Quick, gay, gregarious, crisp, trendy, swinging Maddy. She must have been like a pilot fish in front of a shark. There was definitely something sharklike about Lord Bair's mouth and chin. Quickly he checked any further thoughts that would lead to contemplation of a physical relationship.

'How do I see the merchant banking rôle?'

'As a catalyst, sir?' It was Tim again.

'How's that?'

'The job of making money work to achieve other people's aims and ambitions.' Tim was working hard. 'Here, abroad! Getting it together, the big conglomerates, the third world!'

'Exactly!' Lord Bair scowled. 'Not so keen on the third world bit, though. Too many of these black beggars coming round with the hat these days. Banking Bolsheviks!' said Lord Bair, counting on pudgy fingers, 'Blacks! Buggery in the basement and Bats in the Belfry. Wogs! Japs! It's all going mad, the whole world! Who controls the highest world councils? Wogs and blacks! And, by God, they're beginning to control the money supply now! I can tell you –'

'Desmond!' Tim Bealey's face had turned a suet colour.

'Millions of pounds going in and out of this place every day and the world like a bloody inflatable raft in a force ten!' roared Lord Bair.

'Colour and anecdote,' murmured Rupert, who had started making notes.

'How about the BB history, sir?' Tim Bealey said faintly.

'Started with Castlereagh,' Lord Bair said grandly. 'Remember Castlereagh? Chief Secretary for Ireland at the time of the Union, Foreign Sec at the Treaty of Vienna. My great-great-grandfather was of service to him.'

'All in the BB brochure, chairman!'

'Ah, but it doesn't say he was the most hated man in Britain at the time, but he was! The real prophets are always misunderstood at the time as Epoch Powell said to me the other day.'

'Enoch?' Rupert said mildly.

There was a knock at the big double doors which opened from outside to allow the entry of Miss Faughsquar carrying an ice bucket with a gold and green bottle neck protruding. Her number two carried a tray with three large glasses.

'Ah!' Lord Bair looked happier. He removed the half-spectacles. 'We generally find a spot of the eye-brightener useful at this sort of time! It's an old BB tradition. Tim, you can do the pouring.'

Miss Faughsquar retired with her assistant and Lord Bair raised his glass. 'Damnation to our enemies!'

'The original BB toast!'

Tim Bealey emptied half his glass. 'What about your real love, chairman. Down to the sea in ships?'

'Know about sailing at all, Potter?' Lord Bair had emptied his glass in one.

'I like messing about with them,' Rupert admitted. 'I've a small gaff-rig boat on moorings at Beaulieu.'

'Well I'm damned!' For the first time Lord Bair looked properly at him. He put on the half-spectacles and turned round one of the silver picture frames on the desk. 'There she is, Nicholson forty-five! I keep her at my place at Beaulieu. You must come and do a bit of crewing with us. Pity you didn't mention it earlier. We could have had an interesting chat.' He picked up a brass bound marine chronometer among the flotsam and jetsam on the desk then put it down. 'Alas, I must be off!'

'Diving?' Rupert asked innocently as he and Tim also rose.

Lord Bair stopped in full flight across the blue carpet. His bulky body still, the heavy head turned. 'Who told you that bit?' He glared at Tim Bealey. Then the big double doors with the engraved three-leaved symbol swung shut behind him.

'Have some more champagne,' said Tim Bealey. 'You know, I really think I shall have to insist I see this piece you're doing.'

At the gloomy entrance to the bank, under the neo-

Georgian pillars, the driver waited with one of the younger porters.

'Where's the guv'nor going then?'

'Hilton Hotel.' The driver, whose uniform was similar to the porters but included a peaked cap pulled down to his nose, looked sideways at him. 'You new here?'

'Three months.'

'Best no questions asked at Bair Brady!'

'All right, be like that! Just the Hilton don't sound like his lordship's style. No more than that motor car. Bleeding old black Ford! Should be a Rolls.'

'When you've been in merchant banking a bit longer, my lad, you'll know its horses for courses, see? We got eight cars. There's Rollses for Arabs and Datsuns for Nips, see? And my guess is, his lordship is going to the Hilton to see some Yanks. If it was big, they'd be comin' here for lunch, up in the dining room. But sometimes it starts small, see? They like hotel business, the Yanks. Take a suite and think it impresses him. Watch it, son! Here he comes!'

The young porter swung smartly round. The glass doors revolved. The driver ran down the steps and opened the rear door of the car. Lord Bair got inside, the chauffeur slid in front, and silently, motorised and isolated, the chairman of Bair Brady moved into the outside world. A submarine slipping from sight into a sea of traffic.

At the Park Lane Hilton, the doorman tipped his delicately shaded fawn top hat as Lord Bair hurried into the shadows of the hall. Inside, he paused only to watch the car go. When he was certain that it was round Hyde Park Corner, he re-emerged, breathing rather heavily.

'Cab, sir?' enquired the top hat, who had been trained to express no surprise at anything. He waved across to the waiting rank.

Inside the taxi, Lord Bair leaned over to the glass partition and gave an address in Earls Court.

He paid off the taxi at the junction with Cromwell Road and walked the remaining blocks past houses of fading gentility and peeling white paint. One or two had been turned into pretentious little hotels, with replanted young trees along the pavement. He turned off into a quieter road, and slipped into a porch where he rang an illuminated bell.

A buzzer sounded and let him in. The hall inside was empty as usual, and he mounted the dark, carpeted staircase, puffing by the time he reached the second floor. On the darkened landing another door was already open, the gap of faint pink lamplight filled by a strong, upright bulky figure.

'So! You are late!' As always, Lord Bair felt his insides churn at the flat, slow guttural voice. He kissed the plump, well-ringed hand that was offered for tribute and heard her close the door behind him with chain and bolts. These sounds, too, were familiar, pleasantly exciting, anticipatory.

The vast bottom, swaying gently above the black leather thigh boots, led the way into a living room where the windows were heavily curtained and the pink-shaded lamps sent her shadow, hugely magnified, swinging round the empty walls. Lord Bair took off jacket, tie and waistcoat.

'You vill kneel!'

'Frau Drogger! Madam! A drink first, I beg you!'

But she had already picked up a plaited, black leather whip from the small table with its clutter of other interesting items. He got down to his knees with slow care.

'You hef bin a very naughty boy, I think!'

'Oh, very bad, madam! So very bad!'

The fat woman advanced with mincing gait. The swollen white thighs that bulged above the patent leather stopped within inches of his face. Tremblingly Lord Bair began to kiss them. First one then the other. Looking up in between, he saw vast black knickers surmounted by twin leather-covered domes. Through peephole fronts the nipples protruded like football inflators, Lord Bair thought, with daring irreverence.

'You hef bin proud! Vicket! Now you vill be humple, small!'

He licked and kissed and slurruped feverishly at the dumpling flesh. The face above looking down at him with satisfaction, was undoubtedly hideous; a swollen white mask with a scarlet slash for mouth, eyelashes like spiders' legs and a golden mass of spun and lacquered hair. A spider! She was a sort of spider! And he was a fly, powerless in her sticky web.

'Now you get your drink! Komm!' She pulled him forward on his knees by his hair to the table. The glass was filled from a flat, round bottle. 'Cognac!' The fat witch's cackle made the man on his knees shiver inside, although the liquor, quickly downed, burned most comfortingly. His first wife, Madeleine, would have a laugh like that as she got older. Strange, the thoughts that went through his mind at such moments.

'I get cognac from other client!'

They both knew what was to follow the fortifying cognac. The laugh was now darkly sinister. Frau Drogger loved to speak of other clients. It made them all so jealous. The whip cracked and snaked around the well upholstered rear. The wrist cuffs were snapped on and he was pulled upright over the table.

'I have been a wicked boy, Madam!'

'Yes, yes! So I tie you to the table!' He felt the whole weight of the footballs and the soft, fat spider body across him. Now she was breathing rapidly. 'Panz *down*! Now ve are ready! Tell me you must be punished!'

'I need it! I have been proud and overbearing!'

The plump and beringed palm fell with regular and professional skill on the noble rump, followed by the strap and presently again, the long whip. So that Lord Bair, at last alternately bellowing and pleading, felt the strange relief of being the dominated one; the pain and pleasure syndrome that took him back to the beginning, to Irish nannies and governesses, warm laps and strong arms and the first of the scents and sounds of submission. Before his world was full of burdens and chairmanship and responsibility, guilt, remorse and boredom.

3

At Dolphin Square it was drinks party time again. Maddy Bair's drawing room overlooking the Thames showed the sky over London at its evening best. Artistically shredded, citrus yellow clouds, deep purple, yet sunlit above the tall chimneys and high-rise blocks on the south bank.

Maddy on the tangerine sofa, kicked off her shoes and tucked up her unmatchable legs.

'Pure Turner,' she said happily. 'Don't you think so, Pot darling? Let's stop looking and have a private drink now, because they will all be late as usual. There's a box of gin in the airing cupboard by the loo rolls. We shall need another bottle.'

'You've changed the pictures again,' Rupert said sadly. He had just come in. 'That big one there, it was in the dining room?'

'Wasted. I love it. Sort of Walt-Disney-Turner.'

'My God, what's that?' Rupert recoiled in genuine horror from a new *objet d'art* on top of the red-lacquered Chinese chest of drawers. It was a photograph of Maddy's daughter, Audrey, framed by a ring doughnut. But it appeared to be a real doughnut. He saw on closer inspection it was made of plastic, but the inner ring of red jam was very realistic as were the sugar grains.

'Mummy sent it!' Maddy said rather distantly. 'Sweet – sort of.'

'Gin,' Rupert said, moving on determindly. 'Lots of it!' He went out by the drinks table, remembering, as he took bearings from another repositioned picture, that the airing cupboard was down the passage to the left of the bathroom.

When he returned, there were already two guests in the drawing room, brought in by Nancy who acted as door maid for drinks parties. It was Ruthy from the gallery and a sharp-bearded man in a pale mustard-coloured suit who laughed continuously. He stood in front of the windows as though he had painted the view, stroking his Van Dyke beard. He looked vaguely familiar.

'Norman Crimp. The Editor of *Groin* – you've met him. And, Pot darling,' it was Maddy's warning voice, 'be nice to him. He's a regular bread cheque at the gallery these days.' She helped him put ice in the drinks.

'You have such odd clients. How does he afford your stuff?'

'Rolling in it.' Maddy's made-up cheeks glowed in the technicolour light coming through the windows. 'Buys stuff he can salt away, small precious pieces. Gugi takes some of them to Swiss gnomes for him. Rather a frighten-ed man, Mr C. But so would you be if you worked for the lady who owns the rag, I gather. But she can't do without him, so she pays. How lucky you are that I fixed you up with dear little Curt Epoch!' Sometimes Maddy was con-descending.

'Darling, do you know Sir Wilfred Poult?'

Rupert shook hands with a stooping, grey-haired man who had small eyes closely set on either side of a thin nose, and who withdrew his hand quickly from Rupert's and used it to adjust a drooping bow tie.

'Wilf is *the* expert in oriental stuff, Chinese, Indian!'

'Maddy's introductions are an exquisite blend of fact and infatuation.' Sir Wilfred accepted a drink from the tray that Nancy was now bringing round. Rupert saw Gugi arriving still wearing the Australian diggers' hat with corks on strings dangling from the brim. With him was Rudi, in a velvet smoking jacket, looking like a particularly well fed seal, kissing Maddy's hand while Gugi sought to perform on her cheek through the cork curtain.

'She has so many followers. Are you one?' Sir Wilfred's question was said so wearily that Rupert accepted it.

'Are you?' It was no more than fair.

'In a way. I work for the British Museum. A sort of fossil. Maddy to me is a kind of Roman Goddess incarnate.'

'Is it possible to find sexy fossils?' The mustard suit and Van Dyke beard of the editor of *Groin* was suddenly with them.

'What's a sexy fossil?' Maddy's daughter, Audrey, was in their midst offering smoked salmon on cocktail sticks.

'Another gin and tonic for me, darling,' Norman Crimp said to her.

'They start at her age now.'

'Of course. Sex is the beginning of everything.' The thin, worldly face of Sir Wilfred Poult looked bored. 'What have *you* in mind for instance? Besides sex, I mean?'

'Business. Would you do me a fossil article for *Groin*? Illustrated. Say two thousand words. If it was OK, we'd pay about two grand.' Norman Crimp's voice and manner had all the prescience of the editor of the *Church Times*.

'Done,' said Sir Wilf, simply. 'What sort of illustrations?'

'Fossilised pubic hair?' The editor waved a limp hand. 'Or any other sort of fossilised fornication. How about you?' He turned to Rupert. 'I asked Maddy about you the other day!' His laugh was the splendid, deep, clean-living-cricketer kind. 'She said you were just the chap to write a piece for us on the money scene. Copulation means Calculation! She even gave me the title! Very bright, Lady Bair. I like it! You edit *Midas* over here, is that right? My publisher, Tracy Flip, would like to meet you. She has some problems on international business, as she calls it, and doesn't trust anyone. Me least of all! If you were one of our contributors she would automatically want to see you, and you might make an extra bob or two for advice. How about tomorrow?'

'I could manage the morning,' Rupert said.

'What is *Groin*?' Sir Wilfred managed to contort his face and so tilt his nose that it looked as though he might be winking, and thus could be forgiven if it was a foolish question.

'I often ask myself!' Crimp's laugh was getting monotonous. 'But I'm only the editor. It's the biggest selling men's magazine in the world.'

'Good Lord!' Sir Wilfred now looked at Rupert. 'Did you know this?'

'It seems most men in the world want to screw the best. They fancy themselves in the genuine Rolls Royce class. Leave the rabbits to *Playboy*. We don't want to reduce the essential female to nursery cuddles. We give our readers the aristos. Let them eat cake!'

'Did you say two thousand pounds?' said Sir Wilfred.

Rupert, having checked that the offices of *Groin* were off Curzon Street, decided to walk there. He crossed Trafalgar Square, weaving through the tourists and overfed pigeons. From his column, Nelson stared down Whitehall and Rupert wondered what sort of blind eye he might turn to what he saw in that direction now. The sunlight gleamed on the restored elegance of the Carlton House terraces and by turning right he came out into Piccadilly and so through Old Park Lane to Shepherd Market.

There was no name on the door of *Groin's* offices to distinguish the entrance and Rupert went up a short flight of stone steps and pushed through glass doors where a pink plastic panel merely said: Reception.

In a dusty room full of parcels, a dumpy girl in a hand-knitted pullover sat at an electric typewriter, which she continued to peck at while Rupert looked around hopefully for glamour and excitement.

'I've come to see Mr Crimp! He's expecting me.'

52

'Uppa stars,' said the girl. Plainly *Groin* had its functional side. She had a spotty face and wore thick glasses. 'Third Floor.'

There was no sign of an elevator. Rupert, representing money and power on its way for a union with sex, tramped up the stone stairs.

On the third floor things improved. There were smoked-glass doors, Italianate furniture and coral pink carpeting. A tough young man in a Hawaiian shirt took Rupert into a large room with overhead skylights.

Norman Crimp rose from behind a great desk made of clear plastic. The effect was like a goldfish springing out of its bowl, as Norman Crimp had changed into another suit, this one a bright orange.

The desk was on an elevated plinth and the editor had to descend two broad steps to cross the floor.

'I got nervous,' said Crimp, shaking hands. 'The girl said she thought you were from the Church or the bank. Christ, we don't want them in here! So I sent Harold to intercept. OK, Harold. Thanks! Mr Potter is going to do us a piece on the Second Thing Most Men Want Badly – Money!'

'It's first *and* second for me,' said Harold. He eyed Crimp meaningfully and flipped a cigarette out of a limp packet from the breast pocket of the technicolour shirt and lit it with a gold lighter. 'I'll be looking out for your advice, friend!'

'That's just because you get sex free all day and every day,' the editor said coldly. He stroked his little beard. 'Just clear that art work off the settee so that Mr Potter can sit down.'

'Not like you to have the casting couch cluttered, Mr C.'

Rupert stared in fascination at the armfuls of pictures of naked women that were being dumped on the carpet.

'Why don't you just clutter off?' Norman Crimp's normally rounded vowels were beginning to disappear. 'Will you take a glass of champagne, Rupe?'

'Yes to the champagne, but not Rupe, please.'

'Money for old Rupe,' leered Harold. 'How about that for a by-line?'

'So helpful as usual, but no champagne for old Harold,' said Crimp. He produced a frosted bottle of Bollinger from a refrigerator that was disguised as a bookcase. 'How do you like this place? It used to be a studio. There are two more next to it and they're all rigged up for camera work with artistes' changing rooms and bloody terrific! We like the outside of the place to look inconspicuous. But the bit the *Groin* girls see has to look like a Hollywood film set.' He struggled with the champagne cork. 'Not like the *Playboy* playhouse up the road. Ever been in there? Looks like a hairdressers outside and a hamburger joint inside.'

'Jealousy, jealousy!' Harold reached out an arm. 'Here, give me that bottle. You'll never open it like that.' Limply Crimp surrendered and Harold wrapped a heavy hand round the cork. 'We've got trouble in One.'

Reluctantly the editor produced a third glass. 'What do you mean?' The champagne spilled into all the glasses simultaneously.

'The Hon Cynthia Tamworthy is also having a tiny champagne break with Tony and the other boys in One. Well, the auburn hair isn't!'

'Oh Lord!' Crimp had climbed back on to his dais and into an outsize swivel chair which he used to rotate himself and his glass at the same time. 'Pubic hair!' The editor was back in full vowel and solemnity. 'You know the *Groin* policy!'

'Must be the same colour!' Swiftly Harold emptied his glass.

'Is there any other policy I ought to know about? I mean, as a contributor,' Rupert asked faintly. He sat down on the recently cleared casting couch.

'Pubic hair!' Crimp's voice rose like a preacher, up on his dais. 'Always a problem! Too much and we lose the readers, too little and we lose the newsdealers. Now here at *Groin* we have always understood the dilemma of the authorities, the dichotomy of our times. Is that good?

54

We have to be responsible you see. I have to be responsible! For the publisher, for the trade, for . . .' He ran out suddenly and tipped back his champagne so that some of it dripped on his beard.

'Too much fuzz brings in The Fuzz,' explained Harold, scratching the Hawaiian shirt where it bulged over his midriff.

Another, younger man came into the room. He wore a pink T-shirt and jeans and had a pale, pinched face and floppy blond hair. The rest of his attire hung round his neck in the form of an assortment of cameras, light meters, lenses and leather pouches.

'OK to touch up, Norm? Bob mixed the right colour.'

'I'm not saying it'll pass,' said Crimp severely, 'but I'll see the rushes and the lady!'

The photographer disappeared. Harold also moved towards the door.

'Got to go and get some props for those Victoriana pix. OK to go to a grand? Can't get much for less these days.'

'I sort of thought,' Rupert said as the editor poured the last of the bottle into their glasses, 'that you would have a lot of terribly beautiful women about. Staff, I mean.'

'Doesn't work. I used to in the beginning, but it's nothing but trouble. They get all wound up about sexploitation. And because you must have some fellows on the staff – production, camera, advertising, subbing – they all keep trying to make each other. It's a bit of a hot-house atmosphere anyway. I think that's why our publisher keeps away.'

'I suppose it is.' Rupert looked at the pictures that had been dumped on the floor as he finished his drink. A high-pitched, muffled shriek came through from the other side of the wall.

'Touching up,' said the editor laconically. 'I expect it will be all right. I don't like it though. Not our usual policy.'

'Weren't we supposed to be visiting your publisher?' asked Rupert. 'I don't want to hurry you. But if I really have got to be approved, or whatever – I must be back in my office by this afternoon. You see, my publisher generally phones about then. It's when he wakes up in Washington.'

'We'll go and get the car.' Crimp became all action. He tossed the empty bottle into a waste-paper basket, stepped over the pile of pulchritude on the carpet and headed for the door. 'I keep it in the Hilton garage so we'll walk there.'

Crimp's car was a purple Ferrari. 'Real sexual experience,' he said. Rupert fastened the seat belt and closed his eyes as they went round Marble Arch as though on a slalom course.

'Goes, this thing, doesn't it?' said Crimp chattily. 'I can never understand why the silly bitch chooses to live where she does. She seldom comes to Town but insists on checking everything and everybody, so we all have to go out there. Norfolk Manse the place is called – bloody great Victorian mansion that makes pretend it's in the country, but actually only round the corner from Potters Bar.' He swung the car between a cyclist and an articulated juggernaut, and Rupert's head hit the roof.

'You'll have the Fuzz in the office if you do that very often!'

Crimp looked hurt. He rolled his beady eyes round. 'Not nervous, are you? I suppose you'd better arrive in good nick or she might cut me down to a bicycle. It was one of the things I never got really water-tight in my contract, blast it!'

'Is Tracy Flip married?'

'No. Her father was Indian army. She was brought up out there. When all his lot came home, he messed about for a bit and then hit on the idea of *Groin* about the time *Playboy* and the rest all first appeared. Actually,' said Crimp grudgingly, 'it was a great idea.'

'What was?'

'The tops instead of tarts!' Crimp laughed happily as he swerved to avoid a double-decker bus pulling out. 'Not a new idea but basically a winner. You've got the girl-next-door bit, which the Yanks have always done, one way or another. Or the usual run of pros and models who will pose for anything. Well Colonel Freddy Flip used to read *Country Life*. They do a nice picture of debs and Sloane Rangers about to be spliced. Tracy's Dad hit on the idea of the same thing, titled birds, daughters of belted earls, but with their clothes off.'

'And it came off?' Rupert said.

'Sure! The clothes came off, the idea came off! How could it fail? It seems the world wide, men want the really classy thing, whether its cars, girls or whatever. Circulation now, over a million, the advertisers love it, too!'

'And the girls – of that kind, I mean?'

'When it comes to money, they're very keen. They get around five grand a set of pix!'

'So how much do you pay for an article from someone like me? I heard the figure for fossilised sex.'

'About one grand. It depends. You're not that famous like the old boy. But about that. The policy is straight stuff in the text, see? Helps keep the tone up. At least Tracy pays, I haven't got solo signing rights for that much. That's why she likes to see the straight stuff contributors – doesn't worry about the girls, unless we have a very nervous case, and then she'll look in and jolly them along.'

'How did dad die?'

'Old Freddy? Ate the wrong kind of curry and copped it, poor bloke. He used to like to go back there, when the magazine began to make a bit of cash, and revisit the haunts of the Raj and that sort of thing. He found me in El Vinos when I'd been flung off the *Sunday Globe* and offered me five per cent of the action and good money.'

The editor's little black eyes swivelled wildly as he pumped the purple car into a roundabout and out again.

'And no trouble from fathers or boyfriends?'

'Bit of a stir occasionally. Usually the debs are the ones that call them off! The shipping Greeks started that sort of game you know, at private parties. They'd invite the classy girls and, as well, a couple of the pay-and-play sort. After a few drinks, the pros would go topless and Daphne or Penelope would think: "I've got a pair better than that!" And one thing would lead to another. The domino principle.'

Rupert glanced at the speedometer and decided to keep quiet, and let Crimp concentrate on getting them to their destination. After another fifteen minutes or so, mostly with his eyes shut, he heard the editor say: 'We're nearly there now. When we arrive I shall toot the horn, just to make sure the snakes are locked up.'

'Did you say snakes?' Rupert felt his head touch the roof-lining of the car.

The car turned off the last bit of main road, past a mock-Tudor post office and pub, turned in between tall brick pillars and a wrought-iron gate. In front of a large, red-brick and gabled early-Victorian house, Crimp switched off the engine and the car's twin wind horns split the silence.

'Boa constrictors,' said Crimp, making no effort to get out. He looked glum. 'She lives alone – except for a daily and a girl *au-pair*. She has a policeman boyfriend, bloody great bruiser, I've seen him. Now he could live in. Or a guard dog would be enough. But it has to be snakes! She learned to handle them from some Guru in India.'

The large, white-painted front door opened and a small, pudgy woman in a tweed skirt and striped shirt strode manfully across the drive. Only at this point did Crimp step out of the car.

'All clear?'

Rupert got out of his side of the car and looked around carefully.

'This is Mr Potter!'

'How do you do!'

'I always like to meet our contributors. Norman tells me you can tell our readers and me all about high finance! *Do* come in!' Tracy Flip was all swinging arms and sudden movement. Her bulging brown pug-eyes shining happily, she led the way through the large, timber-ceilinged hall, full of hunting prints and brass warming-pans, into a gloomy and high ceilinged living room.

'Are those bloody things shut away?' said Crimp edgily.

'In the conservatory,' replied Tracy Flip. 'Norman's told you about my little hobby then?' She made an Indian dancer's arm, pointing to the far end of the room. Rupert saw glass panes, dim with heating and wire netting, with the misty shapes of tropical plants and some sort of wooden super-structure inside.

'For a woman on her own they're great! We get no intruders here!' She faced Rupert across a trolley that was loaded with bottles, an ice drum and a quantity of glasses.

'They're Boas – quite harmless if you know how to handle them. I have four. There's Feather Boa, Beau Brummell and Bow Bells! The largest one is called Boa-bor which is short for Borborygmus. I bet you don't know what that means. What'll you have to drink?'

'Scotch, please, neat. No, I don't.' Rupert found his hand shaking as he took the glass.

'It means gas in the intestines. Look it up if you don't believe me. So suitable, don't you think? Why don't you look at them, while Norman and I do a bit of business at the desk there? Then he can use the phone in the kitchen while I find out how much you know about money!'

'Do I get a drink?' Crimp asked sulkily.

Tracy Flip waved a hand at the trolley and retired to a desk in the far corner.

'Can you smell them?' Crimp's whisper was drowned by the sound of squirting soda.

Rupert shook his head and, while Crimp carried his glass over to the corner where he was forced to stand while the publisher sat signing, Rupert strolled with careful nonchalance over to the conservatory end of the room and peered through the separating glass. On the other side he could see gravel, boulders, plants and what looked like gymnasium equipment. There was a miniature pond at the far end. Two of the inhabitants hung motionless on a leafless tree, thick and heavy like striped mooring cables.

'They're not poisonous, you know.' Rupert jumped. She had come up behind him, the pug face earnest. 'Pythons are the same – not poisonous, I mean. They mostly come from Brazil.'

'I'll take the kitchen phone!' Crimp shouted. 'And another Scotch!' He retired with papers and glass back through the hall.

Tracy Flip sat down on one of the chintzy sofas and patted a place beside her for Rupert. 'Are you married? I'm not.'

'No, but I think I shall be soon.'

'How super!' Her expression drooped for a moment. 'I wish I was. Sometimes.'

'Is Norman Crimp?' It was a question Rupert had not cared to ask the editor himself.

'You bet! He was caught early by one of the models. And not the kind-hearts-and-coronet kind either, but one of the others. By the time she'd had three kids and learned about a few of Norman's other escapades, like fiddling me – which I know he's doing – he stayed caught. You work for Curt Epoch? You edit his money magazine?'

'I run the London office.'

Tracy Flip lowered her voice, looking towards the closed door to the hall, and now leaned towards him. 'This is what I really wanted to ask you when Norman said you might write for us. Do you know someone with a rather odd name. Sir Dai Pol?'

'Curt Epoch says he's coming over here, I think. From Hong Kong. He's a financier.'

'Yes, Curt told me, too. He says he wants to buy the magazine. And his London bankers, Bair Brady, have written. I don't like meeting people much, except here. The thing is,' Tracy Flip was twisting a brass bracelet on her wrist and was looking down. Rupert saw the toes of her small, plain shoes were turned inwards. She looked up at him. 'Strictly between you and me, I wouldn't mind selling. I've had offers before and for a lot of money. I'm happy as things are. But this Sir Polly Wolly, or whoever he is, wants to come and see me. Now I don't understand some of the stuff the big wheeler-dealers talk. We've got an accountant, but I thought, if I got to know you, you might sort of help me. Norman wouldn't want to sell, you see.'

'I'll have to think about it – you really need a merchant bank too. Like Bair Brady. Don't you have a solicitor?'

'Yes. Dad's. But I don't trust him – he's a fuddy duddy. When this Pol gets into town, do you think I could give you a ring?'

There came the sound of footsteps crossing the hall floor on the other side of the door and Norman Crimp looked in, his little eyes full of suspicion.

'I'll look forward to getting a sight of your article when Norman sends me the proofs then,' Tracy Flip said coolly.

Later, when both men were in the car, she leaned down to the half-open window on Rupert's side.

'I'll let you know what happens!'

'Did she say what she was going to pay you?' the editor asked as he spun the purple car round, fountaining spurts of gravel stones on to the neat flower beds.

'No.'

'Typical!' said Crimp. 'Wants advice thrown in too! Those snakes are not the only slippery ones in that place.'

By herself, Tracy Flip mixed an outsize Bloody Mary and ate a handful of salted peanuts from a large brass bowl. Like so many other things in Norfolk Manse, it was a relic of the India days.

With the two men gone, she was glad to be alone again. It was the *au pair's* afternoon off. She was Swedish and in no way worried about the inhabitants of the conservatory. Neither was the middle-aged daily help. Her previous employer had been an undertaker and Tracy remembered what she had said: 'After what was kept there, and at all hours and unannounced, miss, well! I'm not worried if you tell me them's not poisonous. Mice I can't abide!'

'They eat mice,' Tracy told her.

61

She made preparations and got everything ready.

In the living room she rolled up the main Kashmir carpet and in its place unrolled a very much smaller, but thicker, prayer mat with its faded coloured symbols. From the corner desk drawer, which was kept locked, she took a screw-top tin and four small capsules. These she mixed with a strong smelling paste from the same drawer. Then she went to the conservatory which she also unlocked with a key from the same bunch.

On a high rack there were poles with different devices at the ends. Into the little metal cup of the feeding pole she slipped a wedge of the paste, and the powder from a capsule. The pole had a device on the end like an extended ice-cream dispenser. Quietly she put a separate, delicious smelling offering in front of each of the sleeping mooring-cables. Slowly, for the temperature was in the nineties, they became interested. She watched closely to see each offering was taken. Important, because the sizes and weights were different.

She had been quite a little girl when her father introduced her to the snake men. From that first time she had been fascinated. Her father had only a condescending interest in the old men, who could do more with their snakes than he could with the dogs he shot over.

But for Tracy it was different. Bit by bit she learned all the old men taught her. Her mother was in almost continuous ill health and hardly cared, although she had protested when the servants told her. But her father had laughed. As she had also learned later, he had enough strange pursuits in a land that specialised in them. The pythons and boas became her friends, the *biranas*, serpent spirits, as the old men called them, her lovers.

It would take a quarter of an hour for the dope to take effect. In India it was opium, of course. Now it was something more effective and ironically, as the opium was illegal, officially obtained from the vet.

Calmly, Tracy Flip poured herself a glass of neat vodka and, after drawing the curtains in the big room and turning on the radiators, went upstairs to undress. Naked she pirouetted and turned slowly in front of a big, tilting looking-glass in its hinged gilt frame. She put her hands on the supports and stood close to its reflection that showed her body white and stocky, her breasts large but flat and her legs short as she stood up on her toes.

'Mirror, mirror on the stand, who is the fairest in the land? Not you, Flippy my love!' It was what they had called her at the school in India. She switched to the Pathan tongue for the rest of it. 'Beauty is in the eye of the beholder! And I am truly beholden! And rich. Because those silly bitches in the magazine make me rich.' She sipped the vodka, and took a bottle of aromatic oil out of a cupboard in the adjoining bathroom. With this, she oiled herself lightly but carefully all over, and after another quick look in the bedroom glass, which showed the oil had given her body a light, gleaming copper colour, she slipped down the carpeted stairs and into the dimly lit living room.

A hidden gas pipe lit the log fire stacked in the big stone chimney piece. Slowly she went through the routine. Incense in little brass bowls. The light dimmer switch by the door. The door key turned. A tiny spotlight went on and lit the faded mat in the centre of the floor. The highest the temperature would go in the big room was eighty or thereabouts, but it was enough. Now all was ready.

At the conservatory door she paused, feet and both palms of her hands together, and briefly intoned the Brahmin of the snake charmers' prayer. Then she opened the door, took down another of the long poles and reached out. This one was more like the elongated implement with which fruit trees are pruned, it had a lever and a wire loop at the far end.

With the skill of experience, she touched the youngest serpent and as it lifted its head she slipped the loop over and used the lever. Unprotesting, its scaly skin slithering on the gravel, it was dragged out into the room. Its supine mates showed no interest. With her free hand she shut the door. The great snake was freed and lifted hand over hand into the round wicker basket that had been placed by the mat, and the loose lid was put over its coils. Squatting cross-legged on the mat before the basket, Tracy Flip closed her eyes and swayed gently. Beside her she had laid the razor-sharp knife that the snake men always concealed in their loincloths or turbans. One stroke could sever a big boa in half.

From the other side of the mat, she took up the other slim metal object of similar length and shape. This was real silver, a collector's piece, the tiny snake flute.

Rocking and naked, feeling her own body with one hand and covering the vents of the flute with the fingers of the other, Tracy, daughter of Colonel Freddy Flip, one of the last of the English Raj, played the high, thin, rapid notes that started the routine she had learned to love. The basket creaked and the thing inside stirred. With her free hand, and still playing, she removed the domed lid.

Slowly the triangular head emerged, the yellow, projecting eyes dulled, blinking. Her own were smarting a little, from the incense smoke that now swirled and filled the air with its heavy scent.

With a slow, superb certainty, the snake moved through the space between them until its head touched her neck, the rest of its body following, until the whole continuing length of it, muscular, sensual, was on the move. The high-pitched, wild notes of the silver pipe rose too, and steadily the snake moved until the entire length of its body was free. Down it went, round the oiled thighs and under, where they lifted from the crossed feet, the snake slithering, caressing, turning.

Abruptly Tracy Flip stopped the magic of the flute. With both hands she lifted and eased the weight of the young serpent, moving it gradually as it twined and recovered, wound and pleasured, easing and tightening, under and around. Like no other physical experience in the world, ecstatic, pagan, for herself alone.

4

As sunset over the river opposite Dolphin Square so improved the view, so sunrise over Mucking Flats, some thirty nautical miles east, enhanced those aptly named banks of the lower Thames.

A crane pointing out across the water at the big white motor yacht, moving silently up river, was like a finger welcoming a thing of beauty in an ugly world.

The man in the crane cabin, isolated from the chill of the early morning, took the cigarette offered by the lighterman who had, against regulations, come up to join him in the cab.

'Bleeding Ayrabs!'

'More likely Yanks. Or Jerries.'

'I see 'em all the time.' The crane driver leaned on the brake handle. 'It's only foreigners got the money for that now! What they comin' up here for anyway? No good that's for sure. No way, mate!'

'Gonta take over the Bank of England!'

'Yeah, and that's no joke!' The crane driver swung the jib round like a toy and let the cable scream on its winch.

Up on the high, equally insulated bridge of the motor yacht, the owner, Sir Dai Pol, his daughter and the German skipper, inspected the moving crane with equal interest.

'The English are early at work!' The skipper, bulky in his navy quilted jacket, stood before the wheel. He jerked his head. 'Now they haf to work, yes?'

He slid his eyes round cautiously to see if this was acceptable to the vessel's curious owner. Sir Dai Pol who stood beside him, was also tall, seeming more so by the height of his much shorter daughter. She was entirely oriental in appearance, but neat, almost fragile. Her father had contrasting features with a heavy head and waved grey hair. The narrow eyes behind the thick framed glasses and prominent teeth that kept his lips almost permanently apart, were from the East, but the nose was oddly thick and the jaw strong.

'What you see, captain, is decline and fall!'

'It is finished!' declared the captain. He spun the wheel lightly. 'The Port of London! Look at it!'

'It is not Hong Kong certainly.'

'Nor Hamburg!'

'Is it so good there now?'

The Captain remained silent and all three of them watched as a mass of heavy driftwood slid past, water-logged and half submerged, on the starboard side.

'You have navigated up to Tower Bridge before, you said? Once, twice?' Sir Dai Pol's slightly harsh voice seemed to have a split quality, like the rest of him. There were hollow vowels that were Chinese, but there was a tough flatness to the lilt that was something else. The Captain had heard it before somewhere in his travels round the ports of the world, but could not place it.

'Once. The tide is not easy. You can see on there.' The Captain nodded across to the chart table. *Machen immer acht* his German navigational almanac said, and he had been doing so since they had left anchorage at Southend at first light.

'I have not sailed up here since I was a boy. It was with my father.' Sir Dai smiled down at his daughter.

'Now I sail up the river with you, Papa!' The thin red mouth showed small, perfect white teeth. The Captain slid his careful glance at the small, high-cheeked face.

He was still not certain she was Sir Dai's daughter. But that was not his business.

'It was the British who built up Hong Kong, sir? Is prosperous, yes?'

'Also Hamburg, I think, after the war, when it was given back to you.'

'Flat! *Ganz kaput!*'

'You would have given London back, captain? If it had gone the other way?' That double voice was soft.

'I was too young to have anything to do with that.' Captain Hoffman looked to his front. It was always the same on these high-pay, big-tip charter jobs. The ship's engineer and the cook-steward were both Hong Kong Chinese and in this man's permanent service. The Captain felt momentarily lonely. He pulled down the peak of his cap. It was best to stick to the job and keep talk to the minimum. Tug-boats, small ships, towed barges, more flotsam and rubbish, oil drums and big timber went past. On this tide he could use the starboard side of the centre channel.

'May we have tea, father?'

'Press the button, my dear. Captain?'

'Coffee, sir!'

In minutes the white-coated steward had brought identical mugs on to the bridge. Green tea in two, opaque black coffee for the Captain who put his mug in the helmsman's special holder.

'I need Channel VHF –' He paused and sat back in the steering chair to look at pencil scribbles on the chinagraph. 'Twelve!'

It was the girl who switched on, and over the rotating whisper of the constant reading echo sounder came the Port of London Authority voice, with its monitor information. The other crew member, the engineer, neat in blue denims, came silently up on to the bridge deck. He made the bow and smile that were automatic, then spoke quietly to the German.

'Plenty rubbish, I think captain! You keep plastic ropes and bags off my propellors!'

The German raised a mock fist.

'Do we have to notify our friends on the radio of our passage?' Sir Dai's smiling mouth had tightened very slightly.

'This morning before you were on deck. At Gravesend, the main clearance station, yes? Then is all clear until anchorage at Tower dock. You requested all clearance to take place there?'

'I did. And you told them no pilot?'

'Not for a ship this size. Twenty metres. Private yacht,' The Captain looked at the chronometer and twin rev counters in front of him. 'I think we are at St Katherine's Dock in three hours now.'

'Come this side, Kitty.' Sir Dai moved across the carpeted section of the bridge. 'I will show you some interesting things!'

He opened the mahogany door on the starboard side of the bridge deck, and preceded his daughter out on to the main deck.

'I don't like the way he looks at me sometimes.'

Dai Pol narrowed his eyes behind his glasses. 'It is the disadvantage of being the only woman on board. When we get into London the men will find their amusements.'

'Ha-ah-ah-ah-ah!' She made the Chinese polite sound, part aquiescence, part sceptical. 'I would like sometimes to made adventures for myself also!'

'If you like the allowance I pay so diplomatically into your account, Kitty, you will consider my interests first. I have already put a thousand pounds for you into a London bank. Do with it as you like! We shall live on board, but you are free to come and go. Unless I need you, as usual. You understand?'

'Do I see theatres and fashions in London? Can I buy jewellery? Clothes? I would like to fly back to Paris!' Kitty's English was as flawless as a private Hong Kong school for girls could make it, but now there was a faint tremor in her voice.

'I will see about an escort. Paris? We may need to go there anyway.'

'Here it is all ugly.' Only the scarlet mouth and the movement of the heavily made-up eyelashes gave life to the mask. The mask would never cry, but the big powerful hand of Dai Pol folded over the smaller one, clenched on the rail.

'See it differently, Kitty! The Vikings sailed up here. You have learned that at school. Then earlier the Romans, two thousand years ago! The river would have been wider than. Marshes, mists, cold! How they must have hated it, too! All of them, raiders, invaders, traders - came this way! And from them bred the strongest nation in the world – for a time. There is some of that blood in you, too. Think of that!'

'And why do we come now?'

'Ha-ah-ah-ah-ah!' Sir Dai Pol making the same response, sucked in his breath. The two of them normally spoke English, but the Canton Chinese he used now amounted to the French proverb: *Plus ça change, plus c'est la même chose*!

'Yes, we shall be trading. I am a gambler. You must not worry if I tell you things are far from good for me in the Colony. I have some plans here that could take care of us if things go wrong. But it is best, I think, if you do not know about them.'

They returned through the door to the bridge.

'I have a phone number,' said Sir Dai. 'On that clip board. Kitty, you can call the Harbour Master on the radio phone. Tell him we're coming, and expect to sail straight in at about noon.'

The high towers of the famous bridge were like some stage set, away ahead of them as the engines eased down to a whisper. Instructions from the Harbour Master came tinnily over the amplifier. Graciously the *Chenn Lo* moved to a pontoon outside the lock gates and the crew passed mooring warps to two laconic youths on the pontoon. Then they moved efficiently, letting down the ship's fenders.

'I suppose that is new – the hotel!'

'Like a *Kriegsbunker*!' said the Captain amiably.

'Look, Kitty, the old dock buildings are beautiful! And the little customs house and those old sailing barges!' Sir Dai had opened the deck doors and stepped out to the rails.

'What's next?' he asked the youths. 'I am expecting gentlemen from my bank to meet me. Are they on the dock? Ah – that gentleman looks like a city bank director!'

A tall, balding man in a brown suit came carefully backwards down the gantry ladder on to the pontoon and stepped on board.

'Immigration!' The sad, moon-like face and walrus moustache looked round the ship's company assembled.

'Sir Dai Pol? Is that you, sir? No very great formalities, sir. Just the usual. We had a signal you were coming. There's a couple of gentlemen from a bank waiting for you, but we have to do our bit first before they can come aboard. Now I'll just have the passports. Very good. Federal Republic and Hong Kong. Just fill in these cards. Didn't clear at Southend? No, well saves a bit of time on the tide sometimes. Now, sir, last port?'

'Marseilles.'

'How was Biscay?'

'Very horrible,' whispered Kitty as the immigration officer flicked through her passport.

'On a lovely boat like this, madam? With stabilisers? Who is Cheng Sun? I see, you. Hong Kong? Origin for all ship's papers?'

'Registered Monaco.'

'Estimated time of stay? Holiday? Cruising UK waters?'

'We shall stay here,' Sir Dai Pol paused. He looked across at the great bridge, and beyond it to the Tower with its flags standing out on the river breeze. 'We shall trade in the City of London!'

'You have paid a month's mooring, I see.'

'Lock gates are opening, sir!' cried one of the youths.

'Fly a yellow signal for customs when you get into the pool. Excise will attend to you inside the dock.' The immigration officer handed back the passports, looked for a long, sad moment at Sir Dai Pol, then reversed up on to the pontoon.

As the tall, white hull of the *Chenn Lo* moved forward, the white painted bridge of the lock was raised. The two youths, now on board, held warps ready for the final mooring.

Ahead of them rose the imposing façade of the old Ivory House, relic of the great days of the Port of London's trade and prosperity, with the row of yachts and cruisers moored to the jetties below.

'Harbour Master 'imself to welcome yer in!' The youth in the prow shouted. A stubby figure in yellow oilskins and boots stood at the end of the jetty. He slowly rotated both arms as though doing morning exercises and the Captain rotated the silver wheel. The ship was suddenly monstrously overlarge for the space. It held motionless on the brown, surging water for a moment, then slid imperceptibly astern, the fenders brushing the wooden pontoon. The youths leaped ashore, warps tautened, the Harbour Master shouted and the Captain, leaning from the open bridge window and, seeing all was well moved his switches. The engines fell silent.

Along the jetty, Tim Bealey and Rupert strolled together.

'I thought you might like to see them come in – as you're going to be with the old man when this customer comes to the bank you might as well see his gin palace moor up. That's obviously Sir Dai Pol.' Tim glanced into a folder he was carrying. 'He's got an appointment for tomorrow.'

'How did he get his K?' asked Rupert. 'Making money, I suppose?'

Tim Bealey consulted the folder again.

'Water actually. From the notes I've got. They're bloody short of it in Hong Kong. He has always got on with the Chinese Commies, trading on a working class background bit. And he succeeded in pulling off some real deal that secured water supplies.'

Rupert looked up at the tall shape of the *Chenn Lo*.

'I think I'd rather sail at Beaulieu.'

From the ship's rail, slightly above them, Sir Dai Pol studied the reception committee. Neither of these two was Lord Bair, he guessed.

'Bair Brady? Won't you come aboard, gentlemen?' he called.

'That's right, sir!' Tim called up. 'I'm afraid Lord Bair couldn't make it. Very upset because he's a dead keen yachtsman himself. Hopes you'll understand. He has a date with you tomorrow morning!'

Rupert began to step on to the gangplank that had been put down at the stern, but the Harbour Master stopped him. 'Sorry sir, not until customs have been aboard!' He pointed to the small yellow burgee wavering dolefully from the stumpy masthead of the yacht.

The two Revenue men stepped up the gangplank, through the doorway and on to the bridge. Sir Dai Pol disliked them instinctively. Certain people reacted to his Chinese half in a way he could see on their faces, although these two had the poker-player profiles of their profession. He played the same game but the Welsh in his blood rose: these were people he did not want trouble with.

The technique seemed to be that while the fat one went quietly through the passports, referring now and again to the ubiquitous clipboard of papers, the thin one with bony cheeks and sliding eyes searched about the vessel.

'You are Sir Dai Pol?'

'Not looking like my photograph, I fear!' A kindly smile.

'That's all right, sir. It's just a question of knowing all the ship's complement is here. Do your crew speak English, sir?'

'Of course. Captain Hoffmann has skippered us over from the South of France. I needed someone who knew European waters.'

'You have the ship's papers?' The Captain handed over envelopes and books.

'You are the registered owner, Sir Pol?'

'Correct.'

'Port of origin, Hong Kong?'

'I think it says that. We fly Monaco registration.'

'Commercial cargo, nil. Who skippered the vessel from Hong Kong?'

'I did. I had two more of my own crew. This is the engineer and the cook. All I need now. The other two were flown home from Nice.'

'And your daughter?'

'She flew out to join me at Marseilles.'

The plumper of the two, who was reading the log entries, ran a pudgy finger slowly down an open page.

'You made a number of stops in the Middle East?'

'Inevitably – I had some business calls. Would it help if I gave you this letter? It is from Bair Brady, the City bankers. They vouch for me and my interests here. Those are two of their people on the jetty.'

'That's all right, sir. We looked you up in Who's Who, sir. We know who you are.'

'The devil you do!' Sir Dai Pol stiffened, his spectacles glinted but he managed a laugh.

'Routine, sir, just routine.'

'We'll take a quick look round the vessel then, sir.'

Dai Pol knew every inch of his yacht. From where he sat he could tell in several ways and from small sounds what was happening as they moved into the cabins. He knew, and he knew these men knew, that there were a hundred ways he could conceal small or large contraband. No real quantity of dope was in question, and his two Chinese crew knew what was at stake if they played foolishly with that. The Captain had been vouched for and would not risk his certificate. He pressed a bell with his foot under the table. The steward appeared instantly.

'Champagne. Five glasses!'

The cork popped as the two customs men reappeared. Kitty slid round the end door and stood behind her father. She lit a cigarette in a long, ivory holder. Sir Dai Pol saw his glass filled and now, without rising, waved to the two men. 'If your duties are complete?'

'Fraid not, sir. On duty!' The two pale faces looked pious in the dim light.

'Arms, sir?' there was a pause. 'The steward has shown us your pair of shotguns there. Not to be used ashore without a UK licence, sir.'

'Come – surely you gentlemen know the season?'

'Nice vessel you have here, sir,' said the pudgy one. 'That model of it there! Very nice.' The man moved casually across the carpet. Sir Dai spoke quickly in Chinese and the steward pressed a switch illuminating a six foot model of the *Chenn Lo*. It was the main feature of the stateroom, a superb copy of the boat with all the main features to scale.

'You could sail that on the Round Pond, sir!'

'Ah, yes! Kensington Gardens!'

'We'll leave your clearance certificate on the bridge. Don't forget to consult us if you have any problems!' The cod fish eyes of the thin officer looked at him ironically. 'Our office is at the end of the main jetty.'

They were seen up on to the bridge by the steward and Rupert and Tim Bealey, coming round the moorings from the opposite way, met them at the gangplank where all four tangled unhappily.

'Ah! The gentlemen from Bair Brady! This is my daughter, Kitty. There is some champagne being poured in the main stateroom.' Sir Dai Pol turned and led the way.

There was a new briskness in his manner now. 'I hope you will join us! The delay has been most irritating. We can discuss business in advance of my coming to the bank. The Romans and Vikings had a much easier time of it. Do I look as though I was going to kill and plunder?'

Rupert returned to Dolphin Square where Nancy opened the door. 'They are in the little room. I acquired some champagne at work which I gave to Lady Bair and if you want some of that you'll have to hurry.'

'Thanks. About champagne I feel a sort of back to back relationship,' Rupert told her.

74

In the little room where Maddy kept all her books and a typewriter, Rupert found Maddy with Polly Flinders sitting at opposite ends of the small, rose-coloured settee. They were wearing long dresses and twirling the stems of their glasses in an atmosphere of exclusive confidences.

'Darling Pot! I thought you weren't coming in tonight?'

'How do you mean *in*?'

'We're going to the ballet and you don't like ballet.'

'Well, I shall probably stay here and get on with things. I'm trying to write an article about your former husband's beastly bank. It's not easy. It makes me feel sort of neutered.'

'Poor darling!' Polly, having kicked off both shoes which lay at angles on the floor, stretched out an elegant stockinged foot and touched Rupert's leg. Rupert jumped, bumped into the glass coffee table and the empty champagne bottle rolled over and joined the shoes on the floor.

'I don't think you ought to do that to my Pot!'

'By proxy. You couldn't reach.'

Rupert went out into the hall, put some whisky in a big, cut-glass tumbler and returned, squeezed himself into a small, elegant armchair and took a big gulp.

'Darling, Wilfred Poult is taking us to the ballet. I wonder what's happened to him?'

Rupert wriggled unhappily in the tight-fitting chair. 'Poult! I understand he got his K shooting defenceless Zulus or something. Why should he take you out when he knows that I, that we – that we're going – oh, Christ!' Rupert sought more consolation from his glass and tried to pull himself together.

'Good champagne?'

'Fortnum's best!'

'I had some midday. With your Chinaman.'

'Have I got a Chinaman?'

'The one Bair Brady fixed to come and see you at the gallery. I only learned that today.'

'Oh! Yeah, I remember now, Ruthy told me.' Maddy moved her small, flushed face from side to side, stretching her gently curved neck like a swan looking for something. 'Isn't he some sort of mandarin? Title?'

'Sir Dai Pol – half Welsh, the rest Chinese. Atavistic rather than aristocratic, I would say.'

'What's that?' Polly cried.

'Never mind, darling. Pot uses clever words because he makes his living with them.'

'Why can't I make a living like Poult? Calm, cultured, buffered by the British Museum and stealing other men's women to stroke their knees at the ballet?'

'You can stroke my knee now,' Maddy said, slowly pulling up the hem of the long skirt.

'I think the mandarin may have a job for you, Polly. Escorting his daughter. Papa wants the bank to take care of that.'

'For pay?'

'Banks pay.'

When Polly disappeared into the bathroom, Rupert finished his drink and stood up. 'I'm off!'

'Where are you going, Pot?'

'Down to the sea in ships! Can't wait. I'm going to spend the night on the boat down at Beaulieu. Had enough of town. Back tomorrow sometime!'

'Pot – darling!'

'Have a good ballet!'

He banged the front door of the flat and pressed the button for the lift. If Sir Wilfred Poult came out of it when it came up, probably reeking of some ancient hair lotion, he would throw him down the stairs, he thought.

The *Chenn Lo* lay to her moorings, sleek, silent and shuttered. The Captain, his duties temporarily finished, had gone ashore to a room reserved for him in the Tower Hotel.

Sir Dai Pol sat with his daughter in the stateroom with only the big model still illuminated at the far end.

'He can find a girl, which is what he wants, and keep away. I have told him to report by telephone every morning and evening.'

'Are we on the telephone?'

'The usual plug in, also electricity, air conditioning, hot water – all you want, without running engines.'

'What is happening to Shee and Yat Sen?'

'The meal will be served. Shee has already been shopping in Limehouse. Then they will go ashore. There is now a flourishing quarter in Soho I am told. They have friends there.'

'Must it be tonight you require me, papa? Because I am tired.'

'It is tonight, my daughter, as I told you.'

The small, perfect-featured white face with its narrow eyes and short black fringe, drew on a cigarette in the holder and looked across the stateroom table through the smoke cloud. 'Sometimes I think I hate you.'

Sir Dai Pol returned the look with a strange, mocking expression. 'If I die in curious circumstances, lawyers in several places have envelopes with several names to investigate.'

'And I am one of them?' Kitty's smile was much the same as her father's, but she reached across the table with bangles clattering round her wrist and took playing cards from an ivory box.

'Then I had better do your fortune!'

'It will be dark in half an hour and then you will change. I shall take a bath and then we have dinner.' Dai Pol rose.

'So clever, my papa! Always everything is arranged.' Kitty rested long, painted finger nails on the cards. 'It is here again. The ancestors are on your side.' She riffled the cards together listlessly. 'Why do you send me to one of the best schools at home? And then, when after all you are only half Chinese, you use me for ancient rites which here in London, I believe, could get you in prison. Perhaps the Tower that is along the water?'

'How charming you are, Kitty!' Sir Dai Pol had two high spots of colour on his cheeks. 'Nobody is locked up in the Tower these days. I have long ago explained to you the old Chinese code that is, as you say, half of me. Your mother was a prostitute. She married me. My father, who was indeed only a sea cook from Cardiff, also married a prostitute. You are not a whore, principally by virtue of my efforts. But in grateful recognition of that, you receive a great deal more money from me than either your mother or grandmother did for the ritual in which they trained you. My dear, it is up to you!'

Kitty shook the bangles down her thin arms. 'Incest!'

'The Tao of Love does not say so. In Cardiff? Or here in London? I wonder. I prefer my Chinese ancestors to my Welsh ones. I am away from your mother, who has for a long time been a sick woman. But the demands of my life of all kinds do not change.' His voice was flat and harsh.

'I too belong to both worlds! I have been taught a convention that rejects the giving of pagan pleasure as a duty!'

'Ah, that is a special part of the pleasure!'

Dinner, served in silence by the steward Shee, involved the many little bowls, recreating all that was traditional. There was duck and pork, peppers, rice, hot sauce, fish, peaches. Dishes in silver, wood and china, and the warm linen towels. The stateroom lights were dimmed. Sir Dai Pol drank sparingly, a strong, clear rice spirit. Kitty drank water, with a slice of green lime. Shee, the steward, obelisk of face, a dim white shape in his house coat, cleared away, leaving half a bottle of champagne peeping like a gold phallus out of its bucket.

Kitty retired and Sir Dai Pol went up on deck. He smoked the first of the special cigarettes, looking round the dock, lit with patches of colour and pools of light reflected in the water. The classic outline of the old Ivory warehouse was etched against a pink sky, its clock tower high above the masts and spars of the older boats. The water gurgled and lapped against the wooden piers, sliding sinuously brown and oily towards the lock gates. Turning his head, Sir Dai studied the heavy outline of the bridge, with its towers and girders over which heavy traffic flowed ceaselessly, headlights flashing on the river under the black arches.

78

He acknowledged the salute of Shee and the engineer as they slipped down the gangway like shadows and along the quay, then went back through the bridge doorway.

Returning to the big stateroom, he saw that the ports were covered by the electric blinds and silk curtains. Kitty had lit candles which stood in heavy silver holders on the floor, tall as altar pieces.

At the far end of the stateroom, seeming to move in the soft light of the candles, stood his special chair, positioned on a low dais. This was an antique piece, black lacquer with flat carved arms, shaped and made comfortable with cream silk seat and back. Sir Dai Pol trailed his heavy manicured fingers affectionately along the ebony arm as he moved past it, his feet sliding noiselessly across the carpet as he went into his cabin.

Presently he returned, changed into a heavy, crimson brocade gown that reached down to the thin ornamented slippers, and slid into the chair, his eyes seemingly closed behind the heavy glasses, noting the two joss-stick burners placed on the floor on either side. Their thin, drifting smoke, like twin charcoal lines were already cloying the air. On a small table beside him, was the long stemmed pipe and a jade jar, and from it he took the soft wad, between finger and thumb, kneading the substance into a small ball and adding it to the pipe bowl. He leaned back in the big chair.

Like all ships, the boat had its own fractional movement, even at rest. A hundred minute noises, whispering creaks and chafings, timber easing, metal alternately resistant and pliable. Now soft music rose above these sounds, low enough to be contained in the curtained, carpeted cabin, the strange, unearthly ancient Chinese love-music played on simple traditional instruments. It was disturbing, and yet soothing, the high plaintive wire-taut sounds and the wind instruments arousing, the intermittent brass cymbals and bells punctuating. And underlying all, a deeper note, the oldest of all insistent rhythms.

Suddenly, silently, Kitty was there. She wore a short kimono of rose-coloured raw silk with tiny red flowers, and a silk flower of the same colour was in her short, soft black hair. Without speaking she poured from the champagne bottle on the table, into a single glass. Barefoot across the intervening space, she came with downcast eyes, candlelight imparting to her movements the wavering, water-like effect. In front of the chair she knelt on a small tasselled cushion, and held up the glass.

From the pocket of his gown, Sir Dai took a capsule and broke it over the glass. Kitty twirled the stem between painted finger tips and, still kneeling, lifted her head to drink, so that the gown yawned open, showing the curve of the small white breasts.

Presently she set the empty glass down to one side of the dais, and watched. Slowly and carefully, her father warmed the bowl of the long pipe in the nearest candle flame. The flame drifted into the bowl. Neither spoke. To the aphrodisiac scent of the joss sticks was added another – thinner, faintly acrid.

Sir Dai exhaled, and the smoke stalked the moving lights of the candles. Slowly his free hand moved under the chin of the kneeling girl, and gently lifted the pale, still face. Her eyes were already changing, the pupils pinpointing, the mouth opening, the small fine nostrils dilating.

'The Tao of erotic kissing, Wu Hsein – you know it,' intoned Dai Pol, like the start of an incantation. 'The harmony of Yin and Yang. And with the help of the little white powder, you will take a long time!'

The small pink tongue tipped between the painted lips and his big hand touched her cheeks, gently drawing her head forward between the open knees as the gown fell away to each side. Fractionally he eased forward in the big chair, inhaling from the mind-stealing pipe.

Up on deck, Shee the steward, had returned, silent as a shadow. Carefully he removed the plug from the peephole he had drilled in the woodwork, and lowering his head applied one slanted eye to the aperture.

5

Lord Bair looked round the faces at the morning meeting with no sign of pleasure on his own ruddy features. The programme for the day was in his hand, provided by Miss Faughsquar who sat, pencil poised over a notebook, at a small side table.

'This fellow, Sir Dai Pol, I'm to see at eleven thirty. Who is he?' Lord Bair fidgeted and eased himself on his elbows in his grandfather's chair. 'Who's briefing me on that?'

'Partly me, Desmond.' Daimon, his cousin and senior director, sat next in line at the board table. 'Tim was the welcoming party yesterday when he came into port. Sailed his own yacht over.'

'Bloody gin palace, I suppose. Where's he moored?'

'St Katharine's Dock,' said Tim Bealey. 'Yes, not exactly a junk.'

'What's he want from us?'

'Facilities. Company flotations. Sean knows more about the Hong Kong end. Obviously loans come into it, some short, some long.' Daimon moved a sheet of paper across the table. 'He had a joint venture with us in Singapore once, but that's merged with International Bunkering.'

'So it's back to back?' Sean said.

Lord Bair felt the old, familiar sense of drifting. He sat

upright which made him wince.

'Arms length?'

'We've dealt with his banking and property.' The darkly saturnine Sean flung an elegant arm over the back of his chair. 'Bunkering have a shoring up situation with at least three of the Greeks and we've a two year loan with option there.'

'You've got the glasses on that one then?' Lord Bair tried.

'They didn't look too good but now bottomed out, I'd say. Should be all right.'

Lord Bair fidgeted and winced again. Damn the old cow! She had really put too much into it. He turned to his cousin.

'What's he want from us, Daimon? For these ventures?'

'Parameters? Five to ten.'

'Really?' said Tim Bealey. 'And you reckon he can cover that?'

'Short term from Hong Kong, then Swiss Canton and Central Basle.'

'Trouble with Hong Kong,' Sir Mick Muldoon took a short black pipe out of his pudgy face, 'is that I don't like the Hang Seng Index. They're jumpy about the Colony lease.'

'Are we into that?' Lord Bair looked profound.

Mick Muldoon sucked on his pipe.

'What does this chap have himself?' It was Miles, the young Brady nephew.

'Property. But it's all a bit cross referenced.'

'I've done some homework on that,' Tim Bealey said. 'Holding companies have a negative cashflow, especially Pol Front Realty.'

'Damn it, who *is* the chap?' Lord Bair roared. 'How's he get his K? Is he in *Who's Who*?'

'The answer is, yes he is, and I got a bit more by telex.' Mick Muldoon scratched his chin with his pipe stem. 'A bit odd really. He did some deal with the CPR. To secure water for the colony.'

'Canadian Pacific? Why did he get into that?'

'Chinese Peoples' Republic, chairman. According to my source, he's always got on a lot better with the CPR than some of the other tycoons. Water is desperate in Hong Kong.'

'So you think he's safe?'

'I think he's all right, sir.'

'I don't mind the chinks,' said Lord Bair moodily, 'it's the bloody blacks we've got to look out for! They've let us down left right and centre!'

The various members of the Board looked thoughtful. Tim Bealey lit a cigarette. They all knew the Chairman on this theme. It could go on. Miss Faughsquar rose from her table, passed him a slip of paper and returned to her chair. The message was simple: five minutes more. Lord Bair consulted his agenda.

'We've dealt with Chicago Grease. That French Nationalisation is going to be a – what did you call it Miles?'

'A bloody bore, sir!'

'Exactly!' Lord Bair looked out of the tall, neo-Georgian windows beaded with gentle rain but already shining in the sun. He felt a nostalgic, almost pre-natal, drag for such weather. A long way in the past was Ireland, and a long way from the boardroom was his boat, and sea spray to wet his face and the sooner he was on it again the better.

'There's the Nimbushi Systems loan.' It was young Erin. 'First tranche due up today!'

'First factory in Ulster, chairman! We're with the Shinbum Bank.'

'The Shinbum?' It was not difficult to remember that one. 'Has that bottomed out, eh?'

'They're the transfer party. It's yen-based.'

'Give them until tomorrow,' Daimon said. 'There's a time lag element.'

'The Japs are all right!' Lord Bair said authoritatively. 'But the bloody Germans have got us into trouble with those joint Polish loans. I want it put in the minutes that it's Zimbabwe I don't like, and those new black buggers there!'

'The Parson and I saw two chaps on the Algerian gas pipe line deal,' Daimon said soothingly. 'We're with Societé Exploitation Sud. They're black as coal, but Arabs. Spoke better English than I do.'

'Not difficult,' said Mick Muldoon. 'I've always thought that French accent of yours was too good, Daimon!'

'Good enough for the Common Market!'

'Arabs are all right!' Lord Bair declared. 'Must keep in there, of course. Any other business, gentlemen?'

'The editor from *Midas* joins us for the session with Sir Dai Pol, chairman,' Tim said as Lord Bair rose from the table. 'You agreed he could see how the working of these things goes. You remember he's doing an in-depth article about BB.'

'In your office at eleven-thirty, sir.' Miss Faughsquar pulled back his chair.

'Well don't let him prod too much!' Lord Bair scowled. 'I don't trust any of these media meddlers!'

Back in her own office, Miss Faughsquar swept a cushion off the small settee that was meant for visitors.

'Of course he wouldn't say anything, the poor old sod,' she explained to her colleague, as she moved swiftly into Lord Bair's own office. 'He thinks I can't see he's got them again. Piles!' she explained. 'Bloody beastly if you've ever had them!'

Sitting in his taxi on the way to Bair Brady, Rupert felt an unusual sense of peace. The night on the boat had been like a small holiday. A pity that Maddy did not like boats. But if she went to the ballet and opera with that aged art fancier, at least it gave him a break.

He had bought the *Financial Times* and the *Daily Express*. In the one he noted that Bair Brady's bullion dealing subsidiary had done something to please the South Africans and upset the Third World. While in the other there was a gossip account of the ballet first night and those attending, including Lady Bair and Sir Wilfred Poult, who was described as The Eminent Ornithologist. Someone on the show-biz column had the right sense of humour!

'Was it Prune Lane, Guv'nor?' asked the cabby, sliding back the glass divider.

"Prawn Passage,' Rupert said. 'A quid if you can find it by eleven o'clock.'

In the ante-room office at the end of the Stormy Passage, Miss Faughsquar was all tight smiles and efficiency. 'Take that seat on the sofa, Mr Potter! I'll try and speed things up. Mr Bealey is on his way. Lord Bair is on the telephone to the Old Lady.'

'Really?' Rupert was astonished. 'His present wife? Or – actually the old one?'

'Of Threadneedle Street, Mr Potter! Upon whom we all wait – even you!'

Tim Bealey came through the outer door and glanced above the double panelled ones that led to the Chairman's office where the two miniature ship's lights were mounted. The green one went on. Miss Faughsquar led the way to the big double doors and pushed them in.

'Red light on until you want the Inscrutable Orient, Chairman!' she said briskly. 'We've got him caged up below!'

Lord Bair appeared to be sitting on the edge of his high backed chair behind the collection of bric-a-brac, but not exactly with welcoming enthusiasm. He scowled across at Rupert. Beside him sat Daimon.

'Give her a good deal of leeway, don't you Desmond?'

'Bloody good secretary! Doesn't like Japs and blacks and Catholics in that order. Had a sister who was thrown to the Japs in Singapore. Now I don't mind dealing with any of that lot! But when it comes to the Press!'

Unhappily, Tim Bealey shoved Rupert into a chair and pulled up another for himself. 'Could we briefly – '

'This chap is from *Midas*, Desmond. Bit different, really,' Daimon said.

'Do we need *Midas*?' It was as though Rupert was not there.

'You told the publisher he could do an authentic piece on BB, everything confidential, we see the result. Just picking up the way we deal with things. He'll sit in on this Dai Pol chap and the warranty listing with Phiz Pharmaceutical this afternoon.'

'I'm doing this for your Mr Epoch, you understand!' Lord Bair at last appeared to consider Rupert among those present. 'He has done me a few favours – some mutual interests – '

'Is Sir Dai Pol to know I'm not part of the bank?'

'Best thing.' Daimon folded his arms. 'Why are you seeing this character anyway, Desmond? OK, he wants some pretty big facilities, but you wouldn't be on this yourself normally. What's the score?'

'I sometimes think you don't realise, Daimon, that I take a personal interest in every level of the bank. Most of the time. The publisher of *Midas* introduced this client, and Mr Epoch is influential. Knowing people, that's what makes a good banker. You can quote that if you like, Potts!'

'Potter, sir,' said Tim Bealey.

'But all back to back, you understand, Potts!'

'I shall try to follow it.'

'You have met this Pol, Tim? You and Potts got him moorings or something?'

'No, he fixed that himself. I get the impression, chairman, that he could be a fixer. Just an observation. If we are going to stake him.'

'Little oriental with whacking glasses, you said?'

'Big, actually. Although I noticed he wears block heels – to give him height, and combs his hair up. Quite a distinguished bloke, Sir Dai, considering – and I found this out – his old man was a sea-cook on a Welsh cargo boat.'

'Very observant you note, our Mr Bealey!' Lord Bair said to Rupert.

'Would he make a good journalist, Potts?' Lord Bair pressed a hidden bell under the desk edge and rose to his feet.

The entry of Sir Dai Pol was all effect. He was dressed in a black coat and striped trousers and was followed by Shee, bowing and carrying a large box. Lord Bair having failed to offer to shake hands, Sir Dai Pol made a small bow. He looked round at Rupert, Tim Bealey and Daimon and nodded at each in turn. Miss Faughsquar gave Lord Bair a small piece of paper on which was written: 'Champers?'

'In five minutes!' said Lord Bair.

'I hope I can be as quick as that, gentlemen!' There was no resentment on the face of Sir Dai, but the eyes behind the thick glasses almost closed. 'I realise we are very small business. I am much honoured at your receiving me, Lord Bair. Our association through my Hong Kong group is one I esteem!'

To the waiting Shee, he signalled to place the large box on the edge of the big desk. 'I bring a token of my appreciation. Not cigars!' He spoke a few words in Chinese and the smiling Shee, tactfully moving some of the smaller objects on the desk, positioned the box and swept off the top like a conjurer. The base stayed behind and a beautiful replica of a yacht, made of ivory, sailing on a green jade sea, stood shining softly in the light. Lord Bair peered over the half-spectacles.

'By God!' He looked round in genuine wonder. 'That's my boat!'

Shee made one or two adjustments to the mast, the miniature stays and the rigging.

'A Nicholson 48, I think!' Sir Dai Pol smiled, the wide lips peeling back from his big teeth. 'For you, my dear Lord Bair, as between sailors!'

'You've got something there, Desmond my boy!' Daimon reached out a finger to touch the tiny ivory burgee at the top of the mast.

'Be very careful! Rigging is very delicate! Ivory not so strong!' Now there was an anxious note in Dai Pol's voice.

Shee slid away with Miss Faughsquar through the big doors, and a moment later she returned with the BB Cuvée champagne and tall glasses. The bottle was already open and she poured efficiently, using a white napkin and putting glasses round the table.

'That's a nice new toy you've brought the Chairman, Sir Dai!' She retired with the empty bottle.

'As nanny says!' Daimon remarked meaningfully.

'My secretary has my interests at heart, Pol!' In fact, Lord Bair wondered if Faughsquar ever suspected anything. Presumably she had put the extra cushion he had found on his chair. But he raised his glass, contemplated its stream of thin bubbles, and let half the quantity go down his throat with ease.

'To your good fortune, sir!' Now he was at his most Harrovian. 'How can we improve it?' Gifts from the natives were not usually so thoughtful. The model of his yacht was ingenious.

'I need financial accommodation for up to five million for a short period. Say two weeks.'

'Purpose?'

'Acquisitions. New UK business investment.'

'Do we take a stake? Arms length, you understand.'

'Hong Kong security?' Daimon played with a paper knife.

'The two banks you know.'

'Your own property company is big with one of them. Is that underpinning a prior guarantee?'

'I am giving a personal warranty.'

'Golden Carp Finance is not strictly a bank. Pol Property is with Bank of Kowloon, where your real clout comes from.'

Sir Dai Pol's big teeth showed between the thick lips again. These people knew their business. With one finger he delicately adjusted the bridge of his spectacles. 'Gentlemen, you have so many facts at BB! The London merchant banks have lost none of their skill!'

'Must be at arms length, Pol!' Lord Bair said. 'Back to back, you know. Avoid negative cash flow, go for the growth scenario!' He finished his champagne.

'Did I gather the Swiss side comes into it?' Tim said from his end of the desk where he sat next to Rupert, who was doodling on a note pad a sketch of a Chinese junk.

'You don't care for champagne?' Lord Bair had noticed the visitor had not touched his drink. 'I'm afraid it's an old BB tradition. Goes back to when Castlereagh got hold of most of Napoleon's stuff, when the Iron Duke's baggage train was in hock to the bank!'

'I like to drink when I have finished business!' Dai Pol knew that after the night before, the champagne would have a second trigger effect. 'The Swiss Canton Bank will give collateral. They are getting very much less conventional in Basle. They have no ex-colonial hang-ups.' He appeared to study the ceiling. 'I can fix this over there tomorrow, if you cannot. Or with our American friends. It is just that the projects are here in London.'

'Can you tell us a little more what you do have in mind, Sir Dai?' Tim asked quickly. He could see a small thunderstorm gathering in Lord Bair's face. 'BB can help. Lots of contacts. Lots of short cuts.'

'Yes! I propose to make two acquisitions. I have written to the parties and they are interested. One you know is a magazine, a certain type of publication with a very wide international circulation. It will not be cheap. Eventually I shall print it on my own presses in Hong Kong. That is one venture.'

'Yes, we've written to the publisher for you.'

'Ha-ah-ah-ah-ah!' Dai Pol followed with the hissed intake of breath. 'You have done homework!'

'Do you know this publication Tim? Daimon?' Lord Bair looked at the new model of his ship.

'I can speak as an interested party,' Rupert said. 'I know the publication and, in fact, I know the publisher would be interested.'

'Amazing!' said Sir Dai Pol politely, turning now towards Rupert. 'Your people know everything, Lord Bair. I congratulate you. I believe,' he sucked in on his teeth again, 'she could think of something like two million.'

'Is that right for PE?' Daimon said. 'When do you see her?'

'As soon as I can take your cheque to her. Lawyers, details – that can be done quickly, I suppose?'

'BB move pretty fast.'

'And number Two, Pol?'

'I understand your wife runs an art gallery, Lord Bair. I wish to buy it.'

The champagne bubbles went up Rupert's nose and he choked. Daimon laughed, throwing back his head, while Tim Bealey thumped Rupert's back.

Sir Dai Pol crossed his legs. He put his head on one side, smiled and for the first time took a sip from his glass. 'I propose actually to make a number of acquisitions, call them what you like. I need to have an established enterprise with connections. I have heard that Lady Bair has a going concern. Can you act for her interests? And mine?'

'Listen Pol! She's no longer my wife! Lady Bair's affairs are nothing to do with me! My present wife, the Princess Tellquilla owns parts of Paris, some diamond mines, a portion of the Swiss pharmaceutical industry but no art galleries.' Lord Bair looked at him distastefully. 'I can, of course, have nothing against your pursuing your interests with my former spouse.'

'Why do you need money there?' said Daimon.

'Very great profitable prospects.'

'Anything that will get my ex-wife off my pay roll will have my full support!'

Rupert began a new doodle of Lord Bair as a pirate.

'I shall need the funds in Switzerland, without Hong Kong involvement. In fact, in strict confidence. Numbered accounts.'

'No problem.' At a nod from Lord Bair, Tim Bealey made quick notes.

'Anything else, my dear chap?' Lord Bair was now definitely fidgeting about in his chair. 'You'll forgive me, but a number of matters are pressing. We can meet again if you let my people know.'

'I would like to visit the publisher tomorrow. By helicopter.'

'Helicopter?' Tim looked puzzled. 'Where does she hang out?'

'I can brief you on that,' Rupert said quickly.

'Yes. I find it makes an impression of a kind on some people. I understand the publisher lives outside London.'

'I can fix that,' Tim said.

Lord Bair was on his feet. Daimon thrust back his chair and the others rose too. Only Sir Dai Pol was a little slower.

'I may want to sign cheques tomorrow.'

'Daimon, you speak to our people in Basle.' Lord Bair pressed the hidden buzzer. Miss Faughsquar opened the doors.

'Legal, I think now,' said Tim Bealey firmly.

Lord Bair turned, removing the half-glasses, a hand rubbing the seat of his trousers. 'Tell me, what made you come by bloody boat, Pol? Aren't planes quicker for a man in a hurry like you?'

'The Chinese symbol is the tortoise.' Sir Dai Pol smiled. 'It carries its own house. I have always liked that!' The dual voice was slow. 'You remember, of course, who won the race?'

'What I can't understand,' Norman Crimp fretted, fingering his little beard and flinging photographs about the desk, 'is that the silly bitch never told me she would sell!'

'There is a time for buying, and a time for selling.' Sir Dai Pol was sitting in the editor's chair and, to Rupert's amazement, Crimp was not objecting. He was moving about the big room, plainly upset and nervous.

'It's a plot, isn't it? You want me to come out there with you, as though I was for it! What do I get out of this?'

'Your present utterly fantastic salary and perks. This pleasantly large office. The continuation of the stream of beautiful and titled ladies sitting in your office, begging you to take their clothes off and take their pictures.'

There was no smile. The accent, to Rupert's ears, was nearer Cardiff than Canton.

'I have told you already, if you carry out my instructions, I can make the salary more fantastic and add to the perks. If you don't like it, Norman,' Dai Pol shrugged, 'I daresay I can find another editor.'

'Don't look at me!' Rupert said.

'OK!' The editor stalked about the room. 'So you say that you, subject to Tracy signing and your merchant bankers fixing the rest, will be the publisher. So what is he doing here?' He jerked his head at Rupert.

'Mr Potter is here simply as an intermediary. He undertook to introduce us. He is also a witness, if you like. He knows you, he knows me, he has met Miss Flip. My bank has various people to deal with something like this, and I understand they trust Mr Potter.'

'And why the hell do you want to own a magazine like this?' screamed Crimp. 'It must be going to cost you a packet, if I know Tracy! I've looked you up since the bank phoned, Sir Dai Pol! They say you are a gent. You don't entirely talk like one. You want to print the thing, probably in Hong Kong, you say. That's going to cause a lot of headaches.'

'Such as the loss of your present kick-back from the printers?'

Crimp crumbled visibly, then rallied visibly. 'You, sitting there! As a witness! You heard that?'

'I think,' said Rupert getting up, 'I have done my bit, and I can leave you both to it. I have nearly finished my article for you, by the way, so I'll put it in the post.'

'Don't bet on it! I may not be editor by then,' Crimp shouted. But as Rupert sought to leave, the door opened, and the long-haired photographer put his head round the edge. 'This Cynthia Flippingshaw, or whatever her name is, says you promised she could keep her drawers on!'

The editor struck his forehead dramatically. 'Oh my God! You see some of the problems! Get it? Jack, give her a glass of something. Tell her I'm coming!' He took a cigar out of a large box and cut off the end with a pair of golden scissors. Sir Dai Pol swung round gently in the editor's chair.

'That is Lady Cynthia Fallingshaw I imagine. A very delectable person. Well done! This is not an occupation you must give up, Norman. But you cannot see her now because you are coming with me. To – where is it? Norfolk?'

The photographer disappeared. Rupert had his hand on the door handle. 'It isn't Norfolk, that's only the name of the house. Crimp knows.' He looked at his wristwatch. 'And you are due there in half an hour.' He shut the door quietly.

Alone with Dai Pol, Norman Crimp looked at him thoughtfully. 'That's pushing it, but I daresay I can manage! I've got a pretty good car just round the corner.'

Sir Dai Pol got up. 'I have something better, my friend. The car and the driver from the bank are below. We drive to the Titan pad at Blackfriars and take the helicopter! We shall be there comfortably in twenty minutes.'

Exactly fifteen minutes after leaving the little oval helicopter pad on the river, the pilot set the landing lights winking and began to descend towards the paddock behind Norfolk Manse.

'That look like it, sir?' All three were on intercom headphones with speakers.

'Is that the house, Norman?'

'Yes! How much do these things cost? Bloody wonderful!' Crimp spoke to the pilot. 'How did you know how to get here?'

'Map refs, landmarks, instruments.' The accent was transatlantic. The pilot looked old enough to have just left school. His hands moved and the machine seemed to turn on its side and go down like a butterfly. It bounced lightly on the grass and, as the pilot turned off rows of switches, the blades overhead fell to a whispering silence and finally stopped. He opened the door and dropped to the ground, then turned and reached up to help the passengers down.

'You want me to wait, sir, you said?'

Sir Dai Pol nodded. 'Off we go.' He gave Crimp a firm push. 'You know the way.'

But Norman Crimp seemed in no haste. He stood looking at the bubble of glass with its high tail and drooping blades. Then turned reluctantly and shook his head.

'You could buy one of those for the office!'

They stepped across the short grass towards the house.

'Where is Miss Flip?'

'Yes, I was wondering that. I should have thought she'd be out to see us arrive with all that noise. She has a daily and a girl living-in too. Perhaps they're all scared.'

They went through a field gate and took a path that ran curving through thick laurels and dark, overhanging beech trees.

Without warning, one of the thicker branches detached itself from the trees. In a sinister dropping motion it hung round Crimp's neck, and with a desperate, high-pitched cry the editor fell to the ground.

Sir Dai Pol sprang back instantly, even as the snake began its sinuous winding, tightening slowly about the body of the hapless figure on the ground.

Sir Dai stood still. To the misting vision of the wretched editor he seemed to be eyeing him with a detached consideration. Then, as though he had made a decision, he moved. Only his hands. From an inner pocket of his jacket what looked like a fountain pen appeared and was unscrewed. It was doubtful if Crimp saw the needle of the hypodermic syringe penetrate the nearest coil. The plunger slid down and Sir Dai sprang back.

For a moment nothing happened. Then the diamond head swung up and the whole giant coil seemed to stiffen for an instant. Tiredly, gently, the coils began to slacken, slowly unwind. There was no thrashing, only a quiet, rustling collapse.

The small cylinder put away, Sir Dai put his hands under Norman Crimp's shoulders and dragged him clear. The editor's eyes were closed, his face a mud colour.

There came the sound of feet, running towards them up the path. A woman in an anorak and boots rounded the laurels and stopped, panting, her eyes wide. In one hand, Sir Dai noticed, she held what looked like a flute and a small bottle.

'My God! Are you all right? Is Norman all right?'

'Concussed a bit, I should say. Are you Miss Flip? I am Dai Pol. How do you do!'

The lady seemed much more concerned about the only actual corpse in sight. 'Oh, oh, poor Feather! He must have escaped an hour ago! There's a great hole in the glass.' She gave a small scream, dropping to her knees on the damp path. 'He's dead!' She slid her hands along the snake's body. Then she looked up, the spaniel eyes in the small, plain face watering. 'He's dead!' she repeated.

'Heart attack!' Sir Dai Pol shook his head and looked grave. 'We have some experience of these things in the Far East, Miss Flip. A sickness, some impending sense of doom, makes them try to get out. To hide, ready themselves for the end. Instead of which, it fell on your editor here and knocked him out!'

Crimp was sitting dazed on the path. Slowly he massaged his arms, rubbed his head and looked with glassy eyes at both of them.

'Bloody things,' he cried. 'I knew they'd get someone one day!' He staggered to his feet, blinking and rubbing dirt from his clothes. He kicked the coils of the dead Boa.

'Leave it alone!' Tracy Flip said coldly. 'Poor Feather had a heart attack, as Sir Dai Pol said. That can happen to any of us.'

'A stiff drink, Miss Flip, is what is needed. If your staff could arrange that. Then we must talk.'

'Staff! They've all left! And call me Tracy, by the way.' She turned and tramped up the path towards the house. 'As soon as I found that Feather had escaped, I asked them to help me search the grounds. Not a bit! They all went off with my solicitor in his car! Anyway, come on in! I suppose we can still have a chat and a drink.' She stopped. Norman Crimp stayed unmoving where he stood. Then he took a few steps backwards in the opposite direction.

'If you think I'm coming anywhere near that place,' he said in a high pitched voice, 'you can guess again! How many more of those sodding things have got through the hole by now?'

'None, you bloody fool!' screamed Tracy Flip. 'D'you think I didn't block it up at once? Well, if you don't want a drink, you can stay out here.'

'One moment!' Sir Dai Pol put a finger on the bridge of the heavy spectacles. He patted the editor's shoulder. 'You've had enough, my dear chap! Tracy and I can get on with our business, now she and I have met. Tell the pilot he's to take you back to Blackfriars. You can get a taxi from there and your doctor ought to look you over. Send the machine back for me.'

Crimp glared at them both. His little eyes and the goatee beard turning from one to the other. Then wordlessly he turned slowly and walked away round the bend in the path.

Tracy Flip pushed open the back door and began to kick off her rubber boots in the hall. 'Come right in! I meant it, honestly! It's safe!' They heard the sound of the helicopter blades as it started up, and as she led the way, clicking in high heels across the tiles of the kitchen floor, a rush of air tossed the trees and bushes outside.

'Of course I heard you arrive, but I was searching the bedrooms. Not really a welcome I'm afraid. You'll have to excuse coming in this way.' She went through the staff room, out into the hall and through to the big main room. 'My poor Feather! Oh well! After your letter and the bank's telephone call, I got my solicitor here. I don't know whether he's coming back.' They had stopped by the drinks trolley. 'Do you want a drink? It isn't the right time for anything really. Except champagne. That open one is Dom Perignon. I had a glass before I went to look for Feather! It doesn't do to let them know you're windy.'

'So very kind!' Dai Pol accepted the cut-crystal glass which she filled, pouring another for herself.

'I had an idea Chinese people never drank.' She giggled. 'Like Indians! You don't mind my saying that to you? Cheers!'

'To our business together! You realise I'm only half Chinese?' Dai Pol said gravely. 'Also that I am a very wealthy man with many interests in many parts of the world. You said I might call you Tracy?'

He watched, poised carefully as, leaving her glass, she turned her back to go over to the desk to fetch a packet of cigarettes. The dropper bottle that put the tiny squirt of clear liquid in her glass was back in his pocket even before she turned.

'Of course!'

'Let's not waste time then, but get down to the screwing! As my father used to say!' The risk was a deliberate distraction.

'I take it your father, unlike you, was no gentleman,' she said coldly, but with the glass in her hand, nearly half of it was being swallowed quickly. She blew out cigarette smoke. 'God, how I really hate these things! They spoil the taste of a decent drink!'

'My father was from Tiger Bay, Cardiff, my dear!'

'Not Tiger Balm mountain?' She pointed to the opposite armchairs in front of the empty fireplace.

'Oh, so you know Hong Kong?'

Dai Pol had not known what to expect. A tough, American-style Madame; perhaps a hard, French executive type, like some of the cosmetic-trade types he had met. He studied the small pug-dog face, the pullover and plain tweed skirt. Only a faint scent that he had slowly become aware of in the big room, was at variance with convention; the gloomy furniture, chandeliers, the status symbol silver ornaments, the lattice windows.

'You burn incense?'

'I was brought up in India.'

'Ah! So the Boas?'

'In their conservatory behind those curtains.' Tracy Flip eyed him carefully. She filled her glass again, lit a cigarette and leaned back in the big chintzy chair. Through half-closed eyelids she tried to make a quick instinctive summing up. If she had understood the long call from the merchant bank, her solicitor and the letter from the man himself, he had actually come to clinch a sale. To buy the magazine that had so miraculously produced so much money, first for her father, then for her. For him, like buying a car or a pair of shoes.

'I know you're surprised.' She started talking quickly. 'I never had anything much to do with the bloody magazine. As a matter of fact I hate it! I leave it all to Norman Crimp. Norman Creep, I call him!' She giggled again nervously, sipping the champagne. She noticed that he had not drunk since the first salutation. 'I never go into the office if I can help it. I like some of the girls who get into the magazine – you know that was Dad's idea, don't you? They all come from top-drawers. God, how Crimp has played with that in the captions! Titles, gold spoons well down the gullet. The sort of thing I never had!' She realised she was probably saying too much to this stranger, but it was such a relief, and a comfortable, warm, almost languid feeling of confidence was coming with it. 'I mean when you said that bit about screwing, I don't mind. Because men talk like that. They talk to me like that, because they think that must be my kind of business. I hate it. But I'll forgive you!'

'I'm sorry. It was, just as you say, a rather coarse business expression.' Sir Dai Pol's face was now almost expressionless. He watched the level in her glass, and took some folded papers from the inside breast pocket of his jacket.

'So you see I'm not a worldly girl,' Tracy Flip was saying, leaning back in the over-large chintz chair, her eyes bright, legs stuck out straight. 'Not a jet set biz executive! Since India, I haven't travelled anywhere much, in spite of making money.' She frowned. 'I wish my solicitor would come back! It's too stupid! I keep a few harmless snakes to scare away burglars, and now I have no staff and no one to help me!' She looked as though tears were coming to her eyes.

Sir Dai Pol moved quickly. This was the danger with the spiking game, especially with women. It could go either way.

'We don't need him, my dear. He has told the bank your price and how you want it paid and they have told me. I have three simple slips of paper here. An irrevocable document of sale at two million pounds. I think that is excessive but I have agreed to accept it.'

'For two pounds a copy circulation it's not too much –' The warm confidence was back. 'Where's the money?'

'Here!' With solemn formality he put two cheques on the small table beside her. 'One for one million drawn on Bair Brady. The other on the Swiss Bank as you requested. They are as good as a suitcase full of notes. I ask for no warranties, no guarantees, no publicity. I have arranged for ownership of the business to move to a Lichtenstein holding company. It seems Bair Brady have much the same idea as yourself, about owning such a magazine on my behalf, and they have found me an off-shore vehicle.'

'It sounds like a paddle boat!' Tracy wanted to giggle, or cry, she didn't know which.

'Lord Bair and I are both sailors.' Gravely, Sir Dai held out a gold fountain pen with the top unscrewed.

'If you sign there, by that seal, the bank will witness. You take the cheque and deal with them. If you do it like a good girl, you will be free! And a millionaire!'

'And I don't have to see the Creep any more or hide away?'

'He is now my problem.' The fountain pen in her hand moved unsteadily across the documents.

At the Bank the red light shone over the doors outside Lord Bair's office. Inside, a conspiratorial air prevailed while Lord Bair deciphered a curling paper telex message, and lowering his voice, looked around at the closed doors.

'Bring out the chart, Daimon, and we'll just do some calculations! I think a bit of sport is definitely in the offing! Here! Do the translation.'

'Admiralty 2040.' Daimon's heavy face reddened, as he bent to pull open a low drawer and drew out the rolled, heavy sheet of paper. He put it on the desk.

'Not very difficult to find this one!'

Lord Bair was working with a French tides tables and an old paper-backed code manual.

'Listen. *Passage Cherbourg entre neuf onze le dimanche. Debarquement chez vous zero trois.*' The accent was all that Harrow had laboured for in vain. Lord Bair rubbed his hands. 'Always amazed by your grasp of the lingo, Desmond! What's the fix?'

'Forty-three Northing 29 East.'

'Have you got *Reed's*?'

'The tide's all right.'

'No moon, of course. Always no moon. It was like sitting duck last time.'

'The big party, the time before, when they were roped together! That was the best sport! You'd think they might be a bit discouraged by now.' Daimon rubbed a heavy, slightly stubbled chin that bulged over his pin-striped shirt collar. 'I sometimes wonder if we might run into a bit of opposition one day, you know, Desmond.'

'Ready for that, too?'

'Isn't your man away?'

'Yes. That is a bit of a rub. Need three, if there's any sort of backing and filling. Trouble is, I don't think I can get him back very easily. His brother was shot up by the Provisionals, and he's gone home on a vendetta. Doesn't even answer cables threatening to fire him!'

'You can't really do that anyway. Can you?'

'He who rides a tiger can't dismount very easily, I agree.' His cousin put on the pair of half-spectacles and studied the French code book.

'Good chap, our French connection! Nothing like a bit of *pied-noir* to make an effective contribution to the cause. I'll telex it's on then. Good idea that signing as

Banque de Corsica. My dear dragons outside think its a dive for mulcting the French franc. Now, are you out to lunch, Daimon? Because I have a connection for two o'clock.' He glanced over his spectacles at the combined brass ship's clock and barometer on the wall. 'In about an hour.'

Both he and Daimon accepted the element of real necessity in the bank tradition that senior directors were allowed to be mysterious, even with each other, about early negotiation contacts.

'All this damned insider information rot!' Daimon said. 'Hope you're on to something that will tickle things up.'

'I am,' said Lord Bair.

'We need it.' His cousin looked grim for a moment. 'Have you seen the provisional half-year figures?'

'It's Hardy!' said Sir Dai Pol's daughter. She stood motionless with her father in the dim illumination of the bridge deck of the *Chenn Lo.* The green light from the big instrument console reflected on her small, white face, the cigarette in the ivory holder a tiny red glow.

'Hardy?' Her father was suddenly tense. 'Someone you know?'

'The fat customs! The thin one, I think, is Laurel!'

The great majority of other boats, including the tall-masted Thames barges, were still, dark and seemingly unoccupied. The long white hull of the *Chenn Lo* gleamed in the overhead lighting strung along the jetty.

'What can he want this time?' Sir Dai Pol slid open the bridge door and went aft as the officer came ponderously up the short gangplank.

'Came to thank you for the case of whisky, sir! Not strictly permitted but appreciated by my colleagues and myself.'

'Ah, good! It was delivered then. Do you happen to know if the Harbour Master –?'

'The same, sir. I expect he'll be round.' The man's face was in shadow but he had a small, official handlight which he now shone up above their heads.

'My colleague noticed the special aerial that went up today. Nothing to worry about, but you'll need a TV licence if its for more than a month.'

'No, officer. It is not TV. The ship has a TV set but that is not it. Also all the radio and radar you would expect. The fact is I have a special short wave receiver to keep in touch with my business in Hong Kong. It needs that aerial.'

'There was a special odour, sir. No offence, but a mention was made by other vessels.' The chubby customs man had moved along the deck with a surprisingly quick step to the bridge deck door. He slid it open and peered down into the gloom, sniffing solemnly.

'You have made clear the penalty for opium, to the crew, sir?'

'What you smell, officer, is incense,' said Dai Pol easily. 'Some of the more rare joss sticks. I'm afraid it's traditional where we come from!'

'Could be, sir!' The fat customs officer took the few steps back to the outer door, where he turned. 'Often used to cover the other smell, sir. Does a good job!'

'As you do!' Sir Dai's wide row of teeth shone in the green light.

'Goodnight, sir!'

'Goodnight, officer.'

'Come,' said Dai Pol presently. They left the bridge and went below, moving along the companionway to where a door was marked with the international lightening streak code. Inside the two Chinese crew were crouched over banked instrument decks. On the bench a tape spool wound its solemn way. Sir Dai Pol shut the door behind them.

'From tomorrow you will have another. Reception from Two is further.'

The steward Shee finished spinning the tape on the spool that was one of two he and the engineer had been playing with. He put earphones onto a shelf and plucked up switches that turned off small coloured lights.

'Is finished now. I think?'

'The monitor goes on at eight.'

Shee nodded and stood up. The other man pressed a button and the sound of the aerial on the cabin roof retracting juddered faintly above their heads.

'Do not let Hoffmann see or hear the tapes. The Hong Kong story is good enough, even for someone who knows navigational gear.' Dai Pol spoke in Cantonese for another last instruction. Then he and Kitty left the cabin.

'The magazine office?' Kitty asked when they were in the stateroom.

'The editor's desk.'

'How did you do that?'

'He got the model Ferrari. I told him if he was a good boy in his new responsibilities for one month, he could keep it. It is silver plated, heavy. He will not move it. I said it must not disappear. Mr Crimp has made a lot of other company property disappear.'

'How do they work, papa?'

'The monitors? That is very simple. They are short distance, ultra-short wave receivers on a fixed wave length Japanese, of course. But they have one advantage over some earlier models. They only transmit when someone is speaking or there is some noise nearby to activate them. This saves the batteries. There is, after all, no way of replacing them.

'Difficult. In the case of Lord Bair, certainly. Besides,' her father spoke very gently, 'only you and the two men know, so it would not be difficult to tell if there was –'

'Father! Please!'

'There is a lot to learn from the inside of a Merchant Bank. I have telephoned my broker to buy quite a lot of a Japanese stock as a result of one remark. There are other things. The first conversation between Lord Bair and his cousin was most intriguing. Perhaps it was nothing. When I have looked in a French dictionary and our brave Captain has found me a chart with a certain number, I may be able to make some guesses.'

6

The special quality of the sunlight that filtered into the bedroom first thing, Rupert decided on waking, was its wateriness. He knew how the world looked to a trout.

Of course it was the same. Weren't most mornings the same? But last night had been different. He put a hand slowly to his head. The violence there was real. A lump and grazed flesh. A foot rubbed up and down against his pyjamaed leg.

Maddy was awake, the face pink and *gamin* on the pillow. The customary one black eye from shifted mascara was only cosmetic violence.

'Pot! Darling Pot. What happened in the night?' Her voice was slow and heavy.

'I hurt myself. I feel dreadful.'

'Where did you go?'

'I got muddled about banks and boats and ballet.'

'That's alliteration, Pot.'

'I am illiterate and that worries me, too. I can't write all these articles for people. I went to places and had drinks. I couldn't go down to the boat again. I felt lost. I didn't put on the lights when I got back here – it was so late. And I got lost on the landing.'

'How, lost?' The foot stopped sliding. Maddy was always quick to sense some criticism of the flat.

'There's that new lampshade in the hall.'

'My Granny's going away hat. After her wedding! It's beautiful!'

'I thought it was a person!'

'Darling!' The foot came back.

'The pictures!' said Rupert, remembering with horror now, his return in the small hours. 'You changed the big Scottish landscape for that modern thing! Those two coloured blobs in the chromium frame. I turned the wrong way to find the bathroom door. It was the airing cupboard. I hurt myself quite badly!'

Now Maddy reached out a bare arm, pulled the bruised forehead nearer to her and bestowed a gentle kiss on Rupert's brow.

'Is the rest of you in shape?'

At that moment the bedroom door flung open and the beautiful Audrey, already dressed in school clothes, threw herself ecstatically on the end of the bed. Maddy sat up sharply, clutching the bedclothes to her front.

'Audrey! That might have broken my leg!'

'I saw you! You and Pot kissing. Why is he in bed? Are you having babies?'

'Pot has stayed in bed because he is very poor and ill! You can go round his side and give him a kiss, too. He has hurt his head.'

'Oooooh! I will!'

Rupert lay back under a barrage of small, wet kisses.

'I'll draw the curtains,' Audrey said efficiently. The room filled with blinding light and the telephone rang, and Maddy had it to her ear instantly.

'OK. Listen! I'll be in the gallery by ten.'

Nancy was bringing in coffee, hot milk and croissants, and Maddy waved a hand in greeting and Rupert tried to smile. 'Yes! Well, OK! If he gets in before that, you keep him entertained! What's that? Well, like any other. Gee, honey, listen! He's not Chinese! Strictly British. More than British I would guess, if I know that kind of thing.'

'He's not entirely,' Rupert mumbled wearily.

'Would you like some coffee, Mr Potter?' Nancy said.

'Very much.'

'Pot's hurt!'

'I *am* sorry. How is that?'

'Yes, how, Pot?'

'I ran into the new granny-lampshade hat. It scared me.'

Audrey rolled on to the bed squealing with laughter.

'Shut up damn it, all of you! Ruthy, listen.' Maddy was still on the phone. 'Yeah, Pot's whooping them up here, he's just a kid, too. You do that! He has a daughter, yeah, and Polly is squiring her round town. She's met him too, and says he's charming. Sure for the dough. Done through Desmond, sort of. The Bank is behind him. 'Bye sweety!'

Maddy smiled round at the assembled dependants and took a swig at her morning coffee. 'Good morning, everybody!'

'Do you think I could get up?' Rupert said desperately. 'Maddy, I would like to tell you about Sir Dai Pol before you meet him. And could I have my coffee in the living room?'

'Nancy, could you do that?' He felt the bare foot begin to touch his leg again. At least it was something to know she felt that way, although now it was all too late, and nothing could happen, which was probably why she did it.

'Yes, indeed, Lady Bair. Audrey you come with me!'

'Can I have breakfast with Pot?'

'That depends on Mr Potter who is not feeling well.'

'Run along, darling! Bring your wheaties up and Pot will have his breakfast with you.'

When they had gone, Rupert managed to get into his dressing gown which he found under the bed.

'Darling!' Rupert looked at her. 'It's never the right moment!' He had tried before and he would try again. He hoped he looked pale and wounded and dramatic. Perhaps Byronic. 'Could we get over this stage? Could we – well get on with it? Get married! Would you? I mean, could we?'

The telephone's outrageous ring was brief because

Maddy had it to her ear even as Rupert tried to kiss her.

'Wilf!'

'Oh, my God, not the Poult!' Rupert shouted insanely. 'At this hour! It's too much! I'm a reasonable man, but does he think' –!'

'I can't now. Yes, I loved it too! Next Thursday? Look, I'll have to see. OK! Phone me again! 'Byee!' She put down the phone. 'Is that short enough?'

Rupert felt dizzy. It was all a hopeless cause. Maddy was too quick, too clever, too beautiful, in demand, independent. It was madness to think she could ever take him seriously.

'Pot, what's the matter?'

'I'm mad about Maddy!'

'Potty about Pot! Go right away, have your nice coffee, have breakfast with my daughter, but you're not to flirt with her! Then you can come with me to the Gallery, 'cos I want you to help me with this Deed Poll or what-ever.'

'Dai Pol. Sir Dai Pol! You don't need my help,' Rupert said bitterly.

'You've met him. You can introduce him. He wants to do some serious sort of business. Tim Bealey called me from the bank – apparently the guy thought Desmond and I were still married. Now he's decided that doesn't make any difference.'

Maddy had started to nibble her croissant, and was beginning to read through the *Daily Signal* which had come up with the tray. 'Hey, listen, get this! It's a para about Debby Paleggy. It says she's going to make a film in the South of France. Did you know that?'

'Why should I?'

'Oh, Pot!' Maddy sounded genuinely exasperated. 'You were sitting next to her at dinner last week. But never mind. I expect you talked to her about her boobs.'

'Happy Croissant!' said Rupert, trailing out to where Audrey was calling for him.

The hired Daimler took Sir Dai Pol silently and swiftly

out of the docks, past the Tower, where the flags on the masts pointed steadily upriver on the wind, and drove down Fleet Street and the Strand. At Trafalgar Square Sir Dai stopped using his pocket calculator and looked out through the dark-glass windows. Nelson's Column, lions, New Zealand House, Canada House, South Africa House, the National Gallery and St Martin's. None of it had changed much.

'Up the Empire, boyo!' His father had said that. The driver slid back the glass.

'I didn't get that, sir?'

'You can't park in Curzon Street. So you can leave me there. I shall need collecting from Bair Brady at tea time.'

'Tea time, sir?'

'Between four and five. Or has that changed?'

At the offices of *Groin*, Norman Crimp was not at first to be found and Dai Pol waited, sitting in the editor's black leather swing chair. He noticed with satisfaction that amidst the confusion of proofs, letters, glossy pictures, colour transparencies and other stuff on the editor's plastic desk, the silver Ferrari remained in position.

'Testing, testing!' whispered Sir Dai Pol briefly.

Crimp burst in looking distraught, kicked away the telephone directory that was propping open the door and, looking sulky as the new owner of the magazine made no effort to move, flung himself on to the casting couch. He relit a cigar which hung on the edge of a pedestal ashtray. Sparks showered on to his small, pointed beard and, frantically, Crimp beat about his chin.

'Bloody bitches! They try and up the ante when they get into the studio! Agents, mothers, boyfriends are specifically excluded in the contracts! They don't need them. The rich got richer, and these up-market birds –'

Dai Pol held up a hand. 'You are absolutely sure the contracts give us film rights. Including overseas?'

'I sent you a copy to the bank,' Crimp muttered. 'You ought to read it.'

'How did the flight go yesterday?'

'Terrific!' The editor brightened at once. 'Nothing like it! The chopper really tickles them. I told the booby Lady Paleggy the evening before about the French film offer. We lifted off about twelve – smoked salmon sandwiches and champagne as you suggested. The pilot found that little airport near Rheims, no trouble, and the people on the executive jet who took her over were helpfulness itself.' Crimp looked hard at Dai Pol. 'Not French, I would say. There was one young chap, very smooth, said he was assistant to the president. Mafia, I thought.'

'Did you, now? But then perhaps you know the Mafia, Norman? Perhaps they take an interest in some of your currency fiddles over the last years?'

Norman Crimp got up menacingly, came over and stood at the desk. 'What has that little cow Tracy been telling you? All right. So you saved my life, or did you? You're a sinister bastard!'

'For that word, my father once put a knife into someone.'

'Withdrawn.' The shoulders in the creased linen suit seemed to sag. He dropped into the chair facing Sir Dai. 'Just to change the subject, there's a technicality. Who actually owns the bloody magazine? It has to go into the imprint you know.'

'A company in Lichtenstein. You will get a note from the bank. That is no problem. But I am the owner. The bank confirmed that too in your new engagement letter. I did read that.'

'I am an editor, not a business shark,' said Crimp with tattered dignity. He tilted his small beard and drew on the cigar. It had gone out.

'You are a pornographer!' said Sir Dai Pol coldly. He drew out of his inner pocket a thin sheet of paper. 'Now will you listen to me carefully. For the next two weeks you will make all arrangements we have spoken about to provide Groin Films Limited with the ladies on this list. They have all appeared in the magazine at one time or another over the last two years. I hope you know how to contact them. If any of them have married in the mean-time, strike them out.'

'Your film company doesn't like married ladies in the parts? Or the parts of married ladies? Which is it?'

'Spare me your humour. Also your vulgarity, commonness, lectures on pubes, boobs or all the other puerility on which you are an authority. I want to know each day that you have done a proper delivery job for the film company. I shall telephone you.'

The editor was glancing down the list of names.

'You certainly have picked out the top drawer lot. For looks and social cachet.'

'Please copy out the names now and give me the list back! They can travel two at a time if need be, to speed it up. And listen again, Crimp, this is important. You will tell them that they are not to make any personal publicity. Of any kind. Publicity is the sole prerogative of my film company. The young lady yesterday – what was her name?'

'Debby Paleggy.'

'There was a mention that she was film-making in the South of France in one of the more stupid tabloids. Tell any of them if that sort of thing happens, the whole contract will be voided!'

The editor got up and glanced at his heavy gold wrist watch. 'How the hell am I supposed to get out the magazine as well as all this? I wouldn't mind getting into films a bit more myself actually.' For a moment he studied the man sitting at his desk. The oddly featured face, the thick grey hair, the expensive black silk suit and cream foulard tie. He would mention this man, and what he knew of him, in one or two circles – people he could tap in Fleet Street. Carefully, of course, but he might glean something that would right the balance a little. His new contract and more money had been a pleasant surprise. But there had always been perks worth twice as much as his salary, unknown to Tracy Flip or the new owner.

'If any of your Sloane Rangers make real objections or trouble at any stage while you are escorting them, bring them back.' Sir Dai Pol was quickly and quietly on his feet moving towards the door.

'They're not likely to. The strange thing about our upper market sisters,' said Crimp, proffering professional wisdom, 'is that they will do almost more for money than the pros. The majority of them are broke.'

'And Norman,' Sir Dai Pol paused, 'don't talk about me. That would be finish!'

For his next call, a cab, which he caught without trouble in Curzon Street, took Sir Dai Pol to Knightsbridge.

Outside the gallery he stood for a moment on the pavement and read Maddy Bair's brass plate. Then he looked briefly in the window and mentally priced the antiques. Classy stuff but not much of it. He smiled.

From the other side of the window, through a tiny hole in the velvet back drop, Ruthy applied an eye.

'He's here!'

'Let him ring the bell.'

'You said I could sit in with you!'

'Sure,' Maddy said, a little impatiently. 'I reckon that's going to look right and proper. After all, I don't really know what the guy's got in mind. His letter didn't say.'

Sir Dai, having finally studied the panelled and polished door, pushed the bell under the brass plate. It could be all right; it could be too small. His first impression was of something that was a cross between an Amsterdam arms dealer and a Harley street consultant, but London was full of contradictions. The little lady who opened the door had faded red hair and a pale face. It was a face that behind a careful smile was apprehensive. He made a mental note to consider why later.

'Lady Bair?'

'No, I'm her assistant, well, partner, really! Come right in.'

The front door was shut and locked behind him, Dai Pol noted that too. He did a lightning inspection. There were three good pictures on the walls, a Picasso and what looked like a pair of small Gainsboroughs. The small carpet on the floor was possibly original. The desk was early Georgian and the silver inkwell was collectable. Presumably all for sale.

'Maddy – Sir Dai Pol has arrived!'

Presumably this was Lady Bair who now came to the door of the small rear office. Dai Pol made a little bow and followed her in. Ruthy squeezed into a chair between a pile of books and a portable typewriter that were on the floor. Maddy pretended to find Sir Dai Pol's letter and flashed him her most brilliant smile as he sat down opposite her.

'You are Lady Bair?'

'Shall I get out my passport? The photo isn't very good!'

'Now you are trying to embarrass me. It is just that you are – not as I expected.'

'That's because you've met my ex-husband!'

Sir Dai Pol smiled. 'And this lady is your partner?'

'We work together.'

'You are both Americans?' asked Sir Dai. 'Forgive me, but you appreciate that I have business to discuss which is very confidential and well, perhaps it is difficult sometimes for us to be as direct as Americans.'

'The oriental inscrutability?' He was an odd customer, this one. Maddy eyed him carefully. Both Tim and Rupert had given her a little idea of what to expect. The way he had run over her with those narrowed eyes behind the big glasses made her feel as though he had frisked her. As she reached for a cigarette from the packet on the desk the visitor instantly produced a thin gold lighter from his black silk waistcoat pocket.

'OK! So we will both be careful of each other, and your partner will see fair play! I will tell you frankly that when I wrote to you, I planned to include your gallery in my business plans during my London visit. I believed you were the wife of Lord Bair. Because his bank manages my affairs over here.'

'Sure. Go ahead!' Maddy blew out cigarette smoke, moved a bowl of flowers, decided to play faintly bored and half closed her eyes. It was an affectation that made people think she was not all that interested.

'You are no longer married, Lady Bair, but I think perhaps you are serious about your business. Also I understand you specialise in overseas sales and certain kinds of connections.'

The bright cheeks hollowed and the quick sensual mouth pursed over the cigarette. Looking at her, he could begin to understand the special appeal these ladies must undoubtedly have to some of his other customers. The ones who used *Groin* as a shopping catalogue.

'The selling of special stuff through agents – certainly,' Maddy said. 'I have people with good connections in Paris, Zurich, Germany or even further east, and in New York.' She tried a quick shot. 'Why don't you deal yourself, Sir Dai?'

'I have the articles, very special, very expensive. But not the time. It is as simple as that.'

'Do I get it that these special things, *objets* or whatever you want to sell,' Maddy's expression had become totally innocent, 'are yours? Do we get commission? We can place almost anything on the market through Art Appreciation. If we know what it is.'

'These are most exceptionally rare pieces. Very old. Ceramics, bronze, jade, precious jewellery.'

'From China?'

'You are very quick, Lady Bair.'

'Not from Hong Kong?'

'Not from Hong Kong.'

'Nor dealt before?'

'For the first time.'

'How do we deal?'

'If I say ten per cent, you must not rush to tell me that you normally expect twenty or thirty. I know. But this is different. I shall name a bottom price. You will arrange a sale through your people. They and their clients will agree a price – perhaps more, never less. The items are unique. There should be no difficulty. The payment must be abroad and must be to a Swiss bank account. You may have your take where you like. The pieces will not be handed over to the customer until the bank has notified me that the payment is deposited, so we shall both be safe.'

'Well all that's not very unusual, I guess.' Maddy Bair stubbed out her cigarette, eased back her chair, and crossed the immaculate legs. But it was at Ruthy Sir Dai Pol was looking, twisting and untwisting her fingers on the sofa. So nervous the little one.

'How about a cup of coffee, Sir Dai? Or Ruthy! That half of champagne would make three glasses.'

The cork was popped and the glasses filled. 'Could we see some of the things you have to dispose of?' Ruthy said. 'I mean – ten per cent is really way off. Are they here in London?' She began to feel uncomfortable. Sir Dai Pol was still looking at her, and suddenly, intuitively, she knew that he knew about the dark cupboards and the other bits. Shakily she drank her champagne, emptying her glass.

Now he had looked back to Maddy and was brisk and genial. 'I will tell you how it will work. Each piece will come to you here in London – and remember I have paid for that. You will find a buyer. But it must be very quick. I am only here for a very short time. Your people can fly, telephone, cable at my cost. If you cannot transact fast, and see the money reaches the account numbers fast, tell me. I would rather know now. If you can, the first example will be with you this afternoon. It is typical of what I am offering. It will be brought by an unusual courier. The Hon Mrs Flinders. The bank tells me she can be totally trusted. She is also escorting my daughter who does not know London. It seems she travels in a bus, a usefully innocuous vehicle.'

'Polly Flinders, of course,' said Maddy. 'She does all sorts of assignments. Yes, that's OK. She will tell me where she collects from, inevitably. So you might as well.'

'The Chinese Embassy?' Ruthy said softly.

It was Sir Dai Pol's turn to be momentarily taken aback and Ruthy saw the high-boned, putty-coloured cheek muscles twitch, under the black spectacles.

'Lady Bair, we must trust each other. I could locate other people, other galleries, but I was given special reference to you by Lord Bair's bank and a gentleman you may know, Mr Epoch, and I am short on time. If you can evaluate what I send to you this afternoon, I will telephone, and you will get to work quickly. I want no trouble with insurance, breakage, losses, customs.'

'This outfit is not bent, Sir Dai.'

'That is why I have come to you, Lady Bair. I want quick, efficient results. If you play your side of the cards right, you will make a very great deal of money, believe me.'

He rose abruptly, nodded pleasantly and stretched out a pudgy hand. Maddy uncoiled from her chair with accustomed grace and gave him her hand across the desk. Ruthy led the way through the office door into the gallery.

'No hat, no bag?'

'No.' Sir Dai had stopped beside the little reception desk. With a quick, unexpected movement he lifted the telephone to reveal a small plastic box beneath. With one finger he pressed a button that flipped the lid, expertly removed the tape cassette and slid it into his pocket as Maddy came up behind him.

'I think the record of our little agreement will be more useful to me than to you, Lady Bair! And with such an efficient partner to help you, I think everything augurs most excellently! Will you unlock the door?'

Sir Dai dismissed the Daimler at the gates to St Katharine's Dock and told the driver to return at three-thirty. To reach the boat, he joined the people strolling in the sunshine along the waterfront by the Ivory House quay, and stopped for a moment. It was not Hong Kong, but there were similarities. The tall masted barges with their tan sails, the little red-lacquered bridge, the crowded moorings of the small boats, looked and smelled familiar. One needed a base that felt not totally strange, for difficult operations.

When he came up onto the main deck, the screens were erected, lunch laid out and Kitty was at the table with a smiling Shee in attendance.

'For drinking, sir?' Shee used Cantonese.

'The water.'

'Is it going well, papa? You look better in your real dress!'

Sir Dai placed a formal kiss on his daughter's fringed brow and sat down.

'Yes. But this evening we shall have the temple of solace. I think this evening again.'

'I thought it was agreed –'

'You have found the arrangements to your liking? Your money? The shopping? This afternoon you will go again with Mrs Flinders for a small collection for me on your way to the matinée.'

'Yes, papa.'

Shee returned with glasses, ice and mineral water. The bubbles sprang up and danced in the sunlight.

'There is quite a lot on the tapes, sir.'

'I shall run through them after lunch, and you and Cheng Sun will help me. I go to the bank at four after my daughter leaves. You may both have the evening for yourselves. Has Captain Hoffmann reported?'

'He came this morning, papa. He seems happy. He likes the London pubs. I have not been into one yet and he offered to take me.'

'I think probably not.'

'You take a lot of risk, father. Can I not take a little?'

'I have to.' He paused carefully. 'I will take care of you and you will attend to my needs.'

'And if it goes wrong here?' Kitty looked around. They were alone. 'The captain could not be reached so quickly! And the lock gates depend on the tide.'

'The boat would stay,' her father said shortly. 'The helicopter is five minutes away. I have open tickets from several airports. Come, you may serve our food.'

In Bair Brady's number three conference room, Sir Mick Muldoon sat with Tim Bealey over a silver-plated tray of tea things. It was the smallest of the several chambers available for the business of the bank and seemed crowded with only the two of them.

Sir Michael sipped his tea noisily. 'When's this bugger due? Why are we in number three anyway?'

'Afternoon seems to be the time when we fill up with borrowers, I suppose. Besides, this is just a routine check-up. You've met him, haven't you?'

'Yes. Bit of a strange bird, I thought. He's yours and who else's?'

'He seems to have a direct line to Desmond. But this doesn't warrant the chairman, so you and I have drawn. Besides you know the Far East markets better than most. Have you looked into his file?'

'Not since it first went round, no, I can't say I have. Canton Bank and Pol Properties, isn't it? What are we in for?'

'Four now. Up to ten possibly, but warranted. Back in a month, so Desmond ruled its bridging. It was that chap Epoch who runs *Midas* who asked the old man to be helpful, I believe.'

'He seems to be able to lean on him. And a lot of other people I believe.'

The bullet head and navy-blue uniform of one of the porters thrust through the door. 'Sir Pol. Sir!'

'Come in, my dear fellow!' Muldoon eased a chair round. 'Do you take tea? Good! You do it, Tim.'

'Milk? Sugar?'

'Just tea.' Sir Dai Pol smiled affably and Sir Mick Muldoon hunched in his chair looking like an undertaker. It discouraged borrowers. He knew some of the Kongs, but not this one. They tended to grow overnight like those Chinese mushrooms. Tim Bealey was running through some papers.

'Second tranche comes down tomorrow. That's up to four million.'

'Pounds?'

117

'Three in Swiss, as you requested, at market rate. No point in buying forward. What then?'

'I shall have to keep in touch. There could be a quick flow back, at the most a few days.'

'Can we know a bit more about the investment?' Tim could be very charming. 'I know the old man has satisfied himself, but I don't think any of the rest of us know more than the magazine acquisition. Film production someone said?'

'You can lose your shirt on that,' Muldoon grunted. 'Got good people?'

'All my people are top. I am not speaking of the magazine – that is a sideline for the printing presses. I am engaged in some more serious purchases.'

'And they need a lot of cash up front?'

'Up front, through the back door,' Sir Dai Pol said drily.

'And you'll make sure it comes back through our front door?' They all knew it was a cue for laughter. Jolly, hollow, bankers' laughter, as empty as vaults.

'Hi kids!' said the Hon Polly Flinders. She put a brown cardboard box sealed with many bands of tape on Ruthy's desk. '*The* courier service! We try harder!'

Polly was exaggeratedly cheerful and clowned about. She wore an outsize pink beret, a gold lamé jacket and red Russian boots. She made her outsize earrings tinkle like temple bells, and to heighten the effect she pulled the corners of her eyes out.

'You pay me me now! "For velly dangerous mission!" Hi! Maddy. That Gugi I see there? *Groozi!* Isn't that what they say in the alps?'

Ruthy opened a petty cash tin and carefully gave Polly a five pound note. 'Just initial here for me.'

'You won't put the tax man on to me?'

Gugi tapped the box thoughtfully with a manicured forefinger. Then all three looked pointedly at Polly.

'OK! Don't worry! I'm off! The bus is on a yellow line. I know you don't want me. Besides I've got Kinky Kitty out there. You met her yet, Maddy?'

'Is she kinky?'

'Oh, I dunno! Something. Bye all!' Polly's earrings tinkled, the smile she gave them was wholly beautiful, and the Russian boots took her out through the door with all the swagger of a genuine Cossack.

Maddy lit a cigarette taken from the pack on Ruthy's desk and led the way into the little back office. 'Bring that box through here.'

'I'll just lock the door, Maddy!'

'All right. But I'm expecting Wilf Poult.'

'You're to sell this thing, Maddy darling? Am I right?' Gugi straddled a small mother-of-pearl inlay chair, straining his drainpipe black-velvet trousers. 'Are you going to open it?'

'Right now!' With swift strokes of the paper knife, Maddy slit the Sellotape. She lifted the lid. Stringy wood shavings sprang up, and her hands moved carefully into it.

She lifted out an object swathed in clear plastic wrapping. It was not large, and from the way Maddy held it, of no great weight.

'You don't know what it is, darleeng?' Gugi said.

'He wouldn't say. That's why you're here and why Wilf's coming! I've told you, we've got to get a move on. He wants the money fast.'

Maddy unwound the soft plastic as though unbandaging a broken limb, and Ruthy moved the box on to the floor and nervously picked up pieces of wood shaving.

Slowly Maddy held up in her hands a blue-and-white ceramic object.

It was a vase, with two small curved handles like a double jug, and a long neck that flared and closed again at the top. The slim, elegant shape, on which a dragon and cloud design seemed to dance, glowed softly in a blue and white perfection that was like the light of a summer morning, recreated in miniature.

Very slowly, Gugi got up and circled the desk. His long fingers reached out and stroked the twin handles.

119

'Where does this guy come from, Madeleine, darling?'

'Hong Kong.'

'And he wants to sell this?'

At that moment the doorbell rang. Ruthy, who had kicked off her shoes, ran like an excited child and stood on tiptoe to use the peep-hole in the door. 'It's Wilf, Maddy!' She unlocked the door and let him in.

Sir Wilfred Poult, in a crumpled suit and carrying an umbrella that looked like a dead heron hooked over his arm, seemed tense. His rather small dark eyes jumped on either side of his thin nose as he took in the scene in Maddy's office. He took two strides to the desk.

'What have we here?' The umbrella dropped to the carpet as in the manner of an actor playing the lead part, he lifted up the blue-and-white flask gently, in both hands, and edged nearer to the light coming through the back window.

'Bring it out front!' Maddy Bair stepped over to the door, trailing cigarette smoke, and flicked on switches. The gallery lit up from carefully sited flood and spot lights so that everything in it glowed and shone with colour and shadows.

Slowly Sir Wilfred came into the centre of the room, holding the vase in front of him.

'Where did you get this?' he rapped out.

'A foreign client. Wants me to sell it for him.' There was a pause.

'Is it – ah – hot?'

'I wouldn't think so,' Maddy said a little distantly. 'He's a client of Desmond's too. He comes from where the thing was made. Or originally, I would say, some of him does.'

'How long ago?'

'Only a few days, I believe.'

'No, no!' Sir Wilfred was jumpy. 'I mean this!' He held up the vase. 'You! What do you say?'

Gugi, who was fingering the gold chain on his wrist, murmured, 'Meeng! About three hundred and fifty.'

Sir Wilfred Poult bared his yellowing teeth in a mirthless

smile. 'This is so rare that I think you do not know what you are doing! A Moon Flask, early fifteenth century. I can trace the markings when I can get to some books in the museum. An X-Ray would show if there are any cracks. I would say,' he held the flask high in the air, 'there might be one like it, but not so good, in the Topkapi Sarayi – Istanbul.'

'Wilf, darling.' Maddy put a hand on his arm. 'What is it worth?'

'Difficult. Certainly over a quarter of a million pounds!'

There was a crash as Ruthy, who had been tiptoeing nervously round the desk, tripped on her stocking tips and fell against the desk bringing down the telephone.

'Don't do that, Ruthy dear!' Maddy said calmly.

Rupert came to collect Maddy from the gallery. They went to Thierry's.

In the half-dark, the candles on the tables shone in Maddy's eyes and on her face.

'I think I'm going to make a fortune! The Hong Kong Polly Wolly is coming up trumps! Darling, let's have a champagne cocktail or something to celebrate!'

Rupert's hopes rose. 'Next week? I'll get a special licence!'

'Pot sweet! So dear!'

Rupert ordered the drinks, the special mushroom dish to begin with, salmon done in pastry and Maddy's favourite white wine, *Gewurztraminer*.

'Quarter of a million pounds!' she whispered.

'Is that what you've got?'

'It'll come through a Swiss bank. I get ten per cent! And more to come. Darling, so exciting!' She squeezed his hand under the pink table cloth. 'Wilf went to the museum and checked. He was back in an hour. Gugi spoke to Geneva, then somewhere else. Berlin, I think. Now he's on a plane.'

'Why the hurry?' Reluctantly Rupert let go of her hand as the drinks arrived.

'The Pol wants fast deals. Fast, fast! You see there's

something else coming tomorrow. Of course he reckons we should be able to move these things easily because they're unique, priceless. Sort of. I daren't let him know we've never seen that sort of stuff through the gallery! Things Sotheby's and Christie's would give their back teeth for, Wilf says.'

'Then why don't you give the things to Sotheby's? Maddy, they're not stolen, are they?'

'I haven't stolen them. No, and the Pol just doesn't want anything sold here.'

The intimate, candlelit moment was drifting as usual, but Rupert thought he saw a new angle. 'Good luck, darling. So if you're going to be independently rich we *could* get married! And if it doesn't work you could afford to divorce me!'

'Pot!' Maddy looked around. She lowered her voice again. 'Tonight!'

'Tonight? You can't get anywhere to do it at night!'

'On the floor!'

'On the *floor*?'

'Take off my clothes, roll me on the carpet!'

'Two mushrooms! Very hot,' The waitress said primly.

Norman Crimp, smoking a large cigar, picked up some items of female underwear from his desk, almost absent-mindedly, and dropped them into a wire tray basket.

'Bloody photographers!'

'You have taken three, is that right?' Dai Pol was impatient.

'One plus two makes three,' Crimp agreed. 'You must be putting a lot of money into this film. When do we start publicity for it in the magazine? You must also be shooting already. Where did you say the action was? Between Nice and Cannes? I could get down there with one of our chaps and get some stills.'

'Later. When do you take the next one? Who is it?'

'This afternoon. The Hon Daffy Dample. A delightful, chubby girl. Cover number ten last year!'

'Still enjoying the helicopter?' Sir Dai Pol said.

'The pilots think I've got a harem somewhere!'

'Ha-ah-ah-ah-ah!' It was that curious non-laugh which gave Norman Crimp an uncomfortable chill in his spine.

Outside the *Groin* offices, the Daimler was waiting and took Sir Dai Pol straight back to the docks. He had telephone calls to make, and with the *Chenn Lo* linked to landlines, it was the easiest and safest place. Kitty was waiting for him on the aft deck, under the canopy.

'Captain Hoffmann is coming in ten minutes!'

'And you are making another delivery? This morning, you said? In the painted bus? I must telephone, because that is early.'

'Mrs Flinders has to leave London this evening. For another job, she said.'

'An enterprising lady. One might think with so many distinguished fathers for her children, as you have told me, she would not need jobs.'

'It seems they do not give her much money, these fathers.'

'Is there anything on the tapes?'

'I have typed most of it. There is nothing from the bank this morning.' Kitty looked obliquely across the table, the heavily made-up lashes lowered. 'Your talk this morning with the editor I heard, of course.'

'For your own sake, it is best that I do not explain everything.'

'Is it big money?'

'Yes.'

'Men will pay that much for it?'

'It is clever of you, my dear, to deduce so much. The answer is 'yes'. It is almost the one thing, in certain parts of the Middle East, and even in some other parts of the world, on which some very rich men will set no limit. For them, a certain type of woman they have set their minds on, is as though they were buying racehorses. They boast about it.'

'Would you sell me to such men?'

'That is foolish.' Her father frowned. 'I am still puzzled by a piece at the bank. The name of the place, I cannot find on an ordinary map. The French message, you remember? Perhaps the place is in France? It was all very quick, but I think very important. You have written down the latitude and other figures on a piece of paper?'

'It is on the captain's chart table. I think it is the place where the bank man has his house, and his boat. But he also lives in London. Is it true he is married to a Princess?'

'Yes.'

'Is he a Prince?'

'No.'

'I would like to be a Princess,' said Kitty.

Shee came and reported the captain was on board, and Dai Pol went up to the bridge.

'Good morning, captain! All well?'

Captain Hoffmann had his cap on. He saluted as though brushing a fly off the peak.

'Is fine city, London!'

'I hear you are telephoning in as requested – just a precaution, you understand!'

'Is no trouble.' the captain agreed.

'Now listen. I want you to write out for me the tide-table here. For the next week or two. Leave it on the chart table. Now help me with another little matter. I have to visit a business friend here,' Dai Pol took a slip of paper from the pocket of his jacket. 'These are figures giving some nautical position, I think. If we have not got the necessary chart, you will obtain it. Mark the place and leave it for my return.'

'*Jawohl!*' said the captain. 'You wait? It may not take long.'

'I have an appointment at the Ritz and the car is waiting.' Dai Pol considered this information harmless enough, and it would impress the captain.

'I have had the dinner there!' said the captain. 'Excellent. To recommend!'

'One of the very few places that does *Oeuf en gêlée* still, the old Ritz.' Daimon with the menu in one hand and a dry martini in the other seemed cheerful. 'What are banks

124

for? To lend money to our clients so that they can afford to take us to the best places for lunch, isn't that right, Desmond?'

Lord Bair shook out the pink napkin over his lap, looked over his half-spectacles and pretended that he was not sure if he had heard.

'Ha-ah-ah-ah-ah!' Dai Pol signalled the waiter. He had considered carefully the setting for this meeting, and the Ritz seemed right. It was as he remembered it; the dining room reputedly still the most beautiful in London, with its carefully repainted gilt and ornamented ceiling. Most important, there was space between the tables for the discussion of private matters.

'Can't be too long over this one, actually old boy,' Lord Bair said. 'So I shall just have a piece of salmon. Daimon and I have to push on to an appointment out of town this afternoon. So get round to whatever you have in mind as soon as you like!'

Daimon looked at him. His cousin seemed to lose all sense of normal business manners when they were heading for one of these cutting-out expeditions, as he called them. And if something was to be negotiated, he would probably give way, just to get the lunch over.

'Ha-ah-ah-ah-ah!'

Damn strange, that noise the fellow made. Almost sarcastic. Drinking lime juice, too. Probably hoped they'd get tight and he'd stay sober. Obviously he had not heard that Prawn Passage had a reputation for the hardest heads in banking.

'You can put me down for the salmon, too,' said Daimon.

'You are not here too often, I hope?' Dai Pol said anxiously.

'We're only bankers.' Daimon said. 'Mostly we eat at Smokey Joe's.'

The wine waiter stooped over Dai Pol's shoulder, the order was taken, and Daimon produced a crumpled paper from his jacket pocket.

'Cash-flow a little slower than we thought, old boy?'

125

'Negative cash-flow?' Said Lord Bair.

'I don't follow that,' Dai Pol said politely.

'That film business you told us about. Expensive game. Any other backers?'

'Ah, yes, I see! The Middle East, of course, is always a little slow.'

'They're topping up?'

'Back to back?' said Lord Bair.

'It will be coming through your holding company, have no fear.'

'That's been fixed, has it?' Lord Bair wished this damn technical stuff didn't make it so difficult. Fortunately Daimon wasn't as bad as some of the younger directors.

The food arrived and he tackled the cold salmon with vigour. Forget any pudding and they could be away in half-an-hour. He sought to move things along.

'Daimon here tells me you're into commodity dealing. With cash coming in from the other side?'

'It has started.' Dai Pol saw no reason to dispute the idea that his business with Lord Bair's former wife involved commodities.

'Tricky game, commodities!'

'This is not the usual, Desmond,' Daimon cautioned. 'International and high prices.'

'Is my first wife involved in something?' Lord Bair began to recollect that she was. 'Strictly back to back, of course!'

'Lady Bair has been very helpful.'

'Buying and selling,' Daimon said.

'Ah, supply side economics!' Lord Bair said firmly. It was probably the right moment, if ever.

'I shall need up to ten million, very short, until the funds from abroad come in!'

There was a short silence. Daimon pushed the remaining pieces of his salmon round the plate.

'That's downside, I take it?'

'Please?'

'An estimate of the funding,' Lord Bair explained graciously.

'Cash,' said Dai Pol simply. 'In dollars, available in Switzerland in the first instance.'

'Double your first facility.' Daimon tried to find his cousin's foot under the table.

'Then that's topside!' Lord Bair cried triumphantly. Sometimes one might really think Daimon and the others tried deliberately to confuse him. At least this client seemed to use language he could understand. 'Is that in addition to what you've already had, Pol?'

'Total!' Daimon said firmly.

'And for how long, pray? It would have to be at a special rate, you know.'

'I would expect that.'

'Trouble is, you know Desmond, and I don't think Pol here will disagree with me, Mick Muldoon doesn't like the look of the *Hang Seng*!'

'That's the name of Pol's boat, isn't it?' It was like the old man to muddle ship's names with the Hong Kong Stock exchange. 'Pretty luxurious from what I hear, but not security for another five!'

Daimon wondered, not for the first time, how long the main shareholders, in spite of being mostly family, would take this sort of thing. Not that there was much scope for him personally in that, and better to shore-up his cousin. As they were known to be so close together, it might be the push for him too. 'It's the Hong Kong securities market, Desmond!'

'In about a week you will find the return for the first tranche coming back through the Swiss account.' Dai Pol was terse, calm, businesslike. 'That will multiply quite quickly, at the rate of a payment a day, probably. Then the major return will start coming in. All the time you have my security in Hong Kong, as you know, from the first reference.' Pity that nothing really definite had come up on those tapes, so far.

'All right!' Desmond Bair twisted in his chair to a more comfortable position as the plates were presently removed. A quick cup of coffee and they could be away. It was the traditional risk of merchant banking, in his family for generations, and it was not Daimon's fault that his side had been bog landowners. Everything was breeding and common sense and that was why he was chairman.

'You shall have it, my dear chap. For a fortnight! We fellows are here to create business, wealth, employment, confidence! Worldwide! Not to all creeds and colours and that rubbish, but genuine entrepreneurs, like yourself. Isn't that it, Daimon?'

'Brandy, gentlemen?'

'I don't see why not. With the coffee. I must say for this place, you don't have the third world in here. Do you know!' Lord Bair looked indignant. 'I had to go to Simpsons the other day, for some unfortunate occasion, and there were black chaps there, doing deals all over the place!'

Dai Pol signalled the waiter for his bill. For him too, the sooner this was concluded now the better.

'Take it back to the house first, Desmond?' Daimon muttered.

'Can I take it you will put the authority through today? If you are leaving town?' Dai Pol spoke directly to Lord Bair.

'Send it back with the driver, that do? I tell you, Pol! It's not you chaps I'm worried about! Not the old yellow peril! Not counting the Japs, who none of us are fond of, but they'll be brought to heel by oil or strife, or both, before long! It's the blacks! They're multiplying here like mad! Powell is right, they'll take us over! Do you know about the riots? It's only the start, I can tell you!'

'Steady, Desmond!'

'You have many problems here!' Dai Pol's eyes behind the thick glasses seemed almost closed. This would have been useful to have drawn out further, but there was obviously not going to be time. 'In Hong Kong we see the problems of former colonial power all the time. "Birds come home to roost" you say?' His lips were still pulled back, teeth bared against the rim of his brandy glass.

Rupert spent the morning in *Midas* London office, typing out the first draft of his piece on Bair Brady. He preferred to work with four fingers on the office machine than write longhand. With the International Monetary Fund all reports, minutes and correspondence had been hand drafted. As a working title he had typed *Prawn Passage Cocktail*. Epoch would like that.

It was now noon as Maddy called it. He reached for the phone, dialled the gallery number and was put through by Ruthy who never asked how he was, or even who he was. Was she against all men, or just someone who might divert Maddy from the true path of Art Appreciation?

'Hi!'

'Any chance of lunch?'

'Sweety, I'm having lunch with Rudi! He's doing the next sale.' She made her voice low and breathy. 'Guess what?'

'You love me?'

'The next consignment's coming in. The first one's been sold!'

'When do I see you then? This evening?'

'Darling, I'm terribly sorry, but there isn't a bed tonight. I meant to tell you earlier. Bella phoned after you left this morning and she's flying in from Paris.'

Something snapped in Rupert's mind. 'Why the bloody hell can't she stay in a hotel?' he shouted.

'Darling, she's my sister-in-law.'

'Not any longer!'

'Pot, behave!'

'And after last night! My God, have you no soul, Maddy?'

'Last night ought to last you a bit, surely!' Her voice was prim, severe. 'Listen, I must go. Wilf's here, and he's looking at a – what is it, Wilf? A Ducai drinking vessel!' Maddy's voice lowered again. 'Three hundred thousand, Wilf says! Rudi fancies Berlin!'

'I'm so glad they're listening,' said Rupert. 'I shall go down to the boat. I may stay there a few days. I may even drown myself.'

129

7

At Waterloo Station Rupert studied the departure board only briefly. He needed the express train to Bournemouth via Southampton. Then, from Brockenhurst, a quick taxi and he would be on the river.

He got a corner seat on the train and closed his eyes. But somehow in the click of the wheels and the other noises of the carriage, he could hear Maddy's voice still. A bachelor boat was all very well, but why did she never come down with him? And what had he got on board for supper? He needed a real mate, one who took care of the ship's stores. With luck he could pick up bread and eggs at the little store in Brockenhurst that stayed open late.

After the train, the taxi dropped him on the road beyond Beaulieu, and he walked down the track that led to the Bucklers Hard yacht harbour where he kept the inflatable dinghy. The yard was quiet, work had stopped, but the oldish night watchman, patrolling with alsatian on a chain, greeted him.

'Evenin', sir! Not much of a breeze. Bit of mist about, too. You going out, sir?'

'I might go down the river. See how I feel. Have you got the key to the shed?'

The man pulled a bunch of keys from his trousers pocket, walking along with him.

'Saw your boat the other day when I was bringing a ketch in for a scrape. Black hull, clinker built. *Cuckoo*, isn't it? Proper little sailer, that sort. I wouldn't mind having a boat like that meself.' He unlocked the shed door and Rupert, putting down his carrier bag of stores, lifted paddles off the rack.

They went down the pontoon where the rows of prams and dinghies were hauled up. An above average number of repair patches made identification of his own easy, and together he and the watchman dropped the inflatable on to the water.

Rupert crouched on the thwart, the watchman threw down the painter, and Rupert headed into the fairway with the water slapping against the rounded rubber bows.

The *Cuckoo* came in sight, one in a line of other boats on the less expensive moorings above the yard, and he swung the dinghy round, bumping the black and weathered hull, rising carefully to make fast the painter to the stern cleat. This done, he lowered the bag of stores first into the cockpit, then clambered aboard.

He stood and looked and listened for a moment. Water slapped on the boat's side, a curlew cried, high, repetitive and lonely, and from somewhere nearby came the honk of a Canada Goose.

The weather was distinctly uncertain. There was a small, sulky breeze, but only just.

He unlocked the cabin hatch, dropped inside and sat down on the edge of a berth. This was always a pleasant moment when the city suit was exchanged for jeans, pullover and deck shoes. There was not full head room on the *Cuckoo* and, still sitting, he reached along a shelf for a can of beer. It would be warm, but he could not keep the tiny refrigerator going. The electrics on board were not the *Cuckoo's* strong point. He went out into the cockpit, drinking straight from the can, listening to the halyards on the metal masts of the more modern boats tinkling hopefully. There was certainly thickening mist but perhaps it was drifting.

Rupert drained the beer and chucked the can through

the cabin door on to the bunk and reckoned he would motor down river and test the wind. At this time of the season it was hardly dark until ten, and there was no point in coming aboard to sit and brood. He looked at his watch. Three hours. He lifted the engine hatch and turned the master switch. Then he dipped the fuel tank; it was three-quarters full.

Most of his sailing was single handed, and the only tricky bit was leaving and picking up moorings, but it was no trouble in this sort of weather. The decision made, he felt suddenly cheerful. Inside the cockpit door he caught sight of the photo of Maddy, pinned to the bulkhead above the cooker. The corner-curled photo, drawing-pinned to the varnished bulkhead, smiled back enigmatically.

'Fickle!' cried Rupert, walking the dinghy around to the bows and lying down to make it fast to the mooring buoy. Women, boats, weather, jobs, tide, all were fickle. Women on board were bad luck anyway, as everyone knew. He probably ought to take down the photo. Thinking about them, you lost hold of dinghy painters and they drifted away. Not this sailor! He would get out *Reed's*, check the tide times, start the engine, make up a tinned meat sandwich, open another can of beer, fix foresail and main for a quick hoist later. And forget about Maddy.

For Lord Bair to go on board his yacht was a simple matter of stepping direct from the private jetty at the end of the lawn, already having changed in the house into the right clothes.

'I told Dickson that we might take a short look out. Just as an alibi.'

Daimon was short of breath. He had carried a long wooden chest from the house to the boat. He lowered it to the deck and looked at it distastefully.

'What is this bloody thing, Desmond? You're not going to need it are you? Seriously, I mean?'

Lord Bair gave a piratical wink and slapped him on the

back. Daimon recognised the change of character, a metamorphosis that always made him uneasy. Since they had started these cutting out operations, they did at least give him a hold over his cousin, should it ever be needed.

'You never know with the bloody frogs! You remember they had a go at us with the signal rockets last time!' The change in manner was accompanied by a change in dress, and the chairman of Bair Brady now wore a blue-and-white striped matelot's T-shirt, topped with a padded blue anorak, and red jeans tucked into yellow seaman's boots. Having taken the wooden chest from Daimon and staggered below with it, he returned to the cockpit. ' "We'll drum them up the Channel as we drummed them long ago!" '

'What about the splicer, Mister Mate? Or are you going to be petty officer gun turret? All the usual in the main cabin, Dickson said!'

Daimon was also changed from a city banker. A navy blue seaman's pullover stretched over his corpulent body from neck to knee. Baggy blue jeans hung over the tops of his short black boots.

They sat on the berths around the cabin and Lord Bair pulled away at the wire on a champagne bottle taken from a case under the table. Daimon wrenched an opener round two bottles of Guinness. He mixed the Black Velvet in two stemmed, heavy rummers, the size of pudding basins. Lord Bair put two fingers in his mouth and blew three piercing whistles.

'What the hell's that for?'

'Piping good luck on board, damn you! It might also get us a bit of wind. I don't like the look of the weather outside.' Lord Bair buried his face in the enormous glass and came up wiping the froth from round his mouth with the back of his hand. 'Damnation to our enemies!'

'Good luck,' Daimon said more modestly. 'Maybe they won't turn up!'

'I've never known our man give us a bum steer yet!'

'Two out of six actually.'

'Not his fault. They didn't sail.'

'What is the fix again? I'll put it on the chart.'

Lord Bair took another long pull at the outsize rummer and threw a much folded slip of telex paper onto the table. 'Forty-five East, twenty-six North, five-five both ways. I've looked at it and sheet twenty-four, and you can see what they've got in mind. Somewhere off Durns Point. Not a bad spot. Quiet bit of beach for the landing party, easy walk through the fields. But we'll scupper them!' He eased along the berth until he could swing open the door of the refrigerator and pulled out a bottle, one that was frosty white. 'Yo heave ho and a bottle of Wodka! Chaser glasses on the shelf there!'

'Half for me, old boy,' Daimon said. 'You know the water outside like your own bath-tub, but I've got to do the foredeck work.'

'You have!' Lord Bair splashed clear, cold liquid into the two tumblers. 'We go out under power. No hurry. We've got light until ten and they're not due until elevenish. *Zazdarovia!*'

'What the hell's that?' His cousin's round, florid face hung nervously over the cabin table like a Hallowe'en mask.

'Bloody Russian toast! You forget I went to Moscow? You had to send the chairman because I was the only member of the board who could stand up to the business there the way they drink that stuff!'

'Didn't do much good, Desmond. Never lend money East, I say.'

'The thing in that box in there is Russian!'

'You didn't bring that back with you from there, surely to God?'

'Sometimes, Daimon, I think you're a bit naïve. They go through your pockets, those bastards. No, Kate gave it to me.' Lord Bair burped loudly, then looked aloof.

'You mean your sister Kate?'

'My sister and your cousin, old boyo. Barking mad, of course!'

'Is she still in the big house in Donegal?'

' "Where the mountains of Mourne run down to the

sea." Yes, you know the old place, dripping wet, laurels up the drive, crows in the chimneys. Been in the family for two hundred years. Only Kate would want it. Nobody else.'

'Haven't seen Kate for years,' Daimon said. 'When were you there?'

'This spring. Young Tim and Erin Eden sailed this thing round Fastnet and I flew out to join them for the run home – and stayed a night with Kate. Remember her?'

'Bless her, yes!' Daimon was beginning to feel more cheerful. 'Pudding hair cut, face like a bulldog. Wasn't there a story she was satisfying the MFH and a new young gardener and the sexton all more or less at the same time?'

'Always generous, my sister! Not just romantic – and a patriot, like all the Bairs! Defence of the Realm – out there, of course, they're in the thick of it!'

'Oh, come on, not in Donegal! Not Antrim, is it?' Daimon downed the contents of the tumbler in one, and spluttered and coughed.

'Good thing you didn't have to go to Moscow! Of course old Kate is in it, up to the neck! They use her place as a sort of HQ, rallying point, armament store, field hospital, everything. She showed me what she and the lads get up to when I was there. Radio stuff in the attic, secret bedroom through a wardrobe for those on the run. Do you remember old Uncle Eamon's strong room, built in behind a bookcase in his study? I hadn't seen it since I was a boy. Made at the time of the earlier Troubles, Bloody armoury! She had three of those long case jobs, like that one in there. And she gave me one. Insisted on it. "A bit of heavy stuff will not come amiss!" was her phrase. I asked what the hell it was, and she said it was Russian. Look, you can see it from here, stencilled on top. RPG 7V.'

'What's that, for God's sake?'

Lord Bair struggled to his feet. 'Let's take a look at that weather!'

Outside the grey mist was creeping up the river all around them, clinging to the tall trees on the shore and already half-hiding the outlines of the big house, grey, silent, only a single light in one of the downstairs windows.

'Let's not go out if it gets worse,' Daimon said.

'It'll blow. There's a bit of wind up there now! You can hear those halyards – probably clear on the Solent.'

They moved back to the cabin and the drinks. The rough-wood box sat like a small unfinished coffin on the spare berth. Lord Bair twisted the catches and the lid dropped open. The rocket launcher lay inside, black and functional, the muzzle like a trumpet, at the butt end two pistol grips.

'Is that other bit the thing it fires?'

'One of them. There are four more in the under part.'

Gingerly Daimon lifted the sleek-looking blunderbuss off its cradle and pulled it across his knees. 'How the hell did old Kate get hold of, did you say three, of these babies?'

'Raiding party, on a tip-off! Seems it goes on all the time. Some of the lot she works with have a surprise go at the other side. There are always one or two wounded, and they come to her place. She says they always bring back a load of stuff – small arms, mines and these Christmas novelties. It's nearly always Russian or Warsaw Pact countries stuff. American sometimes.'

'But have you used this pop-gun yourself?'

'I had one go, Kate made me. It was at night. That telescopic sight has got an illuminated granule –'

'Graticule.'

'How do you know?'

Daimon sniffed. 'You forget I actually was a gunner, blast you!'

'Ah! Well, when you put this bit on, you first screw in the rocket charge. It's dead simple, but bloody clever. The rocket has a two stage motor, the first ejects it without much fuss, so that the bloke who fires doesn't catch the back blast, and the second goes off about ten yards away. Range about three to four hundred yards!'

Lord Bair was also happier with ballistics than banking.

Daimon lifted the launcher to his shoulder. 'What happens at the receiving end?'

Lord Bair reached for the vodka bottle. 'It was impressive! I was shown an old cowshed, stone blocks and corrugated roof, you know the kind of thing. It disintegrated! Gone! Practically vaporised.'

'Good God!'

'It'll go through a foot of armour plate, Kate said. A kind of lava of hot metal goes through any sort of tank or fortified thing and it just blows up: phut, destroyed, finished!'

'And the Russkis are giving out these things to their pals all around the place?' Shakily Daimon put the weapon back into the box and closed the lid.

'Not give, old boy,' Lord Bair said sadly. 'Sell! You know the way it goes? What was that syndicate loan we put together last year for one of the Latin American places? You knew what that was for! Where's my glass? Drink their bloody Wodka and damnation to all our enemies, and their liquor helps to pay for it! It's a great world!'

'Where do we stow the thing?' Daimon said shortly. He refilled his own smaller glass.

'She can go on a forrard berth for the time being. Then if we want her, up through the forepeak hatch! Just the place for a quick shot. Rest your elbows on the deck and bang! Kiss me Kate!'

Daimon lugged the box away, and came back puffing and blowing. He knocked back his drink. 'Honestly, we'd better make a move, Desmond! Or call it off. This mist –'

'Bugger the mist! We've got a compass and radar! There's the channel buoy, clear as bloody daylight! I don't want to be stooging around out there for all to see.'

'It'll be dark in an hour or so now, we'll want some seaway round us by then.'

'Right!' They went out into the cockpit and Lord Bair jerked his head round, looking from stem to stern. 'Bend on the mizzen! The number two genny is on automatic already. Leave the ties on the main until we see what wind there is. Probably only use the mizzen anyway, for steadying. Stand by to cast off when I've started up the motor!'

An hour before, Rupert had cleared down the river at the permitted five knots, with the wooden tiller of *Cuckoo* in one hand and a mug of Scotch and water in the other. There was nothing else moving, only the mist.

The old Ford engine drummed away, and the withies that marked the Beaulieu channel slipped by. He passed the old oyster beds and the yacht club's wooden building on the west bank. It looked deserted, the flag on the mast forlorn.

The marks for the river entrance were only just visible and he put the helm across.

With the help of the Scotch, Rupert felt his spirits still rising. The little boat's prow smacked the water, the occasional wave sending its spray back to the cockpit, fresh and salty on the wind made by the boat's passage.

About half a mile out, Rupert put the helm over to starboard and watched the prow come round as he throttled back.

'Damn, damn damn damn!' He often talked aloud when sailing alone and thinking of Maddy again, swore in conscious emulation of Professor Higgins. 'I've grown accustomed to her face.' What would she be doing now. Probably some party where, instead of rigging, the ice cubes clinked in the glasses and the view was across a roomful of people. Not like here where there was almost no view at all and really no other prospect than a rapid return before it got dark. Because this was no longer mist, it was blowing up a full sea fog in the Solent. Which was not the sort of thing for a small craft to hang about in.

Out on the starboard side, he could just hear a timed and muffled sound, the clang of the East Lepe bell. Always sad, even in a good light. "For whom the bell tolls!" For all the ships gone down and lost in the deep. He reached down into the cockpit locker where he had stashed the whisky bottle and replenished the mug, glancing up the mast at the spreaders. Probably a good idea to put on masthead lights and navigation. And to fiddle with the radio and try and get some weather. With reduced throttle the boat had only just got way on.

He knew these mist conditions in which there could be this sudden, dense, grey sea fog between the Isle of Wight and the mainland, and be clear with light airs in the Channel. Or the opposite.

He lifted the hatch and felt for the switches. Up aloft and at other illumination points, nothing happened.

'Oh, for God's sake!' Rupert shouted. He turned the master switch on and off several times. Still nothing. The *Cuckoo's* ancient electrics had been well behaved for some time, but were never infallible. This was total treachery. *Cuckoo* had no chart table or locker, but the few charts he kept were folded above a berth, and he ought to get one out to check several things. First, lash the helm with his own home-made solo pilot, a length of nylon cord, a few turns round the tiller, and then make fast to screw eyes in the port and starboard thwarts.

In the locker, beside the bottle of whisky, was a large old torch. That worked. He checked on the binnacle compass. He was still making easterly, about seventy degrees magnetic, which would be all right for the moment. It would be a good idea to keep clear of Thorn Channel, the main shipping lane.

'Talk about sodding bad luck!' Rupert said bitterly to the clanging Lepe bell, his only companion in the mist which was now definitely thicker all round. He froze. Something close was moving, visible but silent, in the half illuminated opaque. It was the *Cuckoo's* own shadow of the mast and mainsail, flapping on the boom. Or was something near at hand? Or an echo? In sea mist everything played tricks.

'Belay there!' Rupert shouted. His voice rolled away, hollow and unanswered. Hooter! Scrabbling in the cockpit bilges, under piles of damp rope and a bucket, he found it, brought it up and tried it a few times. After some damp had been expelled, it emitted a few mournful sounds. 'More like a bittern than a cuckoo!' Rupert told the Lepe bell.

He got *Reed's* almanac out of the cabin and thumbed through the pages. It confirmed the second Solent tide was flooding, and would reach high water in a couple of hours. Returning to Beaulieu on the ebb, in anything less than good visibility was to be avoided. The mudflats were expansive, imprecise and sticky.

Shivering only partly from the chill of the mist, Rupert turned to the radio, worked on its own batteries. By using the fixed Beacon signal at Southampton and Yarmouth with his handset Helley/Hengist, he drew lines with a stub of pencil on the chart, and made a cross. Blind offshore navigation was not something he laid claim to. He unscrewed the top of the whisky bottle and swallowed hard.

The worst thing was the onset of darkness, which was now apparent, a deepening of the surrounding gloom, the element of light overhead that had been there to start with, definitely gone and the *Cuckoo* almost stationary on a gently heaving circle of black water.

He was virtually hove-to. Should he stay put? He had no sea anchor, but might rig something with a bucket. Probably best to change course, go about, and head westerly again for the river mouth, with the East Lepe bell astern and, when the mist lifted, fumble his way in, risking other craft, mudflats and all.

He looked at his watch. It was now past ten. Rupert decided to make a quick visit to the heads while the helm was still made fast. He had always disliked urinating over the side. It seemed insulting to the sea.

He eased his way, head down, through the cabin and opened the sliding door. He never heard what hit the *Cuckoo*, until it was too late, and the crash sent him reeling back into the cabin. Noise, huge and terrifying, outside the roaring of a powerful engine and confused shouting, and then the hideous sound of rending woodwork. Flung half prostrate over the cabin table, Rupert saw, as though in a nightmare, what appeared to be a glittering dripping silver saw, pointed at the end and with savage teeth, sticking up at him through the bottom side of the bilges. Sea water was pouring in after it, in a thrusting grey fount.

As he floundered round, shouting protest, the evil metal swordfish slowly withdrew, rending and splintering the woodwork as it went. And now the water spout poured in with torrential force, the flood on the cabin floor rising rapidly.

Rupert splashed his way out into the cockpit. Outside all was suddenly bright light as floodlights went on and glittered on the scene. Towering topsides and the white hull of another larger craft were blindingly close.

Rupert stood up in his own rapidly flooding cockpit, grasping the hatch combing and choking for breath. The water was rising slowly across the slats over his boots. A bulky figure in a pullover that came down to his knees, was standing in the prow that loomed above, wielding a dangerous looking boathook.

'I'm sinking, for God's sake!'

'Grab hold of this!'

'Damn you, Daimon, you bloody fool. You were look-out!' The bellowing shout was from a second figure, somewhere amidships on the other yacht. Rupert stared, lurching wildly, so that he nearly went overboard, still half-blinded by the swinging, dazzling white light. The figure was lumbering nearer now, and he saw dancing blue-and-white stripes, a bulky jacket and woollen cap. A familiar heavy, reddened face with bloodshot eyes, stared down at him from the high pulpit above.

'Lord Bair!'

'Who the devil are you!'

'Potter, damn you!' screamed Rupert. He splashed back from the cockpit into the flooding cabin, grabbing up things from shelves and berth. He stuffed them into a holdall, then floundered back into the cockpit and mounted up onto the thwarts, flinging the bag blindly ahead of him.

Then he jumped, reaching for the pulpit rails, and felt hands grab his shoulders, pulling and lifting him up to safety.

They watched the *Cuckoo* sink. The whole thing was over in a remarkably short time and Rupert turned away from the oily swirl in the water, a trench that quickly filled, and felt faintly sick.

'I was very fond of that boat.'

Daimon clapped him round the shoulders, coughed and looked embarrassed. Rupert stared coldly at him, then at the extraordinary figure of the seagoing Lord Bair.

'That was my bloody boat you've sunk! It's all I've got! You bloody man Bair! What the hell are you doing out here, dressed up like that? Sinking people's boats! Do you hear me?' Carried away, Rupert took hold of the quilted jacket with both hands.

'Let go of me you young idiot!'

Rupert, feeling his knees sag, dropped his bag on the cockpit seat and slumped down beside it. He closed his eyes. A faint drumming started in his ears. Lord Bair lumbered back to the helm and opening his eyes again, Rupert realised it was the engines.

The grey, swirling mist pressed all around them, and in the glare of the mast-head and spreader-lights, everything on deck below seemed black and white. It was a nightmare. All totally unreal. As though he had merely changed from one boat to another. Except that the man who was Maddy's former husband, last seen self-important and unctuous behind his vast desk, and now beside him looking like a pantomime mercenary, a pirate from the Barbary Coast, was standing there behind the glittering, circular wheel glaring at him.

'Give Potter a drink, Daimon! I'm not going to mess around here anymore. We'll go about and get on station!' The wheel moved slowly round, and Rupert felt his head going round with it.

'Nasty shock for you, Potter. Tea for shock, but we don't make tea! Try some of this!' Lord Bair picked up from the thwart beside him what looked like a glass flower vase filled with bilge water.

'What is it?'

'Black Velvet! Code name for this operation, my boy. Sets you up.'

'I'll stick to my own thanks!' Rupert fumbled in his bag and found his own salvaged Scotch. His teeth chattered on the neck of the bottle as the liquor burned its way down and he found courage slowly returning and he glared at Lord Bair and then at Daimon.

'What bloody operation? Sinking other people? Sawing them up?' He pulled at his rubber boots which came off with a sucking noise. He poured the water out across the slats, then wrung out his socks and flung them down, and stuck his wet feet back into the boots again.

'Stress of weather, dear boy!' shouted Lord Bair. 'Nobody's fault! Bloody awful sea mist!'

'Don't you keep watch, damn it?' Rupert yelled back. He got up and the clammy boots clutched at his feet. 'I might have drowned!'

'Why weren't you on watch? Eh?' The heavy figure of Daimon stood, head and shoulders out of the cabin hatch, eyeing him carefully. 'No lights! Two of us to your word, you know!'

'I shall be giving Potter a cheque, Daimon,' said Lord Bair grandly. 'You must tell me your loss figures, Potter, and I will settle with you. Leave insurance out of it.'

'We could always push you overboard and say you went down with the ship.'

Rupert stared unbelievingly. Daimon's eyes under the heavy brows were hard, unwinking, the heavy jowls grim.

'What was that bloody spike that holed me?' Rupert said slowly. 'That wasn't weather.' There were a few other things he had noticed. 'And why have you got your dodgers furled? To conceal the name? You've got something hanging over the stern, too, if I'm not mistaken, for the same purpose. They won't like that at Lloyds when I tell them! I'm going for'ard to look at that spike!'

'Don't worry, I'll tell you about it!' Lord Bair tilted

back his head and emptied his pot.

'I told you not to put that bloody thing down until we needed it, Daimon!'

'How should we know Potter would be skirmishing about with no lights? As I said, why no lights, Potter?'

'Wiring, I think,' said Rupert wearily. The mist was still billowing gently about like thin cotton wool as the ship slipped slowly through an oily sea. He glanced along the deck. All of forty feet plus. If he went up to the prow, that might be the moment when Daimon would get the nod to push him in. There were, as he had said, two of them.

Lord Bair was grinning fiendishly. 'Daimon won't shove you in, will you, Admiral? Here!' He swung the empty goblet about and belched mightily. 'Take the bloody helm. I'll give Potter the tour!'

Rolling his way forward he conducted Rupert up into the bows by pushing him from behind. 'Looks like the pulpit top rail, see? But you screw the old swordfish bit on and with the ends of the pulpit arms hinged, the whole lot lowers away below the water line.'

'What the hell for?' Rupert stood back aghast, staring at him.

'Bloody effective!' Lord Bair was already making his way aft, swinging gorilla-like along the stays and shrouds.

'What for?' Rupert shouted after him. 'What's it for?'

'Ramming chaps like you who sail without lights!' Lord Bair shouted back.

'We'd better tell him, Desmond. We're stuck with him now. Lloyds wouldn't like him sailing about without lights, silly sod! Near the main lanes, too. D'you hear that stuff hooting out there now?'

'You've got radar!' Rupert looked wildly up at the top of the mainmast. 'Why didn't you pick me up on that?'

'Not much use with your size actually,' Daimon growled. 'Lot of junk about on the screen anyway, you know. Isle of Wight and all the rest.'

'There are two of you, as you put it so charmingly. You could have kept watch!'

'Daimon was making drinks, old boy!' Lord Bair said solemnly. 'But of course we shouldn't have put on the swordfish so early.'

'What's it for?' Rupert sat down in the cockpit again. 'And this name hiding? You're smuggling, aren't you? You'd better tell me! You seem to forget I work for *Midas*. I could put this in that profile piece!'

'We've either got to call it off, or tell him, Desmond!'

'I'm going to, damn it! The fellow's a patriot, I don't doubt! And hell, he's sleeping with my former wife, isn't he? She wouldn't take him in if he wasn't a gentleman! You are a gentleman, aren't you, Potter?'

'Leave Maddy out of it,' Rupert snarled. 'What are you two up to?'

'All in good time. But it would be bloody unfortunate if, because of you, I had to cut down, or cut off, Lady Bair's financial resources. Because of your sailing about without lights! Eh, wouldn't it?'

'I've told you – leave her out of it!'

'We wouldn't take you back ashore to write a load of junk for that magazine of old Epoch's, would we, Daimon?'

'Bloody media!'

'Let's give the media another drink!' Lord Bair heaved himself down the cabin stairway. 'Still on Scotch, Potter? I'm for a Wodka. You Daimon?'

Daimon looked at Rupert, and now he seemed to be pleading with him.

'Listen to me, old boy! It's really all a bit of sport! At the same time it's a job that ought to be done. An Englishman must defend his castle. Desmond's right! Somebody's got to do it, or we shall all go under!'

As Rupert stared back at him, the air was split by the siren of some sizeable vessel so near that it seemed to be stirring the grey murk around them. They could hear the muffled thump of its engines.

Lord Bair re-emerged from below, both hands clasped round three glasses. 'There you are, now, drink to this! Damnation to our enemies!'

Rupert took the tumbler of what proved to be neat

whisky, and drank quickly but without response. Standing down half below, Lord Bair wiped his lips with the back of his hand, and thumped Rupert on the knee with the other.

'Now! I know what you're thinking – there's too much bloody hypocrisy about!'

'Probably won't find them in this stuff, anyway.' Daimon put the lock on the helm so that he could get at his glass.

'Russian trawlers! Is that it?'

The wash of the large, unseen vessel, it's siren fading astern, moved their boat choppily in the water, and Rupert looked from one rolling head to the other.

'French with illegal nets! Dope runners? You might as well tell me!'

'Bloody blacks, pouring in without let or hindrance all out of control!' roared Lord Bair, almost in his ear. 'The country's being taken over! Rioting and arson! Nothing's safe, Potter! Powell is right! Stop them coming in!'

'That's a job for immigration, the coastguards! How do you know they're coming in? Or do you just cruise about sinking people on sight?'

'We have the pirate's chart! We know,' chuckled Lord Bair and rubbed his hands before picking up the half tumblerful of vodka and emptying it. 'You stay around and you might see a bit of sport! You'd shoot a poacher to stop him, wouldn't you? Well, what's the difference?'

'I don't shoot!'

'Or hit somebody molesting your girlfriend? Like my ex-wife? Eh? Well these bastards are molesting our country! Stealing our heritage! It's only a small effort, if you like, but my own! Direct action!'

'I'm on two hundred and sixty,' Daimon shouted. 'What do you say?'

'Sounds about right? Of course in this stuff the Froggies may call it off. Or heave-to somewhere. But equally they may reckon it's all a great help. Depends if they started off and got caught up in it. They won't want to go back loaded.'

'How do you know it's a French boat? Pirate's chart! Aren't you a bit carried away by all your bloody banking games? Pirates? You're not joking!'

'Give me a drop more in the glass, old boy!' Daimon said. 'It's bloody cold here on the helm. I make it nearly midnight now, so I suppose the temp must be falling. Are you going to helm when we get there?'

'We have a mole! A French mole! A French ex-naval mole.' Lord Bair winked at Rupert solemnly. 'An old chum from de Gaulle days, Algerian banking – they know all right! Actually he get's the leak from a water rat, would you say, Daimon?'

'A mermaid, I believe. What's French for mermaid?' Daimon reached out a hand for his refilled glass.

'Good God!' Rupert looked aghast at Lord Bair. At the woolly capped head at knee level, peering out of the cabin door, the reddened face, the watery eyes. They stared back at him solemnly.

'Moles, rats! You're a bit past *Wind in the Willows* aren't you?'

'Money, old boy! We always get information for money, banks especially. There's big money in smuggling flesh! Very big. They screw those black bastards for everything they've got! Now, if you'll let me, I must just do a bit of calculating here on the chart. I'll get a fix that checks with information received. We should be just about there. Somewhere off Durn's Point, I thought.'

The bonneted head disappeared and Rupert saw the chart table light go on below, and heard the sound of the paper being unfolded.

'Keep your eyes peeled up there, Daimon! And you, Potter!'

The siren of the ship that had passed could be heard no more, but two further away were now crying mournfully to each other.

'Is that a shotgun? The thing in that bag?'

Daimon at the helm glanced down, then stared ahead, his eyes half-closed.

'Twelve bore!'

'I'm dousing the lights,' roared Lord Bair from below. 'Kill engines! Then we can listen.'

In the clammy darkness Rupert sat and shivered. He felt a glass being put in his hand. 'Have another drink, old boy! It's bloody cold!' said Lord Bair.

'Why don't you pack it in?' Rupert said later.

'We've been hove-to half an hour, what do you think, Desmond?' Daimon was humped on the opposite thwart, a drip on the end of his nose.

'Give it another half. They'll have had to go slow, they can't chuck them out too far from the shore.' Lord Bair at the helm, croaked and coughed.

'The stupid buggers wouldn't know that!'

'No, but the old Frogs want it to work. The word get's round if they have a failure. Then no more business.'

'Just how often have you done this?' Rupert had taken a blanket from the cabin and sat wrapped in it with a growing mood of indifference.

'Three, I'd say.' Daimon yawned hugely and rubbed his nose. 'Can't take on the East Coast stuff, you see, Pass that on to others.'

'We did all right that time outside Poole Harbour.'

'And Newhaven.'

'Bloody funny, that was!'

'Why on earth don't you just tell the people whose job it is? They'd act on a tip-off.'

'Ah, but you can't be sure, old boy!' Lord Bair said. 'Now we take care of information received and there's some real action! Besides, how else would we get a bit of action on the high seas in this time and age?' He coughed, thumping his chest. 'Bloody mist!'

'You've already sunk me, isn't that enough?'

'A Peer of the Realm,' Lord Bair coughed again and raised his voice to a shout, 'is entitled to take action to defend it! On his own if need be! Did you know that? It's in the Magna Carta! Never been altered!'

8

'There's something about!'
    'I heard it!'
'Don't want them hearing us first!' Lord Bair heaved himself up on to the thwart, his heavy chisel nose snuffling the darkness.

'Probably some harmless soul like me, and you'll sink them too! I notice you've still left that bloody spike on!'

'Keep your voice down, damn you! There's way on from the foresail, Daimon – the mist is moving, too.'

'You know what the shoals are like off this bit of the north shore! You probably haven't got more than a foot of water under the keel now.' Rupert stood by Daimon, peering at the instruments.

'Twenty!' hissed Daimon, twisting and turning his head as he checked the echo sounder and the burgee at the mast head.

All three of them could hear a faint, low, drubbing note of engines, somewhere off the starboard quarter. It became louder, distinct, then faded away again.

The foresail started flapping, a sound like faintly mocking applause, and Daimon put the helm over.

'They're getting behind us!'

'Put the bloody engine on!'

'If they had lights we'd see them! It's more dark than

mist now – it must be them, the crafty sods! The Solent can't be full of old tubs with duff electrics!'

'Daimon, look!' roared Lord Bair up on the counter as the yacht's engines rumbled into life again, and the boat swung round. Less than a hundred yards away on the beam, the shadowy shape of a motor cruiser, tall with flying bridge, was hove to on the water. A dim light showed figures on the rail, and below the shabby paint-work on the stern, bobbing on the waves, the bulbous shape of a large, empty rubber dinghy.

They had also been seen. Suddenly a searchlight on top of the cruiser's tall bridge snapped on, and a blinding shaft of light swept across the shortening distance that separated them. In the black darkness created behind it, there were muffled shouts and the sound of feet running about on deck.

Lord Bair was off the thwart, leaping heavily into the cockpit, and in a moment had the shotgun out of its slip and on to his shoulder. As both barrels blasted off in the confines of the cockpit, the double explosion was deafen-ing.

'For God's sake, what are you doing?' Rupert screamed and took cover down the cabin stairs.

'Give 'em hell, Desmond! I'm coming about!' roared Daimon.

From behind the searchlight on the other vessel came a higher, vicious crack and something whined sufficiently close over the cockpit for Rupert to draw his head back rapidly into the cabin again.

'They've got a rifle, the bastards!' Daimon, his arms flailing round the wheel in the bright glare of the white light cast dancing shadows on fragments of the mist around them. Lord Bair was reloading feverishly and again the shotgun's double blast roared out. The search-light went out with dramatic effect, leaving total darkness, and from across the water silence.

'Take the helm!' Daimon snarled at Rupert who was creeping out on hands and knees. 'I want a shot! Where's the other bloody gun?'

At that moment a red signal flare streaked lazily towards them through the air, hit the foresail and went careering off. It was followed by a dazzling white one that ricocheted off the hull with a blinding flash and fell hissing into the sea.

'They'll get Kate's cannon if they fire us!' Lord Bair shouted. 'By God they will!'

There was a tremendous uproar as both his and Daimon's shotguns went into action at once and, staggering backwards, Daimon kicked the box of cartridges which shot across the cockpit, spilling the contents into the scuppers.

'Get that one in the stern!'

'Sink the rubber boat!'

'There's one of those black buggers in it already!'

As one of the twelve bores went off again, Rupert saw with horror the apparent collapse of a crouching figure in the rubber dinghy which was still made fast to the stern of the big motor cruiser which was now beginning to move ahead through the water.

'Get your heads down!' roared Lord Bair suddenly.

The rifle shot went through the cabin top with a crash of splintering wood and the sound of broken glass.

'Get the black sods on the deck! Potter! Pick up the cartridges, you spineless newt. Do something useful! Get bows on to them, Daimon!'

But the cruiser was now thundering with a mighty roar of engines at full bore across the water, swinging away in a wide arc, the sea behind it tossing the helpless dinghy high on its wash. So rapid was its departure that one moment it was a gliding, ominous shape, and then there was only mist, with the heavy double rumbling of engines echoing back through the darkness and the violent wash of its going hit the yacht and sent it rocking wildly.

'If that one in the inflatable is dead or alive, he'll soon be out!'

'See anyone in the water, old boy?' Lord Bair, gun tucked under his arm, sounded hopeful. 'Let's have our own spot on!'

151

'Don't think so, not with that rifle! I'll cruise around!' Daimon was rolling with the wheel against the waves. 'Potter, why don't you stop mutinying and get us a drink? You can do the first aid bit, even if you don't fight!'

'Might as well put on regulation lights.' Lord Bair clicked the switches. 'Not a bad action, Daimon, would you say?'

'Second best after Newhaven!'

'We got one, at least probably! Have to patch that hole in the jib.'

'Much mess in the cabin?'

'You haven't stopped them! They'll come back!' Rupert said. He found the vodka bottle and filled the glasses, as much for the restoration of his own morale as theirs.

'Nonsense! You don't know the game, dear boy!' Lord Bair had undone his jacket and happily patted the front of his blue-and-white striped vest. 'Those chaps are shit-scared now, and nothing the Frogs can do will persuade them to go ashore! But like others they run the risk of being pushed overboard!'

'Fetch me some more drink, Potter!' said Daimon genially. He held out his glass.

'They'll be back in France in short order,' said Lord Bair. 'The niggers beginning and ending at Calais! Wouldn't you say?'

Exhausted, Rupert slept on a berth in the main cabin of the *Shamrock* as it returned to harbour, creeping up the Beaulieu river on the ebb tide with all lights shining. As though in a continuing nightmare, he thought at one point he heard the captain and helmsman outside chanting sea shanties. Later it seemed as though he heard Maddy, arguing with her first husband. He sat up, hitting his head, and realised it was Daimon doing the female responses to Lord Bair's noisy version of Barnacle Bill the Sailor and, groaning, fell back in the berth again.

When Daimon woke him, he pulled on the wet boots again and staggered out into the cockpit. They were coming in to the moorings at the Bair jetty.

Rupert realised that by sleeping he had not properly

thought things out. He was suffering from an unpleasant headache from hitting his head and from what seemed like an eternal succession of whisky and vodka. He made no effort to help with mooring and only as he collected his bag, staggering into the cockpit, and sought to go ashore, did the grim reality strike him that he was not stepping off his own boat.

'You will hear from me,' he said coldly to Lord Bair. It sounded like someone else speaking.

'I shall send you round a cheque, Potter. No lights, stress of weather, remember!'

'Bloody good shot in that light, Desmond!' Daimon was tidying up in the cockpit, throwing empty shotgun cases overboard. He straightened up, looking bleary. 'Cheerio, Potter! Was it number four shot?'

'Six, with the second barrel! Leave the rest of it! Dickson can clean her up in the morning.'

'What about Kiss-me-Kate?'

'Yes, pity we didn't try that when they started shooting. Leave it on the forrard berth, I don't want it in the house.'

'Is he staying in the house with us?' Daimon jerked his head at Rupert.

'No!' said Rupert. 'I am not.' He set back his shoulders and stepping ashore gave them both a look of withering disapproval.

'You won't need any excuses, old boy,' said Daimon cheerfully. 'People would think you were inventing it all, to cover up, about your sailing around without lights!'

'I see you've got your gear. By the way, I chucked your ship's papers overboard. Come on, Daimon! For God's sake stop mucking about. Bring the guns. I want a hot bath and a glass of champagne!'

Rupert stalked on with as much dignity as he could muster. His head still reeled as he turned abruptly at the end of the jetty. Their voices fell away behind him.

On the gravel path he skirted some hedges beside the high brick wall, and found himself out on the road. He looked at his watch. It was nearly five.

He wondered whether to knock up Mr Mentin of Bucklers Hard Garage; he was after all, an old customer. But there would be too many questions he was not ready for. To the right, the road went to Beaulieu, and there it would be easier to phone for a taxi and then catch the earliest train up to Town. Rupert trudged on, his feet in the still wet rubber boots making a sound like a lame duck along the tarmac road.

It was still misty and only just light, the first birds making tentative territorial claims. In all truth he was a lame duck. Or very much a fish out of water, with no territorial claims, no boat and no real home. A castaway on a lonely road and certain to get blistered feet.

From behind him came the sound of a vehicle steadily approaching. Its headlights cast a faint flicker on the road, and as it came closer, more light brought colour to the hedges and the road verge.

Rupert turned and, although it was a long time since he had done it, thumbed energetically, peering back at the twin blobs of the approaching headlights. It was some large sort of vehicle, probably a truck.

When it was almost upon him, the driver seemed to swing wide to draw past, revving the engine, then as the truck overtook him the brakes squealed and, with exhaust labouring, it stopped fifty yards ahead, the red tail lights winking. Rupert stumbled along the verge towards a door which was opening on the nearside of the vehicle.

Even as he got there, Rupert stopped, and the grip of unreality seized him again. The shape, the colour, were horribly familiar. The row of windows, the psychedelic patterns on the side of happy flowers and Donald Duck, complete with sailor hat and suit, welcoming a fellow mariner.

'Gee!' It was the warm smile, the loving eyes of Polly Flinders. 'Rupe! For gosh *sakes*! I reckoned whoever was hiking along at this hour was in trouble, but I didn't guess it was you! Come on in, baby! Cummup!' She swung back inside, pulling him up by the sleeve. The door slammed and the engine roared as she got behind the wheel. The bus rolled forward.

Rupert sank speechless on to the seat immediately behind her and closed his eyes.

'How come you're here?' Polly Flinders shouted above the noise of the motor. 'You're in boating gear! You got a boat! I remember!'

'I did have a boat. I haven't any more.' Rupert could just see Polly's face in the driving mirror.

'You mean you sold it? Get a good price?'

'Sunk!' said Rupert tersely. Then wished he had not. But the growing sense of loss was great.

'No! You mean like just now?'

'Last night. The weather was bad.'

'You can say that again!' Polly swung the bus round the bend in Beaulieu village, and changed up the gears with gusto. 'I know it! I've been on the shore all night! Fog! You could hear the ship's foghorns out there. And bangers and stuff, warning each other! Flares, too!' she shouted cheerfully. Rupert sat up. He noticed the tangerine beret tied on with a faded Hermes scarf, the navy duffle coat that reached down to Polly's feet encased in bright yellow seamen's boots.

'Any children in the back?'

She shook her head. 'Only a guy!'

'A father?'

'Nope! A customer.' Rupert detected reticence. 'He's asleep. Kind of exhausted. A black guy but real nice! He's in the bunk, right hand side, so if you want a rest, better try this end!'

They were bowling along at a steady speed. Dawn was breaking over the New Forest which stretched away on both sides. It was promising to be a beautiful morning.

Rupert groaned aloud. 'Polly! Is this one of those business trips of yours? A paying trip?'

'Got to pay with gas the price it is! But I shan't charge you! OK? You can take the kids to the circus or something!'

'Polly! Listen to me. Is it a job like bringing that stuff over for Maddy?'

'Sort of.' Cautiously she was looking at him in the rear view mirror.

'Spending all night up on the shore at Durn Point, Polly?'

'Look, not so many questions. This job is the best payer I've got. Real money! And I get paid whether it comes off or not.'

'If it works, and if you get stopped by anyone,' Rupert said tersely, 'what happens?'

'Nobody stops a school bus like this, do they? I look like a mum don't I? Have you seen me smile? The way the cops like it?'

'Who pays on this job?'

Now Polly was hunched over the wheel, grim in a way Rupert had not seen her.

'That's none of your bloody business! They're very nice people. OK? And if it comes to that, why aren't you safely in bed with Maddy?'

'Bella! Who else? Whenever some Bair relation turns up, she puts them in my spare room.'

'And why can't you sleep with her, or on the sofa?'

'She won't have either.'

'Maddy certainly plays life the way she wants it!'

'I wish she would stop playing with me,' Rupert said wearily. 'If we were married I wouldn't have to be chucked out all the time. And all sorts of things wouldn't happen.'

'She's scared Lord B will cut her off without a penny.' Polly said shortly. 'And let's face it, you haven't got the kind of money Maddy uses!'

For a moment Rupert was silent. 'I don't think he will,' he said thoughtfully. 'Not now. I've been seeing quite a bit of Desmond Bair lately.'

'Weren't you writing an article or something about him? The way Maddy told it.' Polly sounded the hooter at an approaching car.

'That was a police car!'

'Sure! They see a girl driving a fancy bus and they think its cute! It's sort of bread on the waters.'

'Polly,' said Rupert earnestly, 'do you think I have any

chance with Maddy?'

'The way she's going on with this new deal at the gallery, she's going to be a millionaire herself! She could support half a dozen lovers!'

'I don't want to be a supported lover. Just a husband,' Rupert said wearily. He pushed his bag of belongings farther up the seat. 'I think I'll lie down here, if you don't mind. Where are you going?'

'London, does that suit? I must get back to pick up some of the kids, and get them to school. I drop the other guy off at any Underground station. After that,' Polly said, 'as I'm in the money from this trip, I'll buy you breakfast at the Carlton Tower! We can park there. They do a good breakfast at the Carlton.'

When Rupert woke, it was because motion had suddenly stopped. As was now routine, he thought for a moment he was still aboard and afloat, and sat up stiffly, cramped and confused. A small black face, with fine white teeth was smiling down at him which seemed strange. But Polly Flinders was still there, too.

'This is Josh – Dr Patel! My friend, Mr Potter!' Weakly, Rupert reached up and shook hands.

'Josh gets out here! Sure that's OK, Josh?'

'Oh, yes indeed, it will do most nicely!' The other passenger was neatly attired in a light grey suit and carried a dark red attaché case.

Bobbing and turning on his way to the door he continued to smile while Polly swung it open for him. He stepped down carefully onto the pavement outside.

'Sorry it didn't work out!' Polly cried. 'But you know where to find me for next time!' The door shut and as the bus moved off Dr Patel continued to smile and wave briefly, then turned quickly. Rupert saw him disappear into the entrance of an Underground station.

'Kids next!' shouted Polly. 'Just a couple of them, then we'll find breakfast.'

'I don't think I'm dressed for breakfast.'

'Hell, you look fine! We both do – the way people

dress for breakfast at the Carlton Tower!'

Later that morning, in the *Midas* office to where he had retreated, Rupert tried to go to sleep again in the adjustable desk chair. Tilted back with a telephone directory on the edge of the desk for his knees, it was possible to lie almost at full length. The telephone rang almost at once.

'There's a kinda buzz going round Hong Kong you could follow up there!' Curt Epoch's grating voice was, as usual, without greeting. 'There's some kind of trouble among the Kongs!' The telephone whispered with transatlantic amplification. 'Canton shipping and Tiger Wharf have fallen out, and the Hang Seng Index has dropped about 300 points. A few London banks are going to get hurt!'

'Did you get my profile on Bair Brady?' Rupert shouted. 'Are they one of them?'

'It was OK. You got a few nice touches!'

'I could add some more.'

'Forget it! That went to press yesterday. Now listen! Get on to that Dai Pol. He's with Bair Brady.' The line went dead. Rupert groaned and fell back in his chair as the telephone rang again. It was the porter from downstairs.

'Mr Potter, sir! Got a personal delivery here. To be signed for.'

'I'll be down.'

In the reception hall, his rubber boots still flapping as he crossed the marble floor, Rupert found one of the uniformed men from Bair Brady waiting for him. The man looked at him curiously.

'Mr Pother, sir?'

'Potter, actually.'

'Sign here, sir.'

'I'll just see what it is first,' Rupert said warily. He opened the stiff buff envelope.

Inside was a cheque for twenty thousand pounds. With it was a receipt and a return envelope. The wording of the receipt was to the point. That he accepted the

cheque in full and complete satisfaction for damage
caused to his sailing vessel, time and date not specified.
With a shaking hand Rupert signed the receipt and the
messenger's book. There was no question that the poor
Cuckoo would have fetched that money in any other
circumstances.

Madeleine Bair sat with her feet tucked up on the big
tangerine sofa, bathed, changed and scented. She had a
gin and tonic in her hand and looked at Rupert affectionately.

'When did you get in?'

'About an hour ago. Nancy let me in.' It had given
him time to bath and change, too. He paused for a
moment, looking at her over the rim of his own glass.
'I'm rich. We can get married!'

'Oh, Pot!'

'I sold my boat!'

'You sold your boat! To marry me? Pot, darling!'

Torn between what could be made of that, and the
truth, Rupert wavered. 'I had a sort of accident and
collected on the damage. A lot! Do you know who
smashed into me?'

'A sea monster!'

'Not a bad guess. Your former husband!'

'But Desmond's a good sailor!'

'Fog.' Rupert got up and paced about.

'Yesterday? While you were away?'

'Maddy, I haven't got the boat any more. It feels
rotten.'

'Darling! You can live here!'

'Until the next time you chuck me out!'

She looked at him reproachfully. 'Well, buy another
one! Listen, when they've all gone after drinks, we'll
have dinner at darling Thierry's and you can tell me all
about it.'

'Now I can afford it, will you marry me?' Rupert
shouted.

Maddy sipped her drink. She took his hand.

159

'Darling Pot, I'll tell you this. If I don't marry you, then I'll hang up my boots!'

Rupert moved onto the sofa beside her. Your ex-husband – is he a bit potty?'

'Like what? He's got lots of bees in his bonnet.'

'About coloureds and foreigners and defending the realm! That sort of thing?'

'Oh, plenty like that! I thought you meant important things . . .'

'Is that why you left him? You've never really told me.'

'That was the sort of thing I thought you meant. He just walked into my room one morning – it was in the big house in Ireland, and said he didn't love me any more and we would be divorced! Zipps! Just like that!'

'Is that where his sister Kate still lives?'

'She's certainly as nutty as a fruit cake!'

'And that cousin at the bank, Daimon?'

'He was best man at our wedding. He and Desmond were always close. I see him now and again at drinks parties. I suppose you've met him doing the article on the bank. Do I get to see it?'

'It's in the next *Midas*.'

The door of the drawing room opened and Audrey sprang towards the sofa, long hair flying, rolling her eyes and laughing with delicious guile.

'Mummy, I heard Pot say he's rich! And you said earlier you were going to be rich! So I can have a pony, can't I?'

'Listening to other people's conversations is very naughty. How in hell could we keep a pony here?'

Audrey sat on Rupert's lap, and swung legs that were a junior version of her mother's. She put an arm round his neck. 'I love Pot!'

'You can't have him. He's mine!'

'Is it true – about you getting rich?' Rupert said. 'Is that the stuff you're selling through the gallery?'

'Give me a cigarette from that box, darling!' Maddy said to Audrey. 'Sir Dai Pol and his daughter, or whatever she is – Polly isn't sure – are coming. And Ruthy and the

Bealeys and Bella are looking in, and you be nice to her, Pot. She's getting a late plane. And Wilf Poult. Super Nancy has very sweetly got some caviar from the famous left-overs, and you and Pot can pour drinks, darling!'

'OK, Mummy!' Audrey skipped off Rupert's lap. 'But you and Pot must promise to get me my pony!'

'I don't like Poult!'

'He doesn't like you.'

'He's after you!'

'Wilf is being very helpful with all this Chinese stuff.' Maddy lit her cigarette with the lighter from the table and puffed out a small cloud of smoke. 'Listen! How much d'you think that stuff is worth? I had no idea.'

'Then how can I have?'

'Literally millions! I get commission into a Swiss bank for doing the deals. OK, so I have to give some to Gugi and the others who are getting buyers just like that! But at the end of the series, our new friend, Polly Wolly, will be a billionaire. OK, that's not new for him – but this baby will be a millionaire!'

'So my little windfall doesn't count?'

'Pot, darling, I'm tired of being a kept woman, by anyone! I can do without Desmond's bloody alimony. But sure! With a bit of luck it looks as though I could get married again and if he cuts me off I could be OK!'

'Marry me,' said Rupert, with sudden grimness, 'and he won't cut you off either, Maddy.'

Her eyes narrowed behind the cigarette smoke. 'I think you're not telling me everything, Pot! Maybe you know him better than I do these days.' She took his hand again. 'Listen! We've got to entertain the chinky Chinaman now, which is really what this evening is all about. Wilf says we've got to know where this stuff is coming from and he's said he'll tell us.'

'I never have you to myself for five minutes!'

'Thierrys afterwards, Pot!'

'You promise not to invite anyone else!'

'Promise! Hey! There's the front door buzzer!' Maddy cried happily.

9

Drinks parties with a purpose were Maddy's speciality. The preparations seemed to Rupert somewhat similar to the setting up of a minor TV production. Maddy decided in advance where people were going to sit or stand. Lighting was raised or dimmed and flowers were brought in. Some of the flowers did not agree with the pictures they were next to, and either or both were moved again. The drinks table was put out into the hall so that glasses might be filled out of sight of the recipients.

The final effect was achieved by the producer-director herself, who stood in the centre of the room, twirling on the tangerine-coloured carpet, and flinging out her arms at each new arrival with a cry of excitement that made them feel the whole evening was just for them.

The guests came very much one after another, so that Maddy's welcoming cries were more or less continuous. Rupert was kept busy ferrying drinks from the bottles in the hall, and Audrey and Nancy served canapés. The room quickly filled and, as though pre-arranged, Sir Dai Pol and Kitty were last to arrive, making a modest entry.

'Now everyone here, this evening, is family – from the gallery or to do with it, as we agreed. I want you to call me Maddy now, like everyone else, and I shall call you

162

Dai. Now, who don't you know? Sir Wilfred Poult is from the British Museum and has been especially helpful with your treasures. Tim Bealey has met you and Rupert.'

'From Bair Brady? The two young men who came on board when we arrived?'

Sir Dai Pol, with a glass of champagne in his hand, smiled continuously.

'My assistant, Ruthy, you know and that is her husband. Polly Flinders who helps us you know, and she knows your daughter. Polly! Help Kitty here meet some of the people while I move Dai around!' Rupert gave Maddy tonic only, which was the advantage of having the bottles in the hall. He handed Ruthy, who had requested the same, an extra gin, and Sir Wilfred a whisky and vodka and much ice, enough to lead to a fearful headache. He had put a spoonful of brandy into Sir Dai Pol's champagne glass.

'I think I have the wrong drink, Lady Bair!' Sir Dai gave back the glass to Rupert, still smiling. 'It is a fine dry champagne, but I think not as a cocktail, please!'

'Perhaps just some orange juice with it?' said Rupert.

'Bring the bottle, sweety, and let's give it to Dai in a new glass.'

The conversation was the audible jig-saw again.

'Ruthy, how did you get those marks on your wrists, baby?' Polly cried.

'Honestly, I don't know. Some kind of allergy from bracelets, or something, I guess.'

Kitty stopped smiling and looked inscrutable. 'Jade is best for bracelets, I think.' She looked at Ruthy's small, white face and heavy lipstick and rouge and, as Ruthy flushed, Kitty glanced under her eyelashes at her husband, who returned a blank stare.

'That's what we must get for them then, honey!'

'Audrey, sweet, take this bottle of champagne round, it's not too heavy now.'

'What an accomplished daughter you have, Lady Bair!'

'Yes, we saw *Traviata* last night!'

Rupert scowled at Wilfred Poult's reflection in the big mirror. The fat, happy Nancy was at his side.

'They've eaten nearly all the caviar, Mr Potter! Do you want the last one?'

'Did Lady Bair enjoy the opera last night?'

'I can't really say. I was in bed when they got back, and then this morning I had to go to work.'

Maddy was getting people to sit down, some on cushions on the floor, the men perched on the sides of armchairs, Sir Dai Pol on the sofa. Rupert stood while Maddy, spinning her long necklace, addressed the room.

'Listen, folk! As you in the gallery with me one way or another know, we owe a big thank-you to Dai Pol for the truly lovely things he is putting through Art Appreciation. So I am asking him a big, fascinating question. To tell us about them! Where do they come from?' Maddy turned to Sir Dai Pol who sat like a Buddha in a black silk suit, still smiling, but now more carefully, his big spectacles glinting in the arranged lighting.

'Yes. It is proper you should know some of the story of the origin of these unique, precious things; you are selling them. But it is not for gossip, my dear Lady Bair. And I would like your friends to know that.'

'But it's not secret – sort of?'

The eyes behind the big glasses were almost closed. 'You Americans are impossible, so informal, in diplomacy, in business! Quite the opposite to the Orient. That is also your difficulty with the Big Bear country.'

'They're the most secretive bastards I ever met!' Ruthy's husband said loudly. 'When I went there – ' He stopped abruptly as Dai Pol turned his heavy head and gazed at him.

'Quite so, you guess correctly! These treasures come from Communist China.'

'But where?' Wilfred Poult, edgy and impatient, leaned forward on the edge of his small gilt chair and folded his arms. 'Where in China? They have not been collected before.'

'You are wrong. They were collected about two

thousand years ago. For a funeral.'

'A burial? Smuggled out?'

'Now, Wilf!' Maddy said.

'I will tell you! I may not satisfy our friend, who is obviously an expert. I shall be very interested to hear his opinion of some of the objects! Please relax. The pieces you have, came through the Embassy here. Mrs Flinders and my daughter know that. Any genuine antiques, ancient things from the People's Republic, can only be exported and sold if they have an official approval mark or seal. This is the control.'

'Possible to forge,' Wilfred Poult said.

Dai Pol put his head on one side. 'Very disagreeable. Have people in Zurich, Paris, here, New York suggested that? I should perhaps find others myself?'

'Take no notice, Dai,' Maddy said quickly. 'Wilf is not in business. He's just trying to get background. To help us all!'

'For his cut,' said Ruthy's husband audibly.

'Sort of!' Maddy was now very cool.

'What we have seen so far is all Han,' Wilfred Poult said. 'Not to detract from their brilliance, you understand. Nor their value.'

'Tomorrow you get the last two pieces from the Embassy source.' Dai Pol paused. 'Then there is one more. Very different. Perhaps the finest and most extraordinary thing to come out of China, privately, you understand, since the revolution. What I have to say is for the professor. It came from the same tomb and the Han Dynasty, about two hundred BC to the same AD. Ch'in, the first Emperor, started the Great Wall and, in the way of military pragmatists, he suppressed the scholars and the artists as divisive influences. Maybe similar to today's repressive military bastards, as our friend over there said? The point is, that in the dynasty that followed, some of the most superb pottery, painting, jade work and bronze was created, and in the tombs of the princes were buried not replica wares, but actual treasures.'

There was an uneasy silence.

'What we have seen so far could have been in the National Palace Museum in Taipei.' Wilfred Poult spoke with seeming detachment. 'Disappeared from the vaults. Some countries are beginning to need the right currencies.'

'Ha-ah-ah-ah-ah!' Dai Pol was smiling again, imperturbable. 'But no! The things you have were never part of the Forbidden Palace collection! The Han prosperity took officials to distant regions, very grand Chinese tombs can be found in remote places, furnished with metropolitan riches.'

Dai Pol reckoned he knew Sir Wilf and his kind. They were the English counterpart of the dynasty he was talking about. Privilege, inheritance, exponents of the arts. But with Anglo-Saxon attitudes and from wealth creating systems that were about to become extinct. He could afford to be kind.

'It is for all of you now that I can draw a picture.' He moved an arm round the room as though actually doing so. 'In the autumn, south-west of Peking, the air is clear, cool, dry and sparkling – you have to envisage a valley, about a hundred miles from the city. Not a valley like river valleys in Europe, nor the Scottish glens, so much wider, the hills on either side not so forbidding, this valley, so wide and beautiful, is a place of utter serenity and peace, the mountains so far away as to be painted against the sky. Here princes were buried in succession, in rock tombs cut in the head of the valley. Yes, they have been raided superficially. But so much exists in China like this, that the current rulers have had only time and money to do proper excavations of really very few. In the valley of the kings, north of Peking, only two of the temple tombs there, out of thirteen, have been dug out properly. Their contents alone fill a museum!'

Maddy who had sat beside him on the arm of the sofa, picturesque herself, chin in hand, said quietly: 'Did you do a private dig? Sort of?'

'I have made many visits there. I am persona grata. I have *entrée*.' Dai Pol felt Kitty stir uneasily on the sofa beside him. 'Certain things were retrieved from the lovely valley and I suggested the way to get them into the hands of others who would appreciate them in a tangible form! That is all really, I think!' He rose to his feet and took hold of one of Maddy's hands between his own. 'I think now we must go and, please, your colleagues keep our little talk in the family?'

'That was really very interesting!' Tim Bealey joined them. 'If need be I could mention the background at BB?'

Kitty had slipped across to Polly as her father moved towards the door. Everyone else was getting up.

'My father says, you will please tomorrow bring a pram.'

'A *pram*? You mean a kid's pram? On wheels?'

Kitty nodded. Polly looked thoughtful.

'Someone will lend me one I guess, sure!'

The smiling Dai Pol shook hands with Wilfred Poult.

'I think I have told you nothing you did not already know!'

'See you tomorrow, Maddy!' Ruthy's husband steered her to the doorway.

'Dai, would you and your daughter join Rupert Potter and Polly and me for dinner? Are you doing anything? I mean it's just a little French restaurant nearby, but very good!'

Dai Pol had anticipated having to reveal something as background to their business. There was a lot at stake in his dealings with this woman. Perhaps he in turn could learn more about her former husband, for example.

'So very kind!'

'I must say goodbye to the others and then we'll call up a cab and get over.'

'Darling!' Rupert pulled her out into the hall. 'You promised!'

'Pot listen! The gallery business is important. They're only here a short while. We'll have lots of other times!'

'Treachery!' said Rupert. He looked at her sadly. 'On every side. You know what happens to people who ride into valleys of death?'

'You just stop trying to reason why, Pot!'

When Tracy Flip parked her car in Curzon Street, she neither locked the doors nor gave consideration to double yellow lines but stormed into the entrance of *Groin*. When she reached reception on the third floor she was breathing hard.

'Mr Crimp in?'

The dumpy girl who served the switchboard looked surprised. 'Shall I tell him you're here, Miss Flip?'

'Don't worry!' Tracy went on up to the editor's office and thrust open the door. For a moment she stood looking for him. She had always disliked the man, and one of the real joys of selling the magazine had been the belief that she would never have to see him again. Now she saw that he was in a corner, apparently toying with some sort of gold club, pushing a gold golf ball across the furry turf of his white carpet. Tracy banged her large handbag down on his desk. 'I don't remember you as a golf buff!'

'Trade goods.' Norman Crimp turned, lifting the club. 'Sent in for approval and editorial puff, of course. The end is a facsimile penis, gold plated. Only nine carat, of course. The balls? Well, they're just balls, gold too. I suppose we might do a picture round it.'

'Listen to me, Norman and put that thing down! You won't do any pictures round anything. Least of all movie pictures. Have you heard from the CID? Police? Angela Minkworth's father? Brother?'

Wearily Crimp slunk round to the other side of the outsize desk and flung himself back in the vast, tilting chair. He had also hoped never to hear that voice again. He picked up a half-used cigar from the glass ashtray and carefully relit it.

'Now *you* listen! It's been going on like that around here for years, you know that, Tracy! There's always some damn Daddy-o or boyfriend with a handle, or Mum who is a Duchess and knows the Public Prosecutor personally. That's the occupational hazard of *Groin*.

But the gilt-edged girls get a Debrett Document. The contract is watertight! No complaints, no hassle, all agreed voluntarily.'

'You're a bloody idiot!' Tracy said coldly. 'This one's different!'

Crimp looked at her, taking no trouble to conceal his dislike. He had spent so long looking at so many women, almost all of them unbelievably more beautiful than Tracy Flip, that he was totally immune to all their moods, manners and make-up. With this particular one as his employer, he had developed a certain *modus vivendi*. But she was no longer the publisher. He sat up. His little beard wagged and the sallow cheeks twitched.

'You can get out! You were always a condescending little cow, and you think you can still walk in here as though you owned the place!'

Tracy Flip put two fists on the desk and the editor moved quickly in his chair. Actually there was something like those snakes about her as she moved her head and hissed at him.

'Angela Minkworth! One of the early feature models! You offered her a part in your new film project. In the south of France, isn't it? She was one of the Golden Groins who wouldn't have her picture taken unless the consoling safety of the lady publisher was present too. Remember? So you were getting bored with the helicopter flip to France after doing about a dozen, you said, and would Flip do the flip and the old job of holding her hand?'

'And you got five hundred for it! Which I agree these days you need like a hole anywhere you care to name. But kind, I thought, Tracy! I happen to know what it's like to be without a job suddenly! And better than being bored out of your mind in that phoney country seat of yours!'

Tracy Flip leaned across the desk, almost writhing with fear and loathing. 'Listen you stupid little man! It's not the south of France this action! It's Middle East! It's the Sheiks of Arabee, you silly sod. It's abduction and kidnap! And when I was on that dirty little air-strip, and wouldn't let her go, they dropped us both. Laughing and touching us up like a lot of baboons! The royal bloody bodyguard, that lot! I don't know how many bodies you've sent them, and how many may, or may not, come back, but I think it's called white slavery! And the United Nations doesn't like it! But from the look of the other plane, there's a very great deal of money in it for someone, something a great deal more than your five hundred!' Tracy Flip was panting for breath now, her small fists thumping the desk.

Norman Crimp stared at her. Then reasserting himself, he sought dignity by swivelling in the editorial chair and sucking on his cigar.

'I know nothing about it! *Groin* has a new publisher who is also producing a film which would, of course, certainly require a lot of finance and possibly various backers. I shall take the matter up with him.' He sounded uneasy.

'And how do you do that?'

'I get very little interference from him, as a matter of fact,' said Crimp meaningfully. 'If I need him I contact him through his London bankers. What are they called?' He pulled open a drawer and shut it again. 'Bair Brady!'

'And good luck to you!' Tracy Flip got up quickly and, pacing across the white carpet, kicked one of the golden golf balls. 'I'll tell you something more though I don't know why I trouble! You think you have a new publisher! And probably a new contract? Yes, I thought so! And I sold out for big money OK? Half paid by Bair Brady and half the way I wanted it, on a Swiss bank to my private number, all through some damned holding company organised by BB. Their cheque has gone through, but the Swiss one, also signed by your new boss, has not so far! I reckon I still own half the magazine right now!'

'You push off!' Shakily Norman Crimp got to his feet. He stubbed out the cigar, rubbing it viciously round and round in the ash tray. 'I shall phone the bank and deal with this without you meddling!'

'I think I will speak to Bair Brady myself.' Calmly now, Tracy Flip sat down again, reaching for the ivory-coloured, direct-line telephone that was one of four of different colours on the plastic desk. 'I shall speak to Lord Bair, whom I met, and ask him about pal Pol! Give me the bank number,' she directed quietly, 'and meanwhile you had better be preparing your piece for the fuzz! The way I left the Hon Angela Minkworth, they will be round here any minute!' Holding on to the handset of the telephone, she looked across the top of the desk at a gleaming replica of the Ferrari.

'What's that?'

'None of your business again!' said Crimp wrathfully.

Slowly Tracy put down the telephone, and reached for the heavy object across the desk top and slid it towards her. She tried to lift it but only succeeded in raising the whole thing a few inches before it slipped from her hand and fell over on one side.

'For God's sake, leave my things alone!' screamed Crimp. The sound of his furious breathing, accompanied by indigestion noises coming from the telephone receiver lying on its side, were now joined by a new noise. A thin, high-pitched continuous note coming from the silver car.

Panting, Norman Crimp picked up a long ebony ruler off the desk, as though he would strike anything that made so much as a move at him. 'What's that?'

Slowly Tracy Flip replaced the telephone receiver, and in the silence that followed, the thin noise went on, stopped for a moment, revived, then cut out altogether. Tracy touched the silver car curiously.

'Where did this come from Norman?'

'Give it to me!' The editor exchanged the ruler for another object from his desk top collection, a dagger-like letter opener. Levering and stabbing, he attacked the base of the model. The green under-felt gave way to plastic and the whole of one end came off. Norman Crimp wrenched it back savagely. Both of them stared at the mass of tiny rainbow colours, the circuits and microchips connected to silver discs with perforations.

'Bugged!' Tracy said sardonically. 'Or you could extend the word, in your case I would say, Norman!'

'Oh, my God!' whispered the editor hoarsely. Reaching wild-eyed across the desk, he grabbed up the silver car, now loose from its stand, and flung it across the carpet. One of the telephones, a red one, began to ring steadily. Crimp's hand moved hesitantly to pick it up.

'Who is it? Two of them? Say I'm out! No, no! They can't! They haven't a warrant! I'll want to get my solicitor. Listen, Mabel!' The editor was pleading. 'Just do as I say!'

Tracy Flip rose to her feet. She looked comtemptuously at Crimp, who put down the telephone and was now pulling at his beard.

'I'm off! They don't want me! They don't know me.' She turned on her way to the door. 'And don't worry. I'll tell them you're improving your golf and can't be disturbed!'

At Art Appreciation the atmosphere was also tense as Madeleine Bair presided over a small reception committee that awaited the arrival of Polly Flinders.

'A what? A boy prince?' Wilfred Poult sat back in the Chippendale chair. The end of his chiselled nose twitched. 'Popular jargon, of course! Who called him that?'

'He did,' said Maddy. She looked at a piece of paper. 'This was the extra dope I got last night in the restaurant. But I think he felt he'd already talked too much. When it arrives, we're to telephone as usual. Maybe then you can ask the questions. I think he's pretty anxious about this one.'

'We're all anxious!' Ruthy said. Rupert, looking at her, was reminded of a white mouse. The red-pink colour of her hair seemed to have run into her eyes. The idea occurred to him that the whole scene was like the tea party from Alice. Ruthy was the dormouse, Maddy was Alice, Poult the Mad Hatter. That left him as the white rabbit. The thought made him look at his watch rather pointedly.

'No time, no time! I shall have to go in a minute!' He got up, peering over the back window curtain. 'It's nearly an hour since he called to say she'd left.'

'Just stay by me, Pot sweety, till we're clear on this thing.' Maddy was drifting round the gallery, smoking. She straightened pictures and moved smaller table top ornaments.

'Epoch calls me in the office about this time,' Rupert said. 'He likes to find me there.'

'Did Dai Pol say we had to call him when Polly got here, or the other way round?' Poult asked.

'We call him!'

Sir Wilfred took out a large red-and-white spotted handkerchief and blew his nose. 'Supposing she has a crash? Or that bus breaks down?'

'Pour yourself a drink, Ruthy, and one for Wilf!' Maddy said. 'I wish Rudi or Gugi were back! I really do like the way those guys keep cool. Having them both away at once to get the stuff moving is a bore! Now this damn prince!'

'I'm quite cool, my dear Madeleine!'

'Wilf, what do we do with the darn thing when we've checked it out? I daren't tell him it's all getting a bit above our resources! It's OK for him to tell me the money he wants to get, and Rudi and Gugi don't seem to have any problems, but it's beginning to add up like the national debt! How much have we transferred since Gugi last called?'

Ruthy opened a drawer and consulted something inside it. 'Nearly twelve million.' Her small voice was flat.

'I guessed it was something like that,' said Poult. 'I think I might double my consulting fees!'

'Is this prince a kind of mummy?' Ruthy asked. ' 'Cos that's gonna be sort of yucky.'

'An effigy, my dear Ruth.' Poult sipped his glass of sherry.

'They pickled them or something, didn't they?'

'Only the so called old lady of Cheng Sha. But they

173

couldn't possibly transport anything like that, it would disintegrate.'

Maddy settled on the edge of the desk, swinging an elegant leg and glancing over the curtain rail. 'He did tell me that it's the only piece he brought over himself because of its size and value. He seemed just a bit jittery about it.'

'What bugs me, Maddy, is the money! Gugi and Rudi – and when Wilf went to Paris – get the amount paid in net, and Sir Dai Pol transfers our commission to your account. But a lot of dough hasn't turned up yet. So we've all the air fares and the boys' hotels up on our shirts.'

'Here's Polly!' Rupert moved quickly to open the door. Sir Wilf remained seated, Ruthy sat limply behind her desk and Maddy drew a little more sharply on her cigarette.

'Just let her come in! That bus is on a yellow line. She can't leave it there for long.'

Polly stepped in as though playing the boy prince rôle herself. With a silver scarf wound round her neck, green velvet knickerbockers and a matching velvet troubadour's hat on her head, she stood in the doorway and embraced them all with out-stretched arms, flushed face and happy smile.

'I got it, kids!'

'Cut the drama, Polly,' Maddy said. 'How do we get it in here?'

'I can tell you how I got it, and you can work it out from there! Anybody got a cigarette? Ruthy, baby, what's in that wee glass? We're celebrating, aren't we?'

'Look,' Rupert said. 'Now you're all right, I've got to move.'

'Stay right there, fella!' Polly said. 'You'll be needed!'

'What have we got to do?' Maddy came and stood over her.

'How big is it?' Wilf Poult's eyebrows were down to the bridge of his nose, his head jutting forward.

Polly enjoying it, puffed on her cigarette. 'You know how he said to bring a pram? I thought he was sort of kidding, but I met Angie Minkworth – she's in a hell of a state, Maddy! Someone tried to kidnap her or something – but I remembered she had a baby carriage, so I picked it up. I don't know if any of you have seen the Old Tower harbour spot? The Monte Carlo scene? You have to park way outside and walk in!'

'Get on, Polly!' Maddy was finally beginning to crack.

'Grab the point of the pram? To get something off the boat without everyone seeing? So the Dai himself comes out and he says to put up the hood on the pram and pretend you've brought the baby for us to see! So we get to the boat, and after a bit of play acting, Kitty brings out a shawl and a blanket and they carry a couple of cushions on board. So when its time to leave, those two guys on the boat carry out something swathed in the blanket and I have to fuss around and we get it back to the pram. I make like I'm worried about the kid, and wheel the pram out to the bus.'

'Does anyone see all this?'

'Well, Dai – he's really nice isn't he? – he says just act naturally and the two guys come out presently to help me get the load into the bus. But I reckon it was all for laughs. They could have done it better at night.'

'It's floodlit at night,' Rupert said.

'Let's go!' Maddy stubbed out her cigarette. 'I'll stay in here with Ruthy! You two see what you can do. There are a few interested eyes round here, too, so make it casual.'

Inside the bus the handle of the pram had been lashed to two of the seat backs with a length of rope. Polly put down the hood and Rupert and Wilfred Poult gingerly seized hold of the top and bottom of the bundle which was wedged inside. Sir Wilfred heaved.

'Don't let go!'

The pram rocked, and with Polly following, they staggered for the door, Rupert backing down the steps and on to the pavement, Sir Wilf, bandy-legged, clinging onto the other end of the load. The gallery's handsome panelled door opened to let them through, then shut behind them. The bundle was lowered carefully on to the carpeted floor. Rupert leaned on the desk and Wilfred Poult fell back in the chair.

'Thanks, fellas!' Maddy, with face flushed and lips parted, was looking fascinated at the blanketed bundle.

'I want that blanket and shawl back!' Polly said. 'Hey, open it up! I want to see what we've done all this for! Then I've got to meet Kitty at the Old Spotted Dog.'

'Didn't she come with you this time?' Ruthy asked.

'I did sort of wonder, too. I got the feeling I was on my own. If anything happened.'

'Wilf – you open it up!' Maddy had dropped down to her knees on the carpet. 'I'm sort of scared!'

Bending awkwardly, Sir Wilfred got down beside her. With some help from Maddy in easing away the shawl and blanket, they got to the linen that lay beneath. As he carefully turned and wound the layers of material away, Maddy gave an odd little cry.

The effigy, suddenly revealed, lying on its wrappings, was strange and beautiful, the complete figure of a child, luminous, with soft light reflecting from thousands of pale blue and green jade particles. Inset in the headdress and collar and cuffs were ruby and gold inlay. The ivory coloured mask of the face, with its flat cheeks and closed eyes, smiled with a beatific peace.

Sir Wilfred knelt back and stared down, his hands shaking. Then, creaking at the knees, he slowly stood up.

'Get him on the phone!'

'Gee, that's just the most beautiful thing I've ever seen!' Polly's face had the same sublime expression as the little figure.

'Do I call him?' Ruthy said.

'If I put him on the box, we could all hear. Then you get it on the tape, too,' Maddy nodded.

The group round the desk could all hear the ringing at the other end. It was picked up almost at once. It was Kitty's voice that answered.

'*Chenn Lo*!'

'This is Madeleine Bair.' Maddy sounded calm, but

Rupert could see that her face under the make-up was pale, and knew she was not.

'I give you my father!'

'Dai? Well he's safely arrived. Listen, we're all a bit dazed. Sort of. Who? Well, just Wilf Poult. No, she's on her way to meet Kitty, I think. Now can you tell Wilf some more about what we have, and what you've got in mind for it? Yes, we can both hear at once, he's on the other phone.'

'I do not want to talk a lot on this line.' The amplifier accentuated the hollow mandarin voice. 'The figure that we referred to in our recent conversation –' There was a pause. 'You are listening, professor? It is from the rock tomb at the south-west end of the valley and not officially excavated. It was created for the first Han prince.' Another pause. 'Have you something to write with, Lady Bair?'

'I am writing!'

'Prince Wan Shang – you have that? His wife, Princess Tou Wan and their infant son Wan Tung. Don't worry about spelling. Undoubtedly all three were carried away by the same disease. Effigies of all three were found in the tomb, together with many other statues of servants, animals, many precious things. Some you have already had.'

'Poult here! Tell me this. Will there be any official export bona-fides on this?'

This time the pause was longer. 'No.'

'There are one or two things that make me think more of the Huai style than Han. I shall have to check.'

'Please do.' The voice on the amplifier was flat. 'Is Lady Bair still there?'

'Right here.'

'Please be so very careful! This is the last of our present business co-ordinations. It must be speedy. Not more than a week. I may have to move away from London, but you can contact me through the bank if this link number is out. Is your friend there?'

'He's still on.'

'Ha-ah-ah-ah-ah!' They could hear the hiss of breath.

177

'What would you consider is realisable, for something quickly, in the right quarter?'

'Impossible to say. Utterly priceless. It is private collection only.'

'Exactly. I make a floor of five million and a top of ten.'

'Dollars?'

'Pounds, Lady Bair. I will keep in touch.' The phone went dead and the dialling tone whirred in the box. Ruthy switched off and replaced the receiver on the instrument. Her pink, mouse eyes looked carefully at each of the others in turn.

'I think that little job will be fifty for me!' said Polly cheerfully. She giggled happily. 'Pounds, Maddy! You don't have to give it me now. If he can trust you, so can I!'

On board the *Chenn Lo*, with the thin rattan blinds down, there was soft filtered light in the main cabin and in his white coat Shee moved like a moth round the recorder equipment.

'I think you do not like this tape.' Shee had worked at the Hong Kong Hilton and when he spoke English he addressed his employer as Sir Dai. In Chinese he used the master conjugation. Now he did neither. 'Also there are many calls from Hong Kong. Here is the list.'

'What is on the tape?' Dai Pol also spoke in Chinese.

'Number two has gone. You will hear. There is a woman.'

'And number one?'

'Nothing. Only ten minutes of nothing – assistant lady. But is still fine. Lights show still fine!'

Dai Pol walked across the stateroom and climbed onto his dais chair. He nodded. 'Play number two. Just the piece!'

The cabin filled with the thin, flat voice of Tracy Flip, then the nervous anger of Crimp. Even with the amplification turned up, the fidelity of the recording was perfect. Then, as the equipment played on, scratching and screeching set in, a sonic whooping and audio bumps. Followed by silence, and the running of the empty tape.

178

For a moment Sir Dai Pol sat still. Then he got down to the floor, moving quietly about the cabin. 'I must see Lord Bair.' He was talking to himself. 'That will not be possible quickly. When is my daughter back?'

'With bus lady.'

'The telephone! What time is it in Hong Kong?'

'Evening!'

Dai Pol dialled and almost at once was talking, using the Kowloon dialect. Silently Shee watched him. But Sir Dai Pol's face expressed nothing. When he put down the telephone he knew that Shee had already heard enough.

'Now I must make one more call to the Colony, and then London. It is better that you do not hear these calls, Mr Shee!' Dai Pol smiled. He knew that Shee, in turn, was aware that this handle to his name meant circumstances were unusual. 'For your own sake!'

'We keep number one on?'

'Essential!'

'I monitor every ten minutes.'

'I want Captain Hoffmann to telephone every two hours.'

Shee moved silently out of the room.

The Hong Kong call took ten minutes, and towards the end Dai Pol wrote down on a pad in his tiny ball point writing, some of it with Chinese characters, addresses in London. The next three calls were to the addresses in turn. In the end he made an appointment. Then called Shee.

'I am going to the hotel to take a taxi. I may be one hour, maybe two.'

'Ha-ah-ah-ah-ah!' said Shee politely, with hollowed cheeks.

Sir Dai Pol went to his private cabin, moved rugs, lifted polished deck planks and took out plastic wrapped bundles of currency. He counted ten into a slim, dark-red briefcase, replaced floor and rugs and went up on deck.

On the bridge he looked carefully round the dock, took a small umbrella from a dump bin by the bridge door and walked to the stern to go ashore. He did not take a taxi from the main Tower Hotel doors, avoiding the help of the commissionaire. Instead he strolled in thin watery sunshine over the cobbles and across the street to the Tower itself where there were always taxis discharging tourists.

'Leicester Square,' he told the driver. He actually had need of an address off Gerrard Street, which he knew to be a short distance from the Square.

'Want the north side, guv?' said the young cabby when they got there. The implication amused Sir Dai.

'Please yourself!' But he gave the man the meaner end of the tipping scale that might indeed confirm that his passenger was a Chinatown restaurant proprietor.

In fact the address only mildly surprised Dai Pol. It was a massage parlour. The usefulness of this struck him when a man in a black suit and bowler hat preceeded him in. Another in bib and brace overalls came out, hopefully enacting that the purpose of his visit had been attention to the plumbing.

To the very pretty girl at the desk, Dai Pol gave the name he had been instructed to. He guessed she was from Malaya rather than the Colony or any part of Indo China. He was, in fact, wrong. She and her parents had been born in Stepney. A version of oriental musak played around in the area of the desk with its shadowed, subdued lighting, and he waited, concealing impatience.

Another girl in a very short slip appeared. She led him along the passage, past cubicles and, at the end, through a towelling curtain. Behind it she unlocked a door in which a bunch of keys had been left.

The setting changed. It was dark, and Dai Pol followed her upstairs, along a passage lit only by low wattage bulbs. The girl knocked on a door. A voice spoke and she showed him in, shutting the door silently behind him.

'Forgive the curious precautions. You are Tang Yo?' The voice was that of a much younger man than himself, Dai Pol considered. It came from the far end of a long table, and the face and most of the figure were in almost complete darkness.

'Please sit at that end! You will not see my face and I shall not see yours.' Dai Pol heard the creak of basketware as he settled into a cushioned chair with thin, wooden arms. He put the briefcase on the table in front of him.

'*Da Sun.*' It was the code.

'*Cimbai nu han.*' The first response.

'*Pan po Shenshi!*'

'*Cheng Chan!*'

In the half darkness both men relaxed.

'What kind of arrangement is required?' The younger man now spoke in English, although it was obvious to Dai Pol that this was face-saving for them both. He reckoned he heard his own district of Kowloon in the accent.

Also in English, Dai Pol outlined a number of things about his special requirements. There was a short silence.

'It is possible. You are lucky. It has been done here twice before, but the man is not in London. He has the kraits. They are very small and deadly. How urgent is this?'

'Tomorrow morning at the latest.'

'Have you any suggestions that will help? Give me everything you have got.'

Dai Pol began to talk. He gave location and details, precise information. It was warm in the dark room with the blinds drawn and he found himself beginning to perspire. He guessed he was almost certainly being taped, but that had to be accepted, and the precautions for anonymity otherwise, both ways, were all he would expect. They were not unfamiliar.

'He did best when they were released into a car.' The voice at the other end of the table was smooth. 'Is that possible? Access is easier than a house. He can put sedation into the things so that they become active after a time delay. It is like a fuse for a bomb.' Dai Pol sensed the smile in the darkness. 'An advantage is that a post mortem for a car crash is difficult and a heart attack is presumed.

The symptoms are the same.'

'A crash could hurt other people.'

'Entry to the house is very difficult. There is too much space, it is uncertain, even in a bedroom. You have chosen an effective but unusual method. May I ask why?'

Dai Pol was silent, for a moment only. 'She herself keeps the things. Don't ask me why.'

The brief intake of breath came this time from the other end of the table. Then there was a small movement of the hands.

'Curious and unusual! But now you tell me, also useful. There is one disadvantage to the method, and it is a faint smell. There is a risk of its being noticed by some people, but not in most cars, and certainly not by such a person I would say. It is like with dogs.'

'Do you guarantee success?'

'That is impossible. It works, as you must obviously know where you come from. And in places other than cars. – boats, small dwellings – it is particularly clever in that the thing almost always leaves immediately afterwards and is never seen again. So I am told.'

'That is what I remember,' Sir Dai Pol said drily. But he did not feel dry, the young cold voice made him sweat.

'The loss of such a valuable asset, in a difficult business, is of course expensive.'

'How much?'

'Five grand.'

'Dollars? Pounds?'

He heard a small sigh. The flat accented voice, sounded for the first time just a little impatient. 'We are in England.'

Sir Dai Pol took it easily, feeling suddenly much older than this invisible young man. Older, and cleverer in almost all ways, and able to see farther. He took from the briefcase the plastic wrapped bundles, stacking them on the table.

'This is in dollars, but it is six in pounds. The resourcefulness of your house is appreciated.'

From the other end of the table there was a tiny chuckle.

'The method is called Paradise! I thought it would amuse you to know.'

'I do not follow you,' Dai Pol said politely. He snapped shut the briefcase locks. 'I add the additional amount to make quite sure you give the job your personal interest.'

'It is in the Bible story. Adam and Eve. And everybody was happy. Perhaps you do not know the Bible?'

'I was brought up on it,' Dai Pol said truthfully.

'And there was the serpent.'

'You wish to check?'

'I have your telephone number. I have to have that much. That is all. When all is ready I will call, and use the code once – nothing else. When the job is done, I will call and use it again. After that – Paradise?'

Sir Dai Pol thanked him, picked up his attaché case and left the room. In the gloomy passage he was met again by the young girl, who escorted him downstairs and out into the daylight.

10

L ord Desmond Bair looked guardedly over his half-
spectacles along the boardroom table. It was a full
compliment for the main weekly board meeting. The
row of faces, old, young, sharp, clever, sallow, dark-
haired or fair, distant or close relations, were too experienced to look expectant, keen, eager or anything but
bored.

'May I begin, gentlemen?' Too experienced to be
anything but jovial.

'Chairman!' Usual low key chorus. Only Daimon on
his right hand stirred uneasily. The agenda in front of
them was rough.

'Minutes of the last meeting?'

'Spelling of those Polish banks all wrong, chairman.' It
was bloody Erin Eden, too sharp and too clever. But the
Polish thing was mainly his.

'Tell Faughsquar. Otherwise OK?'

'Phrase two, ball park loss figures eight million, not
eighty!'

'Same again! Matters arising, not on agenda?' But Lord
Bair felt the indigestion rising under his own waistcoat.
The Princess had insisted he had breakfast in her bed-
room. She had brought back Mexican coffee with her.
He gazed at the far portrait of his grandfather for comfort,

184

and saw, for the umpteenth time, that the half-glasses on the old man's nose were crooked. He put a finger to his own.

'First item, whose is it?'

'Mine!' Erin again. 'I think they're going to default or postpone, and France and Marseilles are going along with it.'

'Bloody Reds!' Daimon said helpfully.

'Committee next Monday!' The chairman's notes from Miss Faughsquar were infallibly helpful. 'Next?'

It was almost impossible for old Miles Malhoney to look cheerful. He had a face like a basset hound. 'West Riding Brass and Manchester Muck and Salvage! We seem to have come unstuck a bit. All warranties OK and it went through Tuesday with a good press. Now it looks as though the whole lot has gone to the other side's bankers.' He rolled his eyes and shuffled his papers.

'Mergers and acquisitions?' said the chairman. He had his list but everyone had to have an innings.

'Telemetric and Sparks Inc. Brussells won't play!'

'Video Superpix onto the last warranties.'

'What's the hold up there?'

'Those west-coast lawyers, Scheinbaum, Mackintosh-Sheriff.'

'I could give Scheinbaum a call.' Parson Pinter doodled on his pad.

'Plugged in there, are we?' asked Daimon.

'I took a couple of thousand bucks off him on the Monterey course last month!'

'Does that endear the fellow?'

'I tipped him on Yukon Rock Crush Smelting! They were at thirty-two cents.'

'You didn't tell me?' Lord Bair looked over his glasses.

'House rules, chairman. Not inside!'

'Remind Faughsquar to put those out for me again! That's the trouble with this Banking House!' The chairman leaned back and looked around. He liked to remind the board of its collective affiliations, ancestry, longevity and his own position, at least once at every meeting. 'By the time all your fathers had finished amending the rules, and the lawyers have brought in every bloody government's cock's-only days, there's nothing much in the pot!' It was dependents' laughter, but appreciative, and he glanced at the tall-case clock between the big windows. Ten minutes and Miss Faughsquar would bring in the champagne.

'Bottle Bolts, United Diapers and that Liverpool Dock Board thing are just about OK, Desmond.' Daimon, beside him, had his own list. 'Sean can minute those. The Parson's team has come a cropper on United Diapers, chairman! Day and night stuff on that for nearly a fortnight. You know what the US of A chums are. Ruthless, and they chop and change on the phone with no idea whether its Thanksgiving or Shrove Tuesday!'

'Minutes, without the observations,' Lord Bair said grandly. 'And Sean, my boy, leave out that bit of mine too, about the rules!'

The double mahogany doors opened and Miss Faughsquar and her assistant advanced to the table with silver tray and glasses. Miss Faughsquar carried the two open bottles of champagne. While the glasses were being filled, she put a lengthy telex on top of the chairman's papers. Lord Bair read it quickly, and when the secretariat had left, he scowled and looked magnificent.

'Fortune to BB!' said Daimon in the traditional toast, raising his own glass and nodding around. He knew that if the matter in his cousin's hand was containing more rough stuff, the glass of champagne could not only be delayed but the toast might sound hollow. He was right. Only the chairman failed to raise his glass.

'This piece about us in *Midas*! Out in the current number. Anybody seen it?'

'You must have, sir. I sent it up to your office two days ago.'

'Well, who passed it?'

'I saw it earlier,' Tim Bealey said uneasily.

'Proofs, or whatever the things are called? Script?'

'Sir, you saw the *Midas* chap who wrote it! From their

office here. He spent time with you. It's as much a profile as a banking story.'

Under the table, Lord Bair felt Daimon's heavy foot pressing on his own.

'Remember him well!' He tapped the telex message. 'This is from my friend Epoch. The publisher! He apologises for some differences in transatlantic humour. What's he mean? Eh?'

'You'll have to read it sir. I'd say it's not too bad.'

'Like what?' asked young Sean tactlessly.

'Rather poor puns I would have said.' Tim Bealey pulled the magazine out from his papers. 'I've marked a few paras. Can't say I understand them. "Bair faced is not two faced," for instance. Some reference to shooting in the dark which wasn't entirely complimentary. To use a ram as a bell-wether can lead to mistakes. Clever journalese, I suppose. Bits that were apparently late telex additions. As a matter of fact, sir, I spoke to Epoch myself when I read them, and I think he hadn't seen it himself, and it was passed for press by the editor.'

Lord Bair was breathing heavily. His manner ominously quiet.

'Why did Tim handle this?'

'Tim is media relations officer, Desmond!' Again the shoe pressure. Lord Bair drummed his fingers slowly on the table, looking at Tim Bealey.

'I see! Well, to get back to the main part of Epoch's message to me which is more important. The stuff coming into Washington from Hong Kong looks bad. What have we got?'

'I began to get some of it through this morning,' Sir Mick Muldoon said. 'The Hang Seng index has been going down all last week. Shung Lai Properties went down even faster. Swang Lo Development –'

'Get to the point, Mick!'

'It's all in billions, with the Hong Kong dollar. Hong Kong and Shanghai did a two billion issue – they have more than one stock exchange as you know,' Mick Muldoon said quickly. 'Demand has fallen away suddenly.

Properties are bought out there by progress payments – to sell on expectation of a profit. If it goes wrong it goes very wrong.'

'Like buying in the futures market on margin,' Daimon played cue.

'Are we in that?'

'Some joint loans to some of the fatter cats who can stand it, Chairman.'

Lord Bair consulted the telex, still held between finger and thumb. 'Epoch here says: "Watch Pol!" What does that mean?'

'Chap we had lunch with the other day, Desmond.'

Lord Bair raised his glass at last. The quiet descent of the bubbles down his throat seemed to clear his mind, as always.

'Is he in property?'

'Over there? Yes, very much so.'

'And here?'

'That's me again,' said Tim Bealey unhappily. He shuffled more papers. 'I got his stat sheets out yesterday. It's a bit hard to get a bench mark because a lot is Swiss side.'

'Look,' said Muldoon brusquely. 'I'm Far East. I don't like it. Dai Pol is into us for twelve million!'

'Hong Kong dollars?'

'No, Chairman. Bair Brady pounds. And Swiss francs and guarantees and some curious holdings!'

'Like what, pray?'

The boardroom had become silent.

'The holding we formed, to buy some magazine and a film-making outfit. I haven't looked into it but I think we're safe there. We still own that. He paid first tranche and we hold the rest.'

'I seem to remember we approved ten million top, Desmond?'

'How the hell has it gone to twelve?'

'I shall be looking into that as soon as we're finished, sir.' Tim Bealey was trying to sound calm. 'I think it's technical only. In transmission stuff from Berne.'

'Isn't he titled – this Hong Kong fella?' asked old Parson Pinter.

'Titled!' roared the chairman angrily. He glared about him. 'What the devil does that mean?'

The silence that followed was long. Lord Bair wished the tradition allowed a refill of glasses. His grandfather in the heavy, dark oil-painting on the far wall, now seemed to be staring at him over those crooked spectacles with an expression of amused contempt . . .

Back in his own offices, Lord Bair switched on the light outside for Miss Faughsquar. He grunted, twisting in his tall-backed leather armchair, and taking a cigar from the old wooden box, cut and lit it.

'I want to see that Hong Kong financier, Dai Pol! Right away!'

'You're marked for lunch two hours, Lord Bair!'

'What day is it then?'

'Thursday. One of your Connection Lunches. You could cancel. Someone else could take it?'

'No!'

'Three o'clock?'

'Yes, but get him!'

'Three line whip?' said Faughsquar firmly.

She was startled for a moment. Lord Bair had let his cigar fall on the desk in a shower of sparks.

'Tell him to report here without fail! And if I'm not back, not less than two other directors will see him! We've got to nail Sir Dai Pol! What else this afternoon?'

She consulted a notebook. 'There's a lady called Flip. I have a feeling there's a connection but I can't place it. She insists on seeing you this afternoon and no later. There is a joint company, isn't there? Very vital, she said. Wouldn't tell me, wouldn't take another director.'

'Three-thirty!'

'The Princess called. Black-tie dinner, thirty people, tonight. Then there is an American gentleman on introduction from Mr Curt Epoch, who has an investment project that he says will return one hundred per cent in year one.'

'Five o'clock!'

Primly, Miss Faughsquar closed her notebook with a crocodile snap.

'I'm sure he goes to have those piles treated,' she said to her assistant when she was back in her own office. 'I can tell by the way he walks to the lift!'

Lady Madeleine Bair parked her orange Deux Chevaux in the Brompton Road, opposite the Victoria and Albert Museum. She had never worried much about parking tickets and now there seemed even less reason to bother about the smaller overheads of the business. She moved up the broad Museum steps and into the cool, high-domed foyer.

Following the porter's instructions she got lost, wandering up and down stairs hung with dark carpets. Between Assyrian monsters, Greek glories and Indian relics. The administrative section was on the third floor, and when she found Sir Wilfred Poult's door with his name on it, she tapped and walked straight in.

'So this is your place! I can *smell* knowledge and great learning, sort of! Can I sit here?'

'It's the only other chair, so you'd better.' He seemed less than radiant to see her. The steel-rimmed spectacles made him look older and he had a book in one hand and a ballpoint pen in the other.

'I was just making some notes against your coming.' He took off the spectacles and smiled thinly. 'Not an easy one this, my dear Madeleine! We have checked several authorities.'

'You haven't told people, Wilf?'

'No, no!'

'You said 'we'?'

'Did I? Well, the trouble is that the thing is unique. Utterly priceless. There was an infant son and they were all buried in the vicinity of the Cheng valley. They would have to be effigies, because with any of the diseases –'

'Look Wilf, let's get to it. *You* have got to help find a buyer for this one! Gugi says he thinks he knows someone in Paris, but he's never handled anything at this level. You heard the bottom figure on it. Five million. And I guess that makes it a bargain to the right collector who'll stash it away. Private peep-show to friends only. And who knows. Maybe someone would pay more? A million to us and if we can get that, you can have a third! You know Paris, you talk the language, you have entrée there. Listen! You need never sit in this sump again! What do you say?'

Sir Wilfred Poult, trained all his life to listen and think, listened. But the thinking was difficult. It showed on his face and as he swung about in his swivel chair, Maddy saw his profile, the long nose, whiskery eyebrows, small mouth pursed.

'How do we get it safely over there?' he said. 'Umph? I would not like to wheel a perambulator to Paris!'

'You're getting warm, Wilf!' Maddy was all charm. 'It's the bus again! It's the best way and quite safe! Polly says she's often taken it through customs and we could pretend to be holidaying. Loire châteaux, collecting kids from Paris – anything! They won't look in all the bunks. I could take Audrey and there's Polly's *au-pair*. She'll come for the ride to Paris. Polly says she can park all her brood with the fathers!'

Sir Wilfred Poult's face continued to show conflict. Doubt, caution and a natural wariness fought with self-interest. 'I'll think about it!' He turned round to the desk and selected one from a pile of books. 'Let me tell you more about the Han dynasty.'

'I've got five minutes, Wilf, that's all,' Maddy said shortly. 'You've got until this evening. Pol wants the money in the bank by the latest next week!'

Back in her gallery, she flung her handbag on the desk. 'I've seen Wilf. I think he'll play. He's just a bit dazed. Lost between Han and here,' she told Ruthy.

'I'm worried, Maddy!'

'For God's sake, we're all worried! How do you sell something like that, for Pete's sake?'

'No, something else. I'm bothered about our break-in

protection. OK, so we've got an alarm. But you know it wouldn't stop professionals. And boysey is not on the insurance policy!'

'He's in that rolled up carpet still?'

'Something happened while you were away.' Ruthy pursed her small, red mouth unsmilingly.

'Like?'

'There were two guys here!'

'Not nice guys?' Maddy knew Ruthy. She had been born and bred in New Orleans, worked in Cincinnati and San Francisco. It had been Ruthy's hard headedness that had made the gallery possible. She knew about Ruthy's husband's interests.

'From the Chinese Embassy.'

There was a long silence. The electric coffee percolator that Ruthy had going on the floor by her desk began to make slow, unhelpful, blooping noises.

'We'll move him!' Maddy said crisply. 'He'll fit in the back of the clockwork orange and I'll get Rupert to come and help. I'll take him home! I'm not going to spend the night here. Nor are you, baby! What did they look like?'

'Little men, in rather mean black suits. They looked mean too, didn't smile, just stared around. Asked if we had any Chinese valuables – that was the word they used. I showed them that little snuff bottle we've had for ever in the drawer. They weren't interested.'

'If anybody is watching, we'll throw them off!' said Maddy swiftly. She moved catlike to pick up the telephone. 'I'll get Rupert and we'll put quite a few things in the back of the car – junk we don't care about as though it was routine.'

The Bair Brady reception committee for Sir Dai Pol met in the number two conference room. It consisted of Lord Bair, Daimon and Sir Mick Muldoon.

'I'm not going to give the bastard the run of my office!' Lord Bair was plainly agitated. He shifted continuously in his chair.

The hall porter who ushered in the visitor looked surprised to see the Chairman in number two. 'Here we are, sir!'

'You know these chaps, Pol! Why don't you sit there?'

'Thank you. Ah, ah! So very kind!' Sir Dai Pol's eyes behind the thick glasses were like paper clips. 'I have no papers! I fear I keep too much in my head. I see you have lots of paper!'

Sir Mick Muldoon pushed his heavy, red face forward until it seemed only inches above the table, one eye half closed.

'What's going on in your head in that case? Because we don't really like what we see! There's not much point in beating about the bush, Pol. You've had just on twelve million from Bair Brady resources – the last agreed limit with the chairman was ten, I understand. About four of this was in transit, switching between two main Swiss accounts.'

'Stop there!' Sir Dai Pol raised a calming hand. In Hong Kong calm was routine. Now it was going to be vital. Lord Bair was shifting uneasily in his seat and probably hardly knew what was going on. But this Muldoon had a reputation in the Far East. He could be awkward.

'Only two. And what the Swiss do for collateral is their affair – and mine.'

'Four!' Lord Bair sought to preside. His notes from Muldoon were precise, and this wily oriental was causing trouble. 'The middle-east money that has come in, and gone out, moved from our associates to yours, so that we have no security. I suppose you thought Swiss numbered accounts were inviolate?' Lord Bair's smile was twinged with genuine pain. 'Bankers owe each other more loyalty than temporary clients, Pol!'

'You have the original security from Eastern Oceanic Bank, Tiger Bay Developments and Deep Wharf Deposit! These cover all my transactions.'

'You must think we were born yesterday! You forgot modern communication systems. This banking house was in business in 1720, but we have moved a way since then!'

Dai Pol spread out his large hands and smiled. The heavy face, pock-marked as though with tiny pin pricks, looked very bland. But the eyes remained thin slits in a mask.

'Lord Bair! We too have old established principles in the Colony, possibly your methods are faster than ours. But please remember this is my first time in Europe for many years! I will increase the cover from Hong Kong to make good any deficiency on the Swiss side until that is ironed out.'

'Eastern Oceanic is your bank!' Mick Muldoon said abruptly. 'I didn't know that until one of my younger colleagues tumbled to it, because it's all so tied up, in and out with other holdings. But it's bust! As of this morning!'

'Please be careful what you say!'

'Oh, don't worry! We're all bankers here! We don't mind you making money, as long as we do too!'

'But we don't like losing money!' Lord Bair said.

'The property company is quite big enough to take care of any temporary problems.'

'Your property company – and the construction company – are pledged twice over. To projects that are not going to show profit! They no longer constitute a guarantee.' Mick Muldoon folded his arms.

Lord Bair leaned forward. 'Listen, Pol! Ten million. If you have not got it to us in an acceptable form by forty-eight hours, I shall personally garnishee you world wide!'

'That is not a long time, Lord Bair! It would be a great mistake. I have heard nothing of trouble in the Colony. But, of course, I shall be directing everything to relieving you of anxiety.'

'I would like you to know that I have taken charge of this myself!' Lord Bair got up, and the relief was such, that he was able to sound almost pleasant. 'Forty-eight hours! After that, my Chinese friend, if the last penny is not forthcoming, I shall cut your throat!'

Mick Muldoon followed him out and Daimon was left

to escort Sir Dai Pol down to the main hall. The lift deposited them in the neo-Georgian elegance of the bank's main entrance.

'Lord Bair does not appear to have charitable feelings about the third world?'

'I don't think banking involves any serious charity to anybody.'

Dai Pol bowed almost formally from the waist, and Daimon felt himself curiously obliged to reciprocate as Pol glided away through the revolving doors. Daimon hurried back to the elevators.

Back in his own office and his own chair, Lord Bair looked savagely grand and gloomily vexed. Daimon and Muldoon had been called back to join him.

'Mick you will pull out all the plugs on that Kong! Now! Get him! The Swiss will play, because they're going to need us the same way one day. I do not propose that Bair Brady show a loss of ten million this way! We shall be the laughing stock of the city.'

'We have the privilege of exception from full disclosure requirements,' Muldoon said.

'And another thing,' Lord Bair said vengefully, 'you can let me have young Bealey's contract details! What's he got?'

'Junior director, on the last of his five years.'

'Cost?'

'Forty thousand. Plus, I suppose. Have to be careful these days.'

'I need to make an example around this place,' Lord Bair said darkly. He opened a folder on his desk. 'The next bloody visitor now! Woman called Flip? Know about her? She's another of Pol's winners! What's all this?'

'The Lichtenstein holding company for the porno magazine and film company,' Muldoon said. 'Trouble is, you see, he didn't pay for all of that either, and we're left owing!'

'Anything really rough?'

'You're chairman, Desmond!'

'What do you mean, damn it?'

Well you know, it's rule book again. You're automatically chairman of any bank subsidiary. It's put into the articles as routine, always.'

'Of course there's something wrong with it, Desmond!' Daimon said. 'There were a couple of coppers, CID men, in here this morning, wanting to see an officer of the company! It seems the editor has been running a white slave business on the side! And we own it! Faughsquar has arranged for them to come back this afternoon to see one of you two!'

'What is white slavery?' asked Mick Muldoon grinning.

'Don't be a fool, Mick,' said Daimon savagely. 'It'll end up on your plate, Desmond. The media will love it! You'd better think twice before dropping Tim, he's our press officer!'

'There might be a get-out.' Muldoon had swung the folder round and was looking at papers. 'This woman coming up now, wasn't she the former owner? If there's some doubt about the whole transaction we might hang it round her neck. Moratorium! Warranties not honoured! All null and void!'

'You will both stay here and see her with me!'

At that moment the twin mahogany doors to Lord Bair's office burst open.

An agitated Faughsquar, breathing hard, advanced with the arm swing of a former naval personage. Normally a discreet knock and one door opening silently was her entrance routine, and all three men rose to their feet, slowly, as though moved by premonition.

'Sir! Mr O'Reilly from the garage begs to report there has been a casualty below!' Wren Officer Faughsquar was sufficiently agitated to have done a reversion to former naval procedure.

'What the bloody hell do you mean? Prancing in here like a TV show!' Lord Bair, normally prudently circumspect with Faughsquar glared at her angrily. 'If the garage has got a problem, deal with it, woman!'

Mick Muldoon moved heavily round the big desk and took Miss Faughsquar's arm. 'Just a minute. I'll take care of this, Desmond. What is it, Jane? Those damned underground garages are death traps. The way some of these lunatics come down that slope!'

Miss Faughsquar shook her head, the firm jaw tilted up. 'The lady was coming to see the chairman and had permission to park her car below. Well, she's collapsed.'

'In our garage?' roared Lord Bair.

'I think Mr Bealey is dealing with it. He has called Dr Boggert. Reilly has called the ambulance and the police. And those two policemen who were to see the directors this morning, are here again, so that will make quite a lot of them!'

'Enough!' The chairman of Bair Brady thumped his desk with the flat of his hand, his eyes bulging. 'The place is full of Keystone Cops, doctors and women collapsing, my directors behaving like nincompoops and Chinese pirates looting us stupid! Get out! All of you! This is a banking house and somebody's got to keep it going.'

Lord Bair's wild gaze fell on the gently gleaming ivory replica of his yacht.

'It was that Chinese bastard who gave me that!' He swept it up on one arm, staggering round until he could just about hold the weight. 'D'you think I want to keep looking at it? Take the bloody thing, one of you! Sell it. Company asset! Must be worth a few quid against what that bugger's cost us!'

The tip of the mast poked Daimon in the eye as he took the weight and followed Muldoon who was already half way through the door.

'I'm sorry, Lord Bair!' Faughsquar was standing to attention. 'Shock! For a moment I forgot myself. I think you'll agree this is the first time I have not been able to keep your appointments in an orderly state in all these years!'

'Get me a drink,' said Lord Bair. 'Now! And, Faughsquar, have one yourself!'

'Would it be champagne, Lord Bair?'

'No, it would not. Medicinal – not a celebration! Rum! In the metal beaker.'

When the small pewter pot was put in front of him Faughsquar said: 'Would you wish to continue business, sir?'

'I want that woman. She's vital to get us off the hook!'

'I'll let you know what's happening. Meanwhile there's the American with the special project, sir. There are two of them in your private waiting room. They're early and I've tried to get another director, but they're all out of their offices, or involved with the bother in the basement.'

'Send them in!' Lord Bair jerked back the jigger of rum. 'Somebody had better try and make some money around here. Tell them I'll give them ten minutes.' He breathed out the fumes and slipped the jigger into his drawer. 'Business must go on!'

This time it was Miss Faughsquar's usual entrance. The knock was quiet and respectful, the two doors opened smoothly. Lord Bair's eyes bulged. The man who entered was dressed in a pale lavender-coloured suit, his white hair contrasting with the mahogany tan of his foxy face, and was followed by a shorter figure, who had shaggy grey hair to his shoulders, a shirt with a fruit-salad pattern and open neck which showed a jungle necklace of teeth and fangs. In unison they took the two chairs vacated by Daimon and Muldoon.

'Sir, your lordship! I'm Earl Abrahams, President of Body Beautiful, Inc, and this is Abe Shite, our treasurer. Our mutual friend, the publisher of *Midas Magazine* –'

'I can give you five minutes.' The chairman of Bair Brady was already regretting the business-as-usual act.

'Sure! That's the way we like it too! Get in fast! Do the business! Lay it on the line. Abe, put the project figures on the table for Lord Bair. He can take them in at his leisure. This project for financing, sir, is maybe the surest deal we have put up for mutual progression since our West Coast expansion, and Abe here can put figures to that! We like to finance locally, but we do have American banks right here in the city of London who are interested.'

'Three minutes!'

'OK, that's it, sure, well! Right now, we have secured,

198

here in the city of London, the franchise, that is to say we have taken over, the leasing of all the spare Johns in the Royal Borough of Kensington and Chelsea! That is six hundred and thirty-two, roughly half and half.'

Half and half *what* man?' roared Lord Bair.

'Half ladies and half gents, Earl means!' the short man croaked helpfully. 'Public conveniences. Like for ladies and gents! Only there's nobody to run them! They're closed down. They're *finito*! Empty! Finished! There's nobody will go down there and take care of them. So the councils are closing them all over!'

Speechless, Lord Bair gazed at this pair of freaks on the other side of his desk.

'Didn't I say Lord Bair would be interested, Abe?'

'Prime sites! There aren't primer more gilt-edged property situations right now in the whole city of London than what we have, every one situated in a key position for the last eighty years!'

'You have leases on lavatories?' Lord Bair asked incredulously.

'Signed, sealed and right here! Abe, give the paper on it! Put in those other photostats, Abe!'

'What the hell can you do with them?'

'The new updated function of Body Beautiful, Inc! That's what the public wants, deep down, all the time! To be Beautiful and Different and Very Truly Sought After,' the tanned face was intoning. 'That's the corporation slogan.'

'We took it from your Mr Kipling,' said the one called Abe knowingly.

Lord Bair pressed the hidden buzzer under the desk edge twice, the signal that told Faughsquar to come back with urgent other business for him. Surely his grandfather would never have survived this!

'Pink railings for the ladies, blue for the fellas, gold tips, inside soft lights, music, facial, tanning, pep products – our own. We'll cut you in on those too. Listen!' The President of Body Beautiful, Inc leaned earnestly across the desk, tapping the papers they had presented. 'Each one of these little old holes in the ground is a gold mine! All we need is the backing!'

A loud double bang of the heavy office doors being once more thrown open unceremoniously, brought the visitors' heads round sharply and Lord Bair rose angrily and turned. If Faughsquar was going to make a habit of this, things were really getting out of hand.

It was Daimon who stood crouched in the doorway, his normally florid face curiously tinged. With one hand he waved wildly for the visitors to leave. Faughsquar stood behind him.

'You're not going to like this!' Daimon's voice was hoarse. 'It's not so good down below.'

The visitors seemed to be trying to get a grip on the conversation.

'I don't think the bank should go so fast at this thing, Lord Bair! Take a look at the papers!'

'Get out!'

'Call us! You have our number! You can't dismiss a big, proven idea like this without kicking it around!'

'Leave the paperwork, we'll look at it. Faughsquar!'

'This way, gentlemen!' When Faughsquar used that voice most men moved. Rapidly the two visitors went out through the double doors and Daimon slammed them shut. He turned, pressing his back to the panels and looked at Lord Bair with haggard eyes.

'She's dead!'

'Who's dead! For God's sake Daimon, is this a bank or a bin?' Lord Bair had the rum bottle and jigger back on the desk.

'The *Groin* woman! Had a heart attack in her car in the garage! Desmond listen! You've got to get out of here! Anywhere you like. Out of town! Sail away! The media are already down there like wasps around jam, and the police. They're insisting on seeing you!'

Behind Daimon, Miss Faughsquar had come in and was standing to attention in the doorway. 'I have called the car, sir! The driver is ready now. At the bullion entrance. The front hall is a bit crowded, Mr Bealey says.'

'Not a time for bowls on Plymouth Hoe?' Lord Bair, fortified by rum, was beginning to recover.

'Beaulieu, Desmond! Much better!'

'Well, you come too, old boy! I can't sit down there alone. If I must go.'

It was an hour before they got away, Lord Bair procrastinated. He decided he must call the Princess and make excuses for not attending the dinner party. With prompting from Daimon, he instructed her not to believe anything she might read in the newspapers, and it would be better if she did not try to telephone him as he would be at sea. Yes, it was business.

Faughsquar he commanded to find him one hundred pounds from petty cash. Then he ordered that another bottle of rum and two of champagne be sent down to the car. Daimon told her to block all enquiries as to his whereabouts. Lord Bair refused an urgent application for audience from Tim Bealey.

'I think the whole thing's bloody nonsense. But I agree as soon as you have anything to do with the media it's trouble. Why don't I stay here and you send them all away?'

Eventually the two men were escorted by Faughsquar down the back staircase and through the bullion rooms.

The car immediately headed off through the rush hour traffic, and in the back Daimon hunched low in his seat. As they went through Fleet Street, Lord Bair, who was looking, pointed out the first posters.

PORN QUEEN DEAD IN BANK VAULT!

'That's quick, even for those bastards! But it's not a vault, it's a bloody underground garage!'

'To the outside world anything underground at a bank is a vault!' Daimon said moodily.

'Or a public convenience!'

Daimon stared at him. Desmond had accused him of being fit for a bin. But if the chairman was going to crack up, it probably was his duty to be with him.

11

Number one off the air now!' said Shee laconically. He took off his headphones and stood up. 'They are angry with you, sir!'

Sir Dai Pol moved swiftly into the chair vacated by Shee. 'Do they know what it is? Give me the earphones! Play back the last five minutes!'

Kitty watched as her father's face became a wooden mask, empty eyed. She put a cigarette into the jade holder, lit it carefully and studied the smoke as it drifted up with the air conditioning.

Presently Dai Pol rose from the chair and looked without expression at his daughter and at Shee. 'The banker has set his friends against me. That explains why I can get no sense out of the Swiss. We are moving. Fast!'

'There were six calls on the telephone from Hong Kong earlier, sir!'

'I want Captain Hoffmann!'

'I told him to come,' said Kitty.

'The bastards!' Her father was moving round the cabin.

Kitty knew the reversion to Tiger Bay and disliked it. Even more the mask face, immobile, hostile.

'Peace, Papa,' said Kitty, slipping out of her chair. 'You will get even with them! Hoffmann is on the bridge.'

'Bring him down here. With what I have just heard, we

have very little time.'

Shee summoned the captain, and Hoffmann appeared, with linen cap under his arm.

'How quickly can you get us away?'

'I presume that is why you want me, Sir Dai, so I ask. We wait only for high water. That is the problem. They open the lock gates up to twenty-one hundred. Clearance from the harbour master. You want me to look after that?'

'What is involved?'

'Charges! Money as usual. Maybe we must tell destination.' The captain shrugged. He looked at father and daughter out of the sides of his small, piggy eyes. 'I say we make holiday cruise, Bournemouth, Torquay. Then you tell me the course.'

'I will. But first I have to make one more phone call. How much money do you need?'

'Mooring, water, power!'

'Power?'

'Electricity from the land line. Also telephone. That will be big, I think.'

'I will give you notes in tens. You have a case?'

'I have my *Aktentasche*. Like all good Germans!' The captain seemed to be in good humour. He had been through this sort of thing before.

'High water,' said Sir Dai Pol coldly. 'How long? Can we get out as the tide flows?'

'I will ask what is the soonest depth, yes?'

'The draught, captain! Move as soon as we have an inch of water under us! After one more telephone call we can be disconnected. I will send the money up to you on the bridge. Go ashore now and tell the harbour master's office you want it done quickly. There will be extra money. For the lock keepers too. I look to you to handle it.'

'*Zum Befehl*!' The captain was at his best under a stream of orders.

When he had gone, Dai Pol nodded to Shee who left the stateroom. Then he picked up the telephone, sitting upright in the rotating chair, dialling swiftly.

'Is Lady Bair there? Ah, I didn't recognise your voice! Yes, I have a lot to do. Now, about the boy. You are acting quickly? Paris you said. I would like to know where to reach you there. I am moving about in this next week. Always business. Problems? Sure there are always problems. But I would like to know where to reach you. Yes, I am writing now. An apartment? Wilf Poult? Not in his name? No, of course! OK, I have that. The phone? You have that too?' He was writing slowly. 'Do me one more favour. Lord Bair is away from the office and not in London, I think. Would he be in the country? That is what I thought. Yes, the Beaulieu house, on the river. South of what? Oh, of the village, yes. No, no, I must reach him by phone. Please don't trouble! I can get it. Now listen, this is important. Any financial transaction must be to the New York Bank, the one I gave you. Not Switzerland. Keep that entirely to yourself, of course, and all will be well. A quick transaction would suit us all. I think so, yes! And to you!' He rotated out of the chair and made for the door that led to his cabin.

'I must instruct the captain quickly.' Dai Pol returned with a plastic-wrapped package in one hand. 'If that phone rings before it is disconnected, do not answer it!'

On the bridge he gave the package to Hoffmann. 'You can account for the money later. It is two thousand in tens. Now listen to me carefully. We shall make for the Solent. There is somebody who lives there I must see. Do you have a chart for the south coast?'

The captain pulled open the big chart drawer and flicked on the reading light. 'It will take time, Sir Dai.'

'Right, you get ashore and deal with the formalities. I will look out the charts we have. The tide is right, I think. I want this ship out in half an hour!' The captain left swinging his briefcase, watched by Kitty through the stateroom blinds.

He returned to the bridge in twenty minutes, and stood to attention, pleased with his own efficiency.

'I have paid for one week extra moorings for the

quickness of sailing!'

'No other problems?'

'Not yet.'

'I have the charts. If we go down river on high water and ebb, how long before we are past Dungeness?'

The captain sat down, fat and important, and pulled pad, pencil and calculator across the chart table. He wrote down figures, put his head on one side, wrote some more, then tapped the calculator.

'It will be dark presently. Say about ten knots at sea. Say ten hours?'

'The shipping lanes are crowded,' Sir Dai Pol said. 'I would like to be clear of coastguard signalling, and there seems to be one chart missing. Do you see the North Foreland?'

'Yes, yes! Tides, no problem with our engines! Changing tide at Newhaven, mebbe. Double tides in the Solent, I think. *Na, ja!*' The captain pushed the pad and calculator aside and studied the blue-and-yellow coloured Admiralty sheet in front of him. 'Is only to worry around the shoals. But it will be afternoon, yes? Sometimes there is not much water. Five metres. But that is enough.'

'We can look at the charts again when we are under way, captain,' Dai Pol said. 'Get ashore and speed things up. A hundred pounds to you if you can get us off this mooring in half an hour!'

Captain Hoffmann rose ponderously from the navigator's swivel chair. His service with owners of different nationalities in many parts of the world had taught him never to ask questions. But he knew the signs.

'A small Scotch for myself now mebbee? And two bottles for our friends ashore?'

'I will send Shee with them at once.'

Sir Dai Pol watched as the captain clipped charts down on the table and flicked off the reading lamp. He surveyed the dockside. Only the usual number of curious strollers and dockside loafers were in front of the pale arches of Ivory House.

He left the bridge and went below. To the steward he

passed on the captain's requirements. To Kitty he spoke quietly.

'If anyone comes to see me, do not let them. You will handle that possibility, not the crew. I shall be in my cabin. Only customs have right of search unless police with warrant.'

'The customs have changed,' Kitty said. 'Some days ago. There are two old men now.'

'You notice everything,' her father said with approval.

A large yacht, leaving the St Katharine's moorings, normally attracts interest, but in fact there were few spectators. So quietly did the big boat move in the water as it turned for the lock gates, that even the engines could not be heard from the wharf. Only the cooling water, spilling from the ports and the small, arrowed ripple from the bows showed that it was under way. On deck the two Chinese crewmen coiled mooring warps, then stood idle, faces turned for any signals from the helm. First the red-lacquered bridge rose then, after a short wait, the white-and-black lock gates drew apart.

Out in mid-river, the *Chenn Lo* turned gracefully on the broad swell of dark water as though round an invisible marker. Captain Hoffmann eased forward the twin-throttle controls. A quick rumble of engines, and a drift of blue smoke astern took the boat forward at speed as the bow wave mounted. Behind, in the early evening light, the black ironwork of Tower Bridge arched across the river against a rose-and-lemon-coloured sky and on the North bank, the square windows in the block house silhouette of the hotel reflected the colours.

Down river, different points were already blinking red, white or green, against the coming of dusk, and Sir Dai Pol and his daughter, now changed into nautical gear, joined the captain on the bridge. Both turned to look astern at the departing harbour.

Through the arches of the bridge, the Tower of London made a familiar, grim, black shape against the thin light of the sky.

'I never went to see it!' Kitty said sadly.

'Do what you can for speed, Captain,' her father said. 'But in no circumstances attract attention. If there is a radio check, we are making for Torquay.'

Rupert woke to find Maddy was looking at him with the one strange black eye, from smeared mascara.

He kissed her softly. 'You look happy!'

'I'm thinking of the other man!'

'Who, the hell?' said Rupert indignantly.

'The prince! Remember?'

Rupert moved closer. 'Somehow I don't think he could make love to you like I can. If you go to Paris today, I shan't be in bed with you tonight!'

'Darling Pot! Surely twice a night at your age is enough?'

'Have the prince then!'

Maddy held the bed clothes round her top half. 'Funny! I've often thought of Desmond with his princess! Do you think I should phone him and tell him I've got a boy prince?'

The telephone by the bed rang, but Rupert had almost been waiting for it, and he continued to roll across Maddy to reach it before she did, which left her deflated and unable to speak as he listened. He put a hand over the receiver whispering in her ear: 'It's Ruthy! I'm afraid Maddy can't speak for a minute! Why? Well, have a guess! No, just our usual double act. OK! She's clear now.' He continued to roll. Off the bed on to the floor and got up to unhook his dressing gown from the back of the door.

'Yeah, I hear you!' Now Maddy had the phone, gasping for breath. 'No, he's sober! Well, maybe you're right. Come over here then. And Ruthy do this! Get hold of Polly. She's parked the bus outside Gerald's. That's number two father, right? We've got to know what time she reckons to get us to Dover. If you're quick you'll get her. OK, sweety, bye.'

'Ruthy's afraid to go to the gallery, Pot!'

'Why?'

'She's had nightmares. About Chinamen! Help!' With

her bare shoulders, she peeped at Rupert from under the sheet, the colour mounting in her cheeks. 'Not now, Pot!'

'Now you've had it mended, I can lock the door,' said Rupert coolly.

It was later in the morning, in the moment of unlocking the door of his office, that recalled to Rupert how pleasant life really could be, in spite of its complications and unreliability.

A Cable and Wireless envelope lay on top of the pile of press releases, circulars and magazines in their plastic wrappers, put there as usual by the cleaners who picked up his mail each morning. He tugged at the envelope and ripped it open.

The message on the slip of grey paper in easy-read typeface was to the point:

> YOU ARE FIRED EFFECTIVE TODAY HAND OVER ALL MIDAS MISTER T BEALEY IMMEDIATE INCLUDES YOUR GOLD MIDAS PRESS CARD STOP LOVE TO MADDY AND THE KID CURT EPOCH PRESIDENT.

Rupert sat for a moment, staring out of the window at the blank office wall opposite. Slowly his hand reached for the telephone and he called Maddy. Her number was engaged.

Numbly, he began to open drawers and shut them. He put papers and some personal bits and pieces into his briefcase. He tried the telephone again, and this time he got through. She sounded pleased to hear from him. 'I'm almost scared to pick up the phone, Pot! Desmond is in some sort of trouble. Do you know about it?'

'So am I.' He read the telegram.

'How has Tim Bealey got the job? The money isn't his sort of rate is it? Could it be something to do with Desmond?'

'Your bloody ex-husband could do anything to anybody I'd say.'

'Shouldn't you know though, Pot? Maybe that's why you lost the job. The Press say he's been financing porn and white slavery and all sorts.'

'Tim was his man in charge of the media, so if he does as well for Epoch that will be great! Don't forget to give the kid his love!'

'Who?'

'Audrey! I suppose he couldn't remember her name.'

'She's being taken round to the Princess while I'm away. But I'm wondering if it's such a good idea. It seems her father is away.'

'Is Audrey happy there?'

'Oh hell, she loves it there always. She and the Princess's princesses, or whatever they are, from her other marriages, play with the tiaras and that junk!'

'I'm coming home,' Rupert said suddenly. 'I mean, I'm free! I'm rich, aren't I? I'm coming to Paris with you! I suppose there's room in the bus?'

'It seems like it's a good thing it's a bus we're taking. Oh, and Pot –'

'Yes, darling?'

'I *am* sorry about the job!'

Rupert tried to telephone Tim Bealey at Bair Brady but ran into the usual merchant-banking mystery. Mr Bealey was not available.

Downstairs, Rupert left the office keys with the porter, explaining that somebody else would be coming to take charge of *Midas Magazine* office. Then he walked out into sultry warmth and sunshine in the Strand, and stopped for a moment on the pavement.

He decided to walk back to Dolphin Square. He was going to Paris with Maddy, wasn't he? A few other people might be coming too, but they could certainly get away together. He had all his boat money. He would spend some of it.

He stopped on the way and bought things at one of the new tourist kiosks. A rather fine straw hat for himself. It would strike a rakish note on the boulevards. Maddy would need things for the journey in view of the curious way they were to travel. He found a small straw basket in the same store, and shopped around as he went on to make up a traveller's pot-pourri. A half bottle of Piesporter, a sealed packet of smoked salmon sandwiches, a lace handkerchief, a *Ma Griffe* atomiser, a packet of aspirin and some eye drops, a miniature French dictionary. The little curved basket looked full and exciting. It was the kind of thing Maddy liked.

He crossed Trafalgar Square feeling increasingly carefree, almost on holiday, appreciating anew the fresh whiteness of the National Gallery and St Martins on the far side. One had to walk in London to appreciate it, and he moved on down Whitehall as though he was seeing for the first time the Houses of Parliament, the spires and elevations of the Abbey, the statues in Parliament Square and the flags on the ministries and other buildings. Past the House of Lords and under the shade of the planes along Millbank, then out into the sunshine and stepping along the Embankment enjoying the broad sweep of the Thames as it sparkled past the Tate Gallery. Beyond Vauxhall Bridge he could already see the roof tops of Dolphin Square.

Rupert took the elevator up to the flat and walked into the big drawing room wearing his new straw hat, noting on the way, with surprise and comfort, that no pictures had been changed. Not only Maddy was there, on the cream sofa and he put the travelling basket beside her. Sir Wilfred Poult was in the big armchair, Ruthy on a cushion on the floor and Polly was using the telephone by the window.

'*Pour le voyage!*' said Rupert, kissing Maddy's cheek.

'What is it, Pot? Do take that thing off your head, sweety.' Maddy looked at the basket absently. 'So when are we actually going?'

'The Hovercraft is at eight-fifteen this evening, the earliest I could get with enough room for the vaircle.' Ruthy's English pronunciation was to explain the delay. So we have to be there at least half-an-hour earlier –'

'If Polly would get off that phone –'

'She doesn't have a phone in the bus,' Rupert explained. 'So she makes up for it at all points of call.'

'Pot, darling, how long to Dover from here in that coach of hers?'

'Allow three hours.'

'OK. Ruthy you're coming! And Pot's coming.'

Wilfred Poult in the armchair where he had been putting his finger tips together, gave a start. 'Is all this crowd a good idea, Madeleine? I mean, if we want just to slip quietly across? I thought it was just you and I? And Polly, of course.'

'Ruthy's coming because the gallery is closed. We've told the police we think suspicious characters hanging about could be planning a raid. They like it. Pot is coming because his French is so good it will be a real help.'

'My own may be a bit rusty,' said Wilfred Poult, 'but I would have thought –'

'I'll tell you who else is coming,' Maddy said quickly. 'That's my help, Nancy. She's been crying her eyes out, poor kid. Seems the cops called this morning about some discrepancy in the caviar stocks, they say, at the place where she works. Of course it's not Nancy, but right now she thinks it could all blow over if she took a break. I'll pay her fare.'

'OK, you guys,' cried Polly. 'Finished on the phone! Anybody want it? All set? When do I take the party to Paree?'

Lord Bair lurked to order. He disliked lurking. It was not his style. It did not suit him and he was not going to do it for long, he told Daimon. Even to keep away from the media, in all its forms. Possibly there was some point in deliberately cutting himself off from the Princess, who had been demanding to know on the telephone with renewed frequency, what the hell he had been doing, and what was she to tell her friends, who, it appeared, were also continuously on the telephone.

The lurking had therefore, on Daimon's suggestion, moved on board the yacht, moored to its private jetty.

The move had been made after a restless night in the house, which had included the invasion of Lord Bair's bedroom by an enterprising woman reporter from the *Daily Galaxy* who had got as far as the window on an aluminium ladder. Several young men in leather jackets, some with cameras and flashlamps, had been repulsed by Dickenson and other members of the staff.

'Think it would help the staff, old boy!' Daimon said. 'Then they can say in all truth that you are not in residence. We just lie low, and I monitor calls on the yacht's radio phone. Those Press bastards will soon tire of it and push off. It seems a pity young Bealey had to quit. He could probably have handled them. I'm not used to it.'

Lord Bair lay back on a pile of cushions on a berth in the centre cabin. Within reach, on the cabin table, was a large goblet of black velvet. He had changed into the striped vest and the bottom half of an orange waterproof suit.

'If the buggers find out where we are, what then? Let's sail off!'

Daimon emptied another bottle of Guinness into his own glass. His city suit looked more than ever as though he had slept in it, which he had mostly. It had been a rough night in the house, he had taken the phone calls and it would probably continue as a rough day.

It had started when two men in donkey jackets had appeared at the front door, claiming they would like to read the electricity meters. They had marched into the billiard room where he and Lord Bair were playing a desultory game.

Lord Bair had stormed out to the telephone in the hall, and with some cunning dialled three eights and asked for the police.

'Yeah, call the fuzz!' one of the donkey jacketed pair had jeered. The other, who had half a cigarette glued to his lower lip, removed it. 'Go on, call 'em. They're interested!'

Baited in this way, their quarry had fetched a twelve

bore from the gun room at the sight of which the pursuers had bolted. But none of this had had an elevating effect on the morale of Dickenson, the housekeeper, the cook and the maid.

Dickenson brought a hot lunch on board and on a second journey, a bottle of Beaune and glasses.

'I keep an eye open, my lord! Before I venture out. And I creeps along the laurels. There was a chap the maid spotted from the first floor window this morning! He had a pair of binoculars. Up in the top of that cottage on the road, he was.' Dickenson lingered. 'We had a lot of that in the Fusiliers, my lord, in Malaya, under General Templar! There was several was careless, sir, crossing the compound to the cookhouse who bit the dust and not their dinner! All you ever saw was a flash of light on them snipers' telescopes!'

'You can fetch some horseradish, Dickenson, when you creep again,' Lord Bair said. 'And if there's any more Stilton, we'll have that too. And Dickenson –'

'Sir?'

'When you get near, recalling your interesting anecdote, you had better give a low whistle. Because if anyone else approaches, I shall not hesitate to defend my privacy!' Lord Bair nodded at the shotgun propped by the cabin steps.

Both men had a short nap after lunch, and when they stirred again Daimon peered out through the forepeak hatch, and reported that it was a pleasantly warm and hazy afternoon on the river, which was empty of any moving craft.

'It is a pity,' he said, as his cousin grunted heavily about the confined space, setting up the big glasses again, popping the champagne cork and passing him the opener for the Guinness bottle, 'we can't, I suppose, go to sea, as you said. But it mightn't be a bad idea if we checked with the club for tomorrow.'

'What's tomorrow?'

'Saturday. We could get a late entry for the races and be out of reach virtually all weekend.'

'Better than staying here! Still won't get us off the phone. They're sure to find out we're on board sooner or later.'

'I see you've still got that bloody Kiss-me-Kate thing on the pipecot. I've put it under a blanket. Besides I hacked my shins on it taking a dekko out of the hatch. I might have set it off!'

'What I can't understand,' grumbled Lord Bair, carrying his glass over to the closed lower half of the cabin door and peering out, 'is why there's all this hoo-ha anyway. The lady pegged it in the garage. All right she had a heart attack. Which I agree was odd, as she was not all that advanced in age. But people do. You look as though you might have one anytime, I mean.'

'Thanks! You're right. I'm not feeling that good at all.'

'Just because she was publishing a porn magazine, I suppose?'

'No, technically you were, Desmond. Or rather we were,' Daimon said loyally. 'There was a slip up over that Kong. Hadn't paid for his controlling shares, you remember.'

'That was Bealey!' Lord Bair growled. He took a succession of long pulls from the giant glass. 'I was going to sack him! It seems from what you got on the phone, he beat me to it. That sodding Chinaman won't get away with it though! I've done him properly.'

'The police are on to something else going on through that holding company,' Daimon said grimly. 'Kidnapping and stuff. All rubbish, I expect, but it's what builds circulation. And it won't do the bank any good, Desmond! One of the calls I blocked was from old Derek Weatherspoon. Wanted to know if you were behind the organisation that had his daughter abducted by some Arab lechers pretending to make films!'

'Was I?'

'Oh, for God's sake, Desmond!'

But Lord Bair's attention had drifted. Quietly he went up two steps and craned over the top of the cockpit doors.

'Here, Daimon! Look at this!' With a roar of fury he came down, sliding his glass across the table and picking up the shotgun. 'There are two crafty buggers out there in a rubber boat!' Leaping back up the steps, he burst through the latched doors and out into the open cockpit.

As the first barrel discharged, the deafening sound echoed across the peaceful river outside. Daimon, blocked for exit, heard shouts and frantic splashing and back paddling as the boarding party withdrew. Lord Bair, abandoning cover, lumbered out and mounted, huge and threatening, on deck. Daimon peered out behind him.

'Let that be a warning, damn you! I have reloaded and I shall give you both barrels next time!'

Out on the river was a rubber boat, crewed by two oldish men, one small with spectacles, the other fat, in his short sleeves, with a camera round his neck.

From what they presumably hoped was a point out of range, the fat one continued to paddle while the other shouted back.

'We are from the *Sunday Globe*, Lord Bair! You are Lord Bair? What do you know of the Porn Queen? Was she your mistress?'

'I shall blow you out of the water!' Two cartridges clicked audibly into the breech.

'We are a free Press in a free country, Bair! You are not in the House of Lords now!'

'I shall count to five!'

'Answer our questions and we'll go!'

As the fat man took up his camera the gun blasted off. The shot skimmed angrily across the water with an effect on the surface like a school of leaping fish. The second barrel, discharged higher, resulted in a high pitched scream, and flinging off his spectacles, the smaller member of the free Press flung himself overboard, while his heavier companion thrashed the water wildly with his paddle, bouncing the rubber boat round in circles.

The figure in the water caught on to it, and slowly they drifted away and out of sight up a dyke in the rushes.

There was a low whistle from somewhere nearby. It was Dickenson crouching on the lawn at the end of the jetty.

'Are you all right, my lord?'

The *Chenn Lo* slipped silently and so slowly into the fairway that she seemed almost motionless. On the bridge, where overnight he had taken his turn at the helm while the captain rested, Dai Pol was studying the banks ahead through binoculars.

'We are looking for a big house, you think on port side?' Hoffmann moved the rim of the metal wheel gently through his fingers, his eyes almost continuously on the echo sounder. 'We have mostly three metres, but sometimes is less. We cannot go far up I say.'

'Use the fairway. Sailing yachts displace more than we do, Captain. They have three metre keels some of them.' The binoculars moved slowly round, the long black tubes held against his spectacles, giving him the appearance of a giant insect.

He had already sent Kitty below, and ordered the engineer and the steward to stay out of sight. The river was peaceful in the hazy afternoon sun, but so large a vessel, with its unusual name and registration would have been noted already, several times over. He had made a number of preparations, including changing the name on the stern with a transfer. Shee had done this without the captain's knowledge.

He found the *Shamrock* suddenly, as they rounded the bend in the river. Barely a quarter of a mile upstream were the low white hull, furled sails, and two thin gleaming masts of the yacht whose accurately made replica he had personally supervised when it was made. The model that had berthed so usefully on her owner's desk, lay in reality to her jetty.

'Heave to, Captain! Let her come on in neutral!'

'We only have high water for mebbee half an hour more, Sir Dai. Don't get me stuck!' The captain glanced at the banks on either side, judging the level of former tides.

Slowly the boat drifted on, a great white shape on the water, the only sounds the venting from her stern and the big balloon fenders rolling gently on the hull.

'Will you want me to make a landing?'

Dai Pol did not answer. Through the glasses he had seen first one, then two heads, low in the cockpit of the yacht. Without difficulty, he recognised Lord Bair and guessed the other figure was Daimon. Although he had no fixed plans, this was unexpected. He had hoped to moor up or drop anchor unseen and get ashore. But specifically he was also ready for what was now possible.

Turning, he put down the binoculars and told Hoffmann to keep position. Then he went below to Shee, speaking quickly, giving orders in the waterfront jargon of Kowloon.

The two men on board the *Shamrock* had now, in turn, glasses trained on the almost motionless, stealthy cruiser.

'What the hell's that bugger doing?' said Lord Bair, abandoning caution and standing up in the cockpit.

'Same damn thing, Desmond!' Daimon told him wearily. 'And I'll tell you what I'd put money on! With a charter that size it's got to be TV! That's not some piddling newspaper outfit!'

They both let the binoculars hang from their straps, and resorted to the reassurance of the other glasses, recharged.

'I don't like it. Nothing moving on board. You can never see who's on these bridges with all that bloody dark glass!'

'I tell you what I don't like!' Daimon began to back slowly down the companionway. 'See that flag? That's not a charter job. That's French! D'you know what? I think that's trouble, old boy! That's our pals from the other night's little business, come to even up the score!'

Lord Bair, looking down, saw his cousin's watery eyes viewing him over the rim of his heavy goblet, and noticed the shaking hand. He felt for, and found the barrel of the readied shotgun, and pulled it up into the open, muzzle end first.

'Then they can have a couple of barrels to be getting on with! TV or bloody Frogs, what's the difference!'

The two volleys roared across the water. As the puffs of smoke drifted about the cockpit, mallard and seagulls rose from the banks, crying alarm.

'Come on out, blast you! Get your glasses on while I reload, Daimon. Where are the bloody cartridges?'

The two of them bumped into each other, stooped, crouching, looking for the box of ammunition.

Daimon focussed the heavy binoculars. On the *Chenn Lo*, Sir Dai Pol had slipped down below into the stateroom as the shots fell short, his face the void, expressionless mask.

Shee had made all ready. The replica they had on board, the model of the *Chenn Lo* that normally gleamed quietly in pride of place at the head of the stateroom, was now exposed to daylight. A long narrow hatch in the deck above it was open, and as an electric hoist whined, twin cables fastened to bow and stern tautened. The six foot long model rose swiftly up on to the deck.

Dai Pol ran up after it. In silence, the two crewmen swung it over to the miniature launching cradle screwed to the rails, hidden on the shore side. The cradle was swung out and the model went down smoothly into the water. Quickly the holding cables were lowered and flicked clear.

Black control box in his hand, Dai Pol went and lay full length beside the bridge from where he could see the target.

'From Hong Kong, with love!' He spoke in Chinese, then pressed two switches. 'What is good for a junk, will be good for you, Lord Bair!'

He heard the quick intake of breath from Shee, kneeling beside him.

The radio-guided model, no more than a small shape on the water, sped silently and swiftly near the bank, heading beyond *Shamrock*. Then far away, it sped on round in a widening arc.

Those about to receive a missive, more normally used in the crowded junk harbours, were now on the right wave length. But looking in the wrong direction.

'It's that bloody fellow Pol, Daimon!' Lord Bair croaked. 'I can see him! On the deck there, the bastard! I'll put a non-negotiable instrument over his head he won't like!'

Dropping below, he plunged heavily through the main cabin, emerging seconds later, sending the forepeak hatch shuddering back with a crash, head and shoulders appearing through the aperture. In his arms he cradled the ominous length of pipe, pregnant and swollen at the end which pointed out across the water.

'Desmond, not that thing!'

But it was too late. The initial crack of the launching was not loud, akin to the sound of a rifle. But ten yards out across the water something happened. There was an appalling noise, like a gigantic piece of calico being ripped up, as the missile, rapidly receding, marked its going with a trail of wispy smoke. The two explosions were virtually simultaneous and devastating.

In the enormous double claps of thunder, rent by red light and similar vast balloons of dense black, the *Shamrock* was cut in half, the masts spinning down slowly as the bow lifted out of the water. What had been the *Chenn Lo* was lost to sight in a huge blazing fire ball that roared feverishly on the water. Only vital seconds before, a small slim figure left its decks as Kitty dived expertly over the side.

In the stunning aftermath, as echoes rumbled up and down the river and across the land on either bank, by the reeds at the dyke mouth a low, grey rubber shape emerged timidly, rocking wildly in the artificially created waves.

'Now and again, Sid, you get a break on this job!' the skinny man with the steel-rimmed spectacles and wispy hair said. Shakily he pressed buttons on his pocket tape recorder. 'What price the Falklands! Leave the sodding paddle alone! Get your lens cover off, you prune! Lots of pix you'll get like that!'

'You leave my end to me, mate!' The fat man was

sweating. 'I can't do a blind thing till this lot stops rocking, can I?'

'Get those pix and look snappy!'

'Funny you, Fred!' The fat man was still grasping the paddle and using it more as a lever on the rounded rubber thwart, heaved himself above the level of the reeds.

'D'you reckon we pick up any, if we see 'em?'

'Yeah, I saw her go in, too. Bird wasn't it? You can just see her head there – going underwater mostly, but she's going to come up this side.'

'Doesn't want to be seen would you say Fred?'

'Get that bloody spoon working! We're on the edge now. We'll nip along the bank and get her in the mud as she comes out! Hold on to them bullrushes and let me go first!'

Like an outsize toad the fat man flung himself up the bank and floundered to his feet, Fred close behind, clutching frantically at the wet trousered legs in front of him.

Together they began running and stumbling along the river edge to where both could see a small, mud-blackened figure lying prone, still half in the water. As they slowed, coming nearer, the head lifted, eyes seemingly closed under the wet fringe of hair.

'What'ya gonna do, Fred?'

'Bloody Chink, ain't she?' The fat man halted. 'Want to watch that lot. Likely as not she's gotta knife in her knickers!'

'Don't worry, she's not going to hurt us. I've got the green light special from the old man himself, remember? Twenty-five grand for exclusive special on any murder, rape or drug scoop. Okay? And I get a cut, too.' He knelt down beside the small, still body, lifting the head with both hands. 'Come on love, you're with friends now! Howd'ya like to make twenty-five thousand, eh? Pound notes! All for you?'

The small head between his hands moved. Above the high cheek-bones the almond eyes opened, looking first at one man, then the other. Kitty smiled.

'First let's get your things off, love, you're soaking wet!' pursuaded the skinny man briskly. 'You there Sid?' Matter of factly he tugged open the soaking blouse, holding the tape recorder with his other hand. 'Start telling us, sweetheart! It's deadline this business!'

'I like it, Fred, I like it!' Already the fat man's camera shutter was clicking like a time bomb.

The company inside the bus with the bright exterior of flowers, ducks, hearts and other stickers, was on the whole no less cheerful than the exterior. As they began the ascent of the Dover Hill, Polly Flinders changed gear noisily, using both hands and the speed slowed.

'It was always a considerable incline, this one.' Wilfred Poult, sitting in a canvas-backed chair, nursed a glass of white wine. Some of the others crouched on the edges of the bunks. Maddy had a space on the floor where she had put down a pillow and spread her skirts about her. They had finished the picnic supper but the wine continued to go around. Only Maddy could bring her *salon* with her, Rupert thought. It was a bit like going to Ascot.

'It's all you lot, plus supper, plus that heavy little guy in the back bunk!' Polly shouted, shifting gear again. The priceless prince had been tucked up in one of the children's beds, flanked by a teddy bear and a companionable wax-faced doll.

'Maybe he never did have a teddy bear and now he has got one!' Nancy had said. After that, her main remarks had been about the supper baskets and how much better they might have been if her inconsiderate employers had not so callously turned upon her.

'It was up this very hill, you will doubtless remember, Madeleine,' Poult remarked, 'that Dickens opens Tale of Two Cities. In dense fog, you may recall? The coach, bound for the *paquet* to France, is stopped!'

'Did they have packet trips then, Wilf?' Polly cried, swinging the bus round the second bend. 'Don't worry, kids! We shan't stop!'

'A horseman appears from behind in the fog,' Poult droned on, 'but is not allowed near for fear he is a highwayman. He calls out a message for one of the passengers. "Recalled to Life!" ' He looked round his audience, the kindly curator lecturer. 'I could not help thinking, on this hill, that our friend in the end bunk there, might well qualify for the same message!'

'Isn't that quite a thought!' Maddy said quickly. 'Anyone for a last drop of this bottle? I figure we ought to be all tidied-up before we arrive.'

'What's the plan, when we have crossed over?' Ruthy asked. 'We can't all sleep in these bunks!'

Rupert stood up and stretched. The question had been in his own mind for some time. He guessed there was little hope of what he would most favour.

'It's going to be one hour later, French time, when we get there.'

'The Grand Hotel Clement at Ardres!' Maddy said cheerfully. 'About fifteen miles outside Calais. Recommended by all the best people and I sent them a cable this morning. The bus can park in their courtyard and Polly has said she doesn't mind taking care of the Prince. A platonic relationship.'

As they reached the outskirts of Dover, there was a stop for traffic lights. Rupert, looking out of the window, took Maddy silently by the arm and pointed to a newsagent's shop where the heavy black scrawl of an evening newspaper poster was large enough for all to read: IRA CLAIM PEER BLAST VICTIM!

'I wonder who that would be?' Maddy said.

The lights changed and the bus jerked on round the corner. The next poster they passed had it differently: RED BRIGADE BOAST BOAT BOMBING!

On board the bus there was silence, collective but with individual reflection.

'I hope that doesn't mean they're going to put bombs in boats now, like I mean, ferry boats!' Ruthy said.

'Polly, stop and let's get a paper!' Maddy said.

As they circled the roundabout, on the approach to

222

the hoverport entrance, the next poster was still in position at a newsvendor's pitch, but the vendor had departed. Only his box remained: PLO CLAIM PEER REVENGE KILLING!

A strange, intuitive sense of forboding seized Rupert. Uneasily he looked across to Maddy. She was staring out of the window, biting her lip.

'Isn't there a radio in the front there, Polly?'

'Only a cassette player. Anyone want The Pistols?' Polly shouted cheerfully. She pushed buttons and sudden noise poured back into the bus, drowning all else. The immediate screams of protest made her turn it off.

They had arrived. Polly wound down the window as the uniformed ticket collector approached and Maddy leaned over and passed out the paper wallet. The man opened the door, grinning, counted the tickets and tore off the counterfoils.

'Straight on! Take lane seven through into passports. They're loading for Calais now!' He slammed shut the door.

The bus chugged on to join the end of a short queue of cars that were waiting to be called for emigration and customs.

'I think what I'll do,' Rupert said to Maddy as Polly switched off the engine, 'I'll just push out and get a newspaper at the terminal building. They're always open. We've plenty of time.'

Surprisingly, she gave him a quick kiss. 'Don't be too long!'

'I'm coming too!' Polly skipped through the bus door and down the steps behind him. 'I want a loo!'

Rupert went with her into the main terminal building, and as she disappeared among the crowd, sought out the newspaper and magazine stand. He paid for the paper and without looking at it made immediately for the entrance. Only when he was outside the swing doors again did he allow himself to look at the headlines. They were not difficult to read, taking up nearly half the front page, and as he stopped and took in what followed, the

lines of stark black typeface seemed to jump up at him
and swim wavily across the newsprint.

'Oh my God!' he whispered.

Suddenly Polly was once more beside him, reading
over his elbow.

'Hi! Give me that!' She was clutching him tightly now,
holding his arm, the other hand grasping the paper. The
action caused them both to stagger forward, and as they
went on reading they took a few steps towards the corner
of the terminal building. Even as they rounded it Rupert
pulled her back, and in the same instant they both stared
towards the distant bus where the others could be seen
grouped around the door.

'Wait!' said Rupert hoarsely. 'Look!'

There were other different figures gathered round the
bus too. Men in the uniforms of Customs and Excise,
and three more in plain clothes that in their similarity
were almost identical in their sports jackets and twill
trousers. A white-helmeted policeman arriving on his
motor-cycle, almost silent at that distance, swung the
machine purposefully side-on in front of the bus, propped
it on its stand and was strolling almost casually over to
join the rest.

'Rupe darling!' Polly's voice was surprisingly, carefully
and thoughtfully controlled. He felt her grip on his arm
tighten. 'I somehow think you and I have more we could
win together than we might lose now for other people. I
really do!'

Astonished, Rupert looked down at the small, pink
face upturned by his shoulder. The tip of Polly's tongue
licked faintly at the corners of her soft, wide-lipped mouth.

The grip on his arm tightened even more. Together
they began to walk backwards, turning through the terminal building doors once more, mingling with the crowd
outside, making for the exit on the far side of the hall.
Then they were in the fresh air again and passed between
the dock gates, walking easily, holding hands and without
once looking back . . .